He had dreamed of this

The morning sun spilled through the lace curtains, lighting up Lainie's face as she lay in his arms.

Her eyes flicked open, and she stared at him. "Good morning." Wordlessly Griff drew her on top of him so that she stretched along his length, his hips cradling hers. His eyes met hers, and a spark of desire kindled between them. Every inch of him was awakening, becoming aware of her scent, her touch. It had been so long, too long. He needed to love her.

"Griff?" It was almost a whisper.

"Mmm?"

She smiled down at him, a subtle smile, a knowing smile. "I love you, too."

ABOUT THE AUTHOR

Before writing her first romance,
Anne McAllister wrote short stories for
children and book reviews. She holds a
bachelor's degree in Spanish and a master's in
theology and is now a full-time writer. Born in
California, Anne now resides in the Midwest
with her husband and four children.

These books may be available at your local bookseller.

Don't miss any of our special offers. Write to us at the
following address for information on our newest releases.

Harlequin Reader Service
P.O. Box 52040, Phoenix, AZ 85072-2040
Canadian address: P.O. Box 2800, Postal Station A,
5170 Yonge St., Willowdale, Ont. M2N 6J3

A Chance of Rainbows

ANNE McALLISTER

Harlequin Books

TORONTO • NEW YORK • LONDON
AMSTERDAM • PARIS • SYDNEY • HAMBURG
STOCKHOLM • ATHENS • TOKYO • MILAN

For Rosemary,
who helps me keep my act together.

Published December 1985

First printing October 1985

ISBN 0-373-16132-8

Prologue

May 2

"Griff didn't get mad, did he? Yell at you? Throw things?"

Would that he had, Lainie Tucker thought, but she looked up and forced herself to smile at her best friend Cassie Craig's lighthearted, hopeful tone. "No," she said. "No, he didn't do that."

"Huh!" Cassie snorted. "I might have known." She raised her eyes to heaven, or at least as high as the hospital's social-services office ceiling would allow. "Oh, to have the perfect marriage," she intoned. "Honestly, I don't know how you two do it! Married seven months and never a harsh word, never an anguished moment."

Lainie opened her mouth to protest that exaggeration, but Cassie went right on, "Do you know what Brendan would have done if someone called me out on an emergency seconds before he was due home and we hadn't seen each other in three and a half weeks?"

"Storm the hospital?"

"At least," Cassie replied, her mouth curving into a fond smile at the thought of her husband's impetuosity. Brendan was not known for his mild manners and complacent attitude. He never hesitated to tell anyone what he thought.

Nor, for that matter, did Cassie. They argued, squabbled
and then compromised. Neither of them ever minced words.

"Anyway," Cassie was saying now, "I just finished my
morning rounds and thought I would just stop by for a moment and apologize for having to call you in to the hospital
last night. Ordinarily I wouldn't have done it for a million
dollars, but I really thought Mrs. Hudson needed someone
just then. And it sure as heaven wasn't me! I can deal with
broken arms. The family problems are up to you."

"You were right to call me," Lainie reassured her.

Cassie's brow lifted skeptically. "You sure?"

Lainie nodded.

"He didn't even raise his voice?"

Lainie shook her head.

"Amazing. Simply amazing." Cassie's tongue clicked
against her teeth in disbelief. Then, shrugging, she gave a
little wave and vanished out the door, leaving Lainie sitting
at her desk alone in the still morning light.

Griffin? Raise his voice? Throw things? Get mad?

Lainie rubbed a hand across her eyes, glad that Cassie
hadn't come any closer than the doorway or she would have
seen how red they were from crying.

What, she wondered, would Cassie have said if she had
told her what really had happened when she got home last
night—that she had come back to their apartment from
seeing Mrs. Hudson to discover that Griff had come and,
obviously, gone, all his things gone with him? And that all
Lainie had to show for their "perfect marriage" was a note
in Griff's precise handwriting, telling her that it was clear to
him now that as far as their marriage was concerned,
"things weren't working out"?

Chapter One

When the phone rang, Griffin Tucker didn't know whether to answer it or not.

If it was an irate fan or, worse but entirely possible, Wes LaRue, still enraged because Griff had thrown him out of tonight's baseball game, there was no way on earth he wanted to pick up the receiver. On the other hand, it might be Lainie. His heart quickened at the thought.

It rang again, and he hovered indecisively by the hotel-room door that he had just walked through. What if it was Lainie? Finally. After all this time.

He had lain awake more nights that he could count, rehearsing what he would say to her. He licked his suddenly parched lips, considering the possibility. Then, deciding it was definitely worth the risk whether it was LaRue or anyone else, he crossed the impersonal space of his hotel room, and taking a deep breath, picked up the receiver just as the phone began to shrill again.

"Tucker here."

He tried to sound calm, detached, professional. If it was LaRue, who had been acting strangely since the season began, Griff wanted every ounce of professional detachment he could muster. And if it was Lainie—he swallowed the lump in his throat—if it was his wife, finally come to her senses, she didn't need to know immediately that he had been waiting by the phone for her voice for four long weeks.

"It's Brendan." The gruff masculine voice in Griff's ear both relieved and squelched his hopes simultaneously. "Where the hell have you been?"

"On the town, of course," Griff replied sarcastically as he sank down wearily onto the still neatly made bed and glanced at his watch. Before he met Lainie, that might have been true, but now he came back to his room right after every game. Even lately. Especially lately. Hell, it seemed that all he did anymore was sit in various hotel rooms and watch the phone, hoping it would ring.

He had told himself when he walked out of their apartment a month ago that he was finished with waiting for Lainie, finished running second in her life. But he couldn't control his thoughts or even his eyes, which seemed to wander perpetually to the telephone. It was his greatest fantasy these days to imagine it ringing and to hear Lainie's voice on the other end, first telling him that she loved him and that things would be different now and then asking him to come home.

But in fact it was half past midnight on a hot June night in Cincinnati, and he was just about to start his vigil again. Only Brendan Craig had called to interrupt it.

"The game went into extra innings," he explained unnecessarily. Given his job, Brendan ought to know where he had been, he thought as he rubbed his right hand through sweat-dampened blond hair. He had taken a shower and changed clothes right after the game, but it was a humid night, and the long drive back to the hotel had made him sticky and irritable all over again. That and a couple of remarks one of his fellow umpires made about his tendency to do nothing but lurk in his hotel room, watching the phone, and what another one said about how hard he was being on Wes LaRue.

"What's up?" he asked now, beginning to wonder why Brendan Craig, who had almost never called him while he was on the road, would be calling him in the middle of the night, unless—unless something had happened to Lainie.

"What's wrong?" he demanded, suddenly cold clear through. "What happened?"

"Nothing serious."

"What?" A fist of fear clenched in his stomach.

"Lainie's been roughed up a bit."

Griff's jaw snapped shut. "Roughed up? How? What happened? How is she?"

"She's all right." Brendan assured him quickly, as though he could hear Griff's fear clawing its way through the phone lines. "She's at our place."

"But what happened? Damn it, man, tell me!"

"Lainie's been counseling an abused wife," Brendan began to explain, and Griff shut his eyes, feeling sick, knowing what was coming. "And she gave this woman the notion that there were alternatives to staying home and waiting for the next blow to fall. Apparently, after leaving the hospital, the woman went to stay at a halfway house that Lainie got her into." He paused for a split second, then added, "When his wife didn't come home, the guy went looking for Lainie."

Griff sucked in his breath sharply. In his mind's eye he could see the ever-optimistic smile of his wife. "No problem," he could hear her saying, just as she had said countless times to her mother, her brothers, her clients and even to him. Her hazel eyes would shine with understanding and compassion, and she would say, "Don't worry. We'll work it out."

How many times had he heard her say that to people? *Yeah, sure, Lainie,* he thought now. *See what it gets you? Why the hell didn't you listen to me when I asked you to quit? I know what I'm talking about.* And now she had been "roughed up." Whatever that meant. He thought he could guess.

"Jeez," he muttered. "Oh, God."

"She's not badly hurt," Brendan tried to reassure him once again.

"I'm coming home."

"That's what I wanted to know. How long until you're back in L.A.?"

"It doesn't matter. I'm coming home now. Tonight." It was what there were substitute umpires for—emergencies. And this, regardless of Brendan's reassurances, qualified, he was sure.

"She really is all right," Brendan insisted, a rising note of panic in his voice. "She doesn't even know I called you, for God's sake!"

Griff's mouth twisted, and his stomach tightened into a knot. It wasn't her idea, then? He felt the knot turn into a strangled hollow ache deep in his midsection. So much for waiting to hear from her all these weeks. So much for hoping that she might actually be missing him. She didn't even want him when she was hurt! He sighed. Maybe she was really glad that he had left.

"Oh" was all he could manage.

"Are you sure you want to come?" Brendan persisted.

"Yes."

"Shall I tell her?"

Griff wished that he knew. Even though he knew the minute Brendan called that he had to be with her, he had no idea at all if she would want him. In fact, if he were honest, it seemed likely that she did not. Maybe his worst fears were true; maybe she didn't love him anymore. *Maybe*, he thought hollowly, forcing himself to consider the possibility at last, *she never loved me at all*. The pain of the past few weeks came back in all its stark, smothering reality.

"Has she—has she said much about, um, about—" He groped for a way to ask what he wanted to know.

"About your separation?" Brendan supplied gently.

"Yeah." Griff's voice was low, aching, hating the very sound of the word that Brendan uttered. It smacked so much of hopes dashed, of a future gone awry. He had never in his wildest imaginings thought that within seven months his marriage to Lainie would have come to this.

Separated. He still couldn't bring himself to say the word, though he was feeling rational—which wasn't often, admittedly—he sometimes wondered why. God knew he didn't shrink from facing reality in all the other parts of his life. In fact, everywhere else he was unflinchingly honest. Why, then, was it so hard for him to admit that his marriage was not going to work, that he and Lainie were different in almost every way and that it had become more and more obvious that they were better off apart? Lots of people were better off apart these days, he reminded himself. And it was a damned sight better than the sort of marriage that his parents had persisted in for thirty-five years.

"Has she talked about it?" he demanded when Brendan didn't reply at once.

"Some." Brendan was obviously reluctant to talk about whatever she had said.

Griff wanted to press him, but he knew his friend well enough to be sure that he wouldn't get a word out of Brendan unless he wanted Griff to know something. He might be Griff's friend; but he and his wife, Cassie, were Lainie's friends, too. Knowing her and her garrulous nature, he guessed that she might have confided quite a bit to them. He dug his fingernails into the worn corduroy of his jeans at the thought that Brendan and Cassie might know more of what his wife was feeling these days than he did. But with monumental self-control he managed to phrase a question that he hoped Brendan would be willing to answer.

"What do you think?" he asked carefully. "About how she feels, I mean?"

"You don't have to come," Brendan hedged. "I only called because if I were you, I'd want to know. Cassie told me I was wrong, that you—"

"Hell, no, you weren't wrong!" Griff burst out, furious at Cassie's presumption. "Lainie's my wife, damn it! I have a right to know, and I am coming home. Now. As soon as I can get on a plane. And you can damned well tell her whatever you want!" he added angrily.

"Hey, calm down. Take it easy," Brendan soothed. "This is not a matter of life and death, you know."

Griff sighed, his burst of anger fading into a bone-deep weariness and depression of the sort that he had felt growing inside him for weeks. "I know. I know. It's just—just that—" He broke off, overwhelmed by a whole flood of emotions that he had been holding at bay for a very long time: need, longing, desire. All the things that he had intentionally blocked out of his mind since they had split up, everything that he had been telling himself he would get over sooner if he just didn't let himself think about them.

Everything came rushing back now with the force of a tidal wave—all the laughter and loving they had shared during their brief marriage and the sense that in Lainie he had found at last the other half of his soul. It was useless to deny those feelings, no matter how much he might have been trying to, no matter how often he had told himself that their marriage had been based on attraction and infatuation and nothing more.

But if Lainie did not love him—and his nails clenched into the corduroy at the thought—well, he could no longer deny what he felt about her. And what he felt was strong enough to make him drop everything and travel halfway across the United States to be with her at a moment's notice.

"We'll be keeping her at our place, then," Brendan told him softly, and hung up.

Griffin nodded, slumping against the headboard of the bed, the receiver still cradled next to his ear.

"I love her," he muttered in an agonized whisper, and he knew it was still true. "God help me, how I love her."

LAINIE TUCKER was examining her swollen purple right eye in the bedroom mirror with as much critical objectivity as she could muster. It was ghastly; there were no two ways about it.

"It's a good thing Griffin left me," she said over the sound of a whistling kettle to Cassie, who was in the kitchen making her up a pot of therapeutic tea. "Can't you just imagine what he would say about this?"

Even as she said it, pleased at what sounded like a jocular tone of voice, Lainie wondered at the marvels of the human mind. Given time, it could rationalize anything.

"I certainly can," Cassie replied grimly, her view obviously as bleak as Lainie's. "I wish you had stayed at our place," she said, coming into the bedroom and setting a cup of tea on the refinished antique oak commode beside Lainie's bed.

"Nonsense," Lainie said briskly. "I'm in fine shape."

"For a woman with bruised ribs, a sore shoulder and world-class shiner," Cassie agreed. She shook her head at her friend's stubbornness. "Then the least you can do, since you've been obstinate enough to insist that I bring you home, is to get into bed. You are certainly not going to work today."

"Why not?" Lainie asked, though just moving around the room provided her with reasons enough. She felt as if she had been in an avalanche, not simply roughed up by Mavis Leary's drunken husband, Dick.

"You would scare the patients, for one thing," Cassie told her frankly, pulling back the bedspread and giving Lainie a significant look from beneath arched eyebrows, which meant that Lainie was expected to be putting on her nightgown this very minute. "And for another, you need some rest."

"Not really." Not at all, actually. Staying home meant having time to think, and that was the last thing Lainie wanted to do now. Whenever she thought, she thought about Griff. And after four weeks of doing nothing but, she had begun to recognize that there was no future in it. So she wanted to keep busy, very busy, all the time.

But Cassie wasn't having any of it. "Don't argue with your doctor," she said. She plumped up the pillows and piled them on top of each other in the center of the wide double bed. Tactful, Lainie thought. It didn't make it seem so much like only half the bed was hers.

"You're an orthopedic surgeon," Lainie argued amiably as she stripped off her sweatshirt, grimacing at the pain that shot through her ribs as she lifted her arms. "What do you know?"

"Not much apparently, or I would have been able to convince you that you were better off at our place. Brendan is going to have my head when he finds out I brought you home instead."

"You couldn't have stopped me," Lainie replied. She had appreciated the Craigs' offer of a place to stay until she felt better. But how she felt had little to do with sore muscles, and she didn't really want to be treated to anyone else's domestic happiness at this moment. The temptation to feel sorry for herself would have been far too great.

She rummaged through her dresser drawer, purposely ignoring her three sexy nightgowns, which Griff loved and disposed of almost as soon as she put them on, and settled instead for a Berkeley T-shirt left over from her college days. It was faded, holey and not sexy in the least. It was also comforting and homey, exactly what she needed right now.

She tossed Cassie a quick smile over her shoulder, hoping to assuage her friend's guilt. Really, there was nothing Cassie could have done to make her accept the offer. She wasn't an invalid, and she didn't want to be treated like one. What had happened was simply a part of her job. Not a very palatable part, admittedly. But some people had it a lot worse. And to be quite frank, Dick Leary's drunken mauling didn't hurt her nearly as much as the pain she felt when she realized that Griffin Tucker, the man she loved more than anyone in the world, had walked out of her life and was not coming back.

"I'll be perfectly fine, really," she said, turning back to face Cassie.

But Cassie wasn't convinced. "How about if I call your mother and have her send someone over?" One of Lainie's brothers, she meant.

"No, thanks."

That wouldn't be as bad as having Griffin around, scowling and muttering, "I told you so," but it would be close. Lainie had four brothers, and while they generally treated her as one of the guys, the sight of her battered and bruised was likely to bring out their protective instincts. Knowing this, she did her best to be discouraging.

"I don't need a soul," she assured Cassie, who still seemed to be fuming as she paced around the room. Still, at least she hadn't suggested calling Griff. Lainie couldn't have tolerated that.

Cassie shrugged and shook her head despairingly. "You're hopeless," she decreed. "As stubborn and willful as they come. No wonder Griff—" She clamped her mouth shut instantly and grabbed the teacup that Lainie still hadn't touched. "I'll just go warm this up."

"No wonder Griff what?"

Cassie didn't reply, bustling into the kitchen and making a production out of dumping out one perfectly steaming hot cup of tea and replacing it with another out of the same pot. "Orange spice tea is really marvelous, isn't it?" she asked brightly.

"Cassie." Lainie followed her into the kitchen, determined to get the end of the sentence out into the open. "No wonder Griff what?"

Cassie stood with her back to Lainie, her madras plaid shirt quivering with the sudden tension in her shoulders. "I'm sorry," she said. "I think God must have short-changed me on tact. Something else Brendan will kill me for." She turned, giving Lainie a wan smile that faded completely when she took one look at her friend's mulish expression.

"No wonder Griff left?" Lainie tossed the words out lightly, far more lightly than she knew she had any right to, and wondered if Cassie would take a swing at them or let them go by. Her friend's guilty look answered her question.

"I shouldn't have even thought it," Cassie said quickly. "I know he's a jerk. I know it's his fault. I know he's the one who walked out without saying anything and never looked back."

"So do I." Lainie's voice was unutterably weary, and she turned then and padded slowly back into her bedroom, sinking down onto the bed as she came face-to-face with her husband's desertion once again. It ought to hurt less, she told herself. But so far it hadn't.

"I didn't mean it," Cassie said, following her, looking truly worried now. She bent her marigold head down and peered solemnly into Lainie's long, somber face. "It was his fault."

Lainie sighed. "I know it. But I can't help wondering if there was something I could have done."

Cassie bristled. "How could you? You weren't even here!"

Lainie lifted her eyes heavenward. "That, I am sure, was his whole point," she replied. "That I wasn't here. He expected me to be. He wanted me to quit." She closed her eyes, remembering her first day back at work after their Hawaiian honeymoon. She had come home late, exhausted yet exhilarated after a trying day working with her patients, and Griff had dumped the charred remains of chicken

Polynesian into the garbage disposal and suggested that she quit.

At the time she had simply thought he was disgruntled, annoyed that she had been late and his dinner had been spoiled, and she had tried to discuss it with him. That was when she had encountered a small piece of the reality of living with Griffin Tucker. Griff didn't discuss. He said what he thought, flatly and in a tone that brooked no argument, and then he walked out of the apartment. Things either went his way or he was as silent as a clam.

And, she thought grimly, remembering, as well, the chain of events that led to her coming home seven months later to an empty apartment, if you still persisted in doing things that he didn't approve of, the next thing you knew, his walking out was permanent.

"Maybe he's insecure," Cassie offered.

"Griff?"

Cassie shrugged, obviously rethinking that ridiculous idea. Griff was as secure as Gibraltar and just as unmovable. "Well, maybe he's not," she conceded. "But why else would he come back to your apartment, find the note you left him, saying that you were at the hospital and would be back soon, and just pack everything he owned and move away?"

"Because I wasn't doing what he wanted me to," Lainie told her. "I mean, you're married to Brendan, who is sweet and rational and always willing to talk and discuss—"

Cassie rolled her eyes, but didn't contradict her.

"And," Lainie continued, "I am married to Griffin, who thinks that the world has one set of answers, his answers— and one way of doing things, *his* way. And he won't even discuss anything he might disagree with!"

"And he wouldn't discuss your job?"

"No! He wouldn't discuss anything. 'Discussions lead to arguments,' he told me. 'You know what I think,'" she quoted, and every bit of the frustration she had been feeling for months, even from the months before he walked out on the day he was supposed to be coming home from his first road trip, reverberated in her voice.

She turned away from Cassie, clenching her fists on the top of the dresser, feeling once more the sense of helpless anger she felt every time she went over the events of that night, as well as every other day of their marriage, again and again. She had analyzed, dissected, studied, probed and considered every possible nuance in his behavior from the moment they met until the night she got his note telling her that things weren't working out. And she was no nearer coping with it now than she ever was.

How could she be if he wasn't even around to tell her what he meant? And how, she wondered, could he expect that things would ever work out if he was never willing to discuss them?

Cassie looked at her sympathetically, then wandered across the room and stared out the window that looked across the broad sidewalk street on which they lived down toward the wide Southern California beach. "Maybe he'll come back and you can talk then," she said, offering a crumb of hope.

"And maybe pigs will fly."

Lainie walked over to the bed and sat down, swinging her legs up onto it with exaggerated care so that she was able to achieve a semihorizontal position without actually moaning out loud. Then she eased herself back against the mountain of pillows and reached for the cup of tea that Cassie had set on the commode. "He'd better not come back now."

"Why not? I mean, if you want to talk to him..."

Lainie looked down at her teacup, her eyes clouding. Then she lifted them again and looked at the picture of herself and Griff on Maui, a picture that had been taken on their honeymoon and which she had placed by their bed the day they got home. Everything had seemed possible then, but now the smiles she saw seemed like a fantasy—too good to be true. And deep within she wondered if that wasn't the case.

Maybe such powerful feelings as she and Griff had shared, almost from the moment of their first meeting, were destined to burn out quickly. Maybe he didn't really love her. Not in a deep-down, lasting way. Not the way she loved him. She sighed, knowing that she wanted to find out, wanted him to come back so she could ask him.

"But," she said to Cassie, "not now. Not this way." She lifted her head up so that the sunlight caught the side of her face and emphasized her puffy purple eye.

Cassie nodded. "I see what you mean."

Lainie managed a smile, albeit a reluctant one. "It'll heal in time. It really doesn't hurt much." She shifted against the pillows and glanced at the clock. "Thanks for bringing me home. Don't let me keep you from your work or from Brendan."

Cassie turned back from the window and grinned. "Is that a brush-off, or is that a brush-off?"

Lainie laughed in spite of her sore ribs. "Sorry. I didn't mean it to sound quite so blunt. It's just that I have this aversion to your feeling that you have to stand around here and feel sorry for me because Griff isn't here."

Cassie reddened, embarrassed at having her motives seen through so easily. "I just wish you were happy," she said lamely. "Isn't there anything I can do?"

Cassie didn't like emotional upheaval. She didn't see that it was productive at all, whereas Lainie had this perverse notion that she ought to grow from it. Though she had to admit that it was getting harder and harder to find a means for growth since Griffin hadn't come back. "Not a thing," she assured her friend.

Cassie didn't move, still considering her with a tender, almost-maternal look on her face.

"Truly," Lainie said, placing her hand over her heart. "Don't worry about me. I promise not to go to work. I promise not to swing from the light fixtures. I promise not to do anything stupid at all."

Cassie tucked her hands into the pockets of her pleated linen slacks. "Well, all right. But I can just imagine what Brendan will say when I come home without you! Believe me, you're lucky you're going to be here."

"Are you angling for an invitation to stick around?" Lainie teased.

"No, I guess not. Here, I'll refill your teacup before I go, and I'll bring you some magazines." Cassie took the cup and headed for the doorway. "But I really think that as your doctor I should advise you to sleep."

"I think you should have another baby," Lainie told her as she watched Cassie go out to the kitchen. "Your maternal instincts are overwhelming recently."

There was total silence in the other room except for the teacup, which seemed to be doing an inordinate amount of rattling. When Cassie reemerged with the other cup balanced precariously on the saucer and a fistful of magazines in her other hand, Lainie thought the color in her cheeks was unnaturally high.

"Do you really think so?" Cassie frowned as she set the cup down and dropped the magazines gingerly on Lainie's knees.

Lainie, who hadn't been thinking at all really, suddenly took a closer look at her friend. "About having a baby, you mean?"

"Uh-huh." Cassie twisted her hands, her fingers seeking her wedding band and winding it around and around. She didn't meet Lainie's gaze.

"Why not?" Lainie tried to sound casual, surprised at what it cost her. She had purposely avoided thinking about babies lately because during the early days of her marriage to Griff her fantasies had included little brown-eyed, blond-haired children with devastating smiles, and now they didn't seem any more probable than the wildest dream. It even hurt to think of someone, even someone as dear to her as Cassie, being happy enough and solid enough in her marriage to contemplate having a child. But she certainly wouldn't let Cassie know it. She was annoyed at herself for even feeling this way. "Of course," she said positively. "Keith and Steve would love it."

"I wonder. They seem so old now."

They were nine and eleven, Cassie's sons from her first marriage to Michael Hart, a cardiologist who was killed in a plane crash. After her marriage to Brendan, though, he had adopted them as his own.

"Am I too old, do you think?" Cassie seemed to have been giving the matter a great deal of thought. Lainie wished again that she weren't so envious.

"Of course you aren't. You're only five years older than I am!" Lainie was twenty-eight, though recently she felt as if she could pass for a hundred and five. "Does Brendan want another child?"

Cassie shrugged and walked over to study her reflection in the mirror as if she might be able to tell by looking if she ought to get pregnant. "He won't say. I mean, he says it's up to me. I know he thinks he's being noble and all that, trying not to take me away from my work. But I think he really would like one." She gave Lainie a wistful smile. "I would, too, really. I think I've dreamed about having Brendan's child for most of my life."

Lainie stared at her, amazed. That Cassie, whose lifetime goals had always read like an overachiever's handbook, would have spent years dreaming about having a certain man's child was almost mind-blowing. But then, Cassie had known Brendan for most of her life, and to hear her tell it now, she had been half in love with him for decades without really admitting it. And if she felt half of what

Lainie felt for Griff, whom she hadn't even known for a full year, well, yes, then she guessed such dreams were possible.

"I think it's a great idea," she said, and in spite of her envy, she meant it.

"We'll see," Cassie said enigmatically, a faraway look coming into her eyes.

It must be nice to still have dreams, Lainie thought after Cassie had bustled around, making sure everything was shipshape once more, before she finally left Lainie on her own. Her own dreams, which had been so richly textured and beautiful for most of her life—especially after she had met Griff—seemed hollow and lifeless now. She tried to understand how it could have happened that way.

For years she had been bouncy, cheerful, optimistic—always there with a new idea, an improved solution, a better mousetrap, whenever her first plan or dream had crashed or faded. If one thing didn't work, she was always willing to try another, whether it was in building a kite or helping the depressed and hopeless people she dealt with at the hospital straighten out their lives. But since Griffin had walked out on her, her mind had gone blank. She had tasted defeat, and for the first time she hadn't been able to come up with a thing that she could do to help herself.

He had walked into her life almost a year ago and had changed it completely. The current between them had been electric. From the first moment she saw him in Brendan's hospital room where he had come to visit his friend after Brendan's motorcycle accident, she had been drawn to him with a pull that was stronger than the tides. And the feeling had been mutual.

He had taken one look at her and had suggested going out for a cup of coffee to discuss the condition of Brendan's arm. She didn't remember whether Brendan was discussed or not, but the ten-minute coffee break turned into half an hour without her even realizing it, and only persistent paging on the loudspeaker and finally a harried chaplain who tracked her down brought her back to the everyday reality of her life. But not before Griff had made her promise to eat a quick bite of dinner with him and then go to the ballpark.

She had found the man in the umpire's uniform as much of an enigma as the one in the faded jeans and white oxford sport shirt whom she had first met—and just as appealing. She was intrigued by his reserve and the way he suddenly punctuated it with a quick wit and a flashing grin. She suspected there was a lot of depth in him, so much that she couldn't fathom it all at once. From his incongruous lime-green Toyota to his starched white shirts, he fascinated her. Her heart beat faster whenever she thought about him, and when he touched her, her senses flamed like wildfire.

Their courtship had been a blur of long-distance phone calls and occasional days when he got back to town. But it made up in intensity what it lacked in length, and while she knew there were parts of him still hidden from her, she wasn't worried when she agreed to marry him. It would be that much more wonderful after they were married, she thought, getting to know him better, learning all about what made Griffin Tucker tick.

She looked over the picture again, a surge of longing welling up inside her. Then she blinked fiercely and decided it was past time to take herself firmly in hand.

"Stop it," she said aloud, and made herself open one of the magazines that still lay on her knees in the hope that she could find something that would take her mind off Griff. "What's the point, after all, in thinking about him?" She wouldn't try to reach him, because she was really afraid he didn't love her anymore. And even if he did, there wasn't any point, because he never wanted to talk. He had done to their marriage what he did on the ball field—made his decision and then walked away.

Of course she wanted him to come back, to talk about things, to try to "work things out," as Cassie had suggested. But that didn't mean it was going to happen. She had spent a month wallowing in private despair while she was outwardly as capable and competent and overworked as she ever was. It wasn't satisfying at all. And she had to do something about it. Maybe Dick Leary would be the catalyst that would get her moving again. It would be nice if he could contribute something useful somewhere. His marriage to Mavis was definitely not in that category at all.

She yawned, deciding that maybe Cassie was right and that she could do with a bit of sleep. She certainly hadn't got much last night, what with all the poking and probing they had done to her at the hospital and all the questions she'd had to answer for the police. She set the magazines aside and slid down beneath the summer-weight blanket, curling carefully into a ball and shutting her eyes.

But she had barely got settled when the phone rang. Groaning, she inched her way to a sitting position and then edged her way slowly out of bed. It might be Mavis or Claire Hudson or any one of a number of patients who needed her. She had long since given up hoping that it would be Griff. Besides, he was never awake at this time of the morning. His late hours precluded that.

She stumbled out to the living room and reached for the receiver. As she picked it up, she heard the front-door lock click and looked over the see the doorknob turn.

"It's Cassie," the voice from the phone panted in her ear. "I just wanted to warn you. Griff—"

"Too late," Lainie murmured.

A tall, lean, unshaved blond man stood framed in the doorway.

"A pig has just flown in the door."

Chapter Two

"What?" Griffin clutched his suitcase in one hand and the doorknob with the other, his concern for Lainie's welfare and his recent irritation when he discovered that she wasn't at Brendan's, where he thought she would be, was thrown off balance by her strange statement. He supposed he shouldn't have been surprised. She had a habit of disconcerting him.

As he watched, Lainie set down the phone slowly and stood leaning against the wall, looking at him out of her one unswollen eye, not moving an inch. He had played this scene over in his mind all night long—how she would look, what she would say, what he would say. But he had always envisioned it taking place at Brendan and Cassie's house, where the presence of other people would have softened its impact and where all that lay between them would not loom so ominously right from the first.

But when he got there, Lainie wasn't at the Craigs'. He had taken a taxi there directly from the airport, first knocking, then hammering on the door, and had got no response. Frantic, he had paced the length of the driveway, wondering if perhaps they had had to take her back to the hospital. All sorts of dire things crossed his mind, and he was just about to go in search of another cab when Brendan drove up.

Brendan, it turned out, had gone grocery shopping, anticipating that when he got back, Cassie would have arrived with Lainie, and he was just as baffled as Griff. He left Griff to wrestle with the grocery sacks while he went into the house to phone the hospital and came back just as Cassie drove up and gave them the news. Lainie, against the doctor's recommendation, had decided to go home alone.

"How could you let her do that?" Griff demanded, and Cassie had fixed him with a stony glare.

"Fancy you caring," she had retorted in scathing tones that cut him far more deeply than she could have imagined. Just because he didn't visibly wilt, everyone seemed to think he was impervious to everything and that he just didn't care. Well, they were wrong. Sometimes, like now, he cared too damned much.

"I care," he had told Cassie in low tones. And perhaps his weary stance, his unshaved cheeks and the fear still lingering in his eyes sufficiently substantiated his words, for Cassie's expression softened perceptibly, and she nodded.

"Are you going over there now, then?" she had asked him.

"Yes."

"Take my car," she offered. "And be gentle with Lainie, will you, Griff? Promise?"

He had promised.

And so he strove to control his emotions now. Just from the expression on her face—like that of a rabbit looking down the barrel of a shotgun—he knew he had to move slowly. However much he might like to sweep her into his arms and hug the life out of her, however much her ghastly, painful-looking eye might make him want to reach for her to offer comfort and solace, he couldn't do it yet.

What he was going to do—and it was harder at this moment than in any baseball game he had ever umpired—was hang on to every bit of his control.

"Shouldn't you be resting?" he asked carefully, setting his suitcase on the edge of the Oriental carpet and shutting the door gently behind him but not moving toward her at all.

For a long moment Lainie didn't respond. Then, gradually, she seemed to breathe again, and the tension eased in her shoulders, though her regard for him seemed at best uncertain.

"Probably," she replied. "That's what Cassie says, anyway." Her tone was soft and hesitant, not a bit like the normal cheery sounds he had been accustomed to hearing from her, and instinctively Griff took a step in her direction.

Lainie's eyes widened abruptly, and she turned and dashed into the bedroom with a speed that belied the aches and pains her body must be feeling. Griff's jaw clenched, but he followed her.

"Lainie." He stopped in the doorway to the bedroom as he saw that she was huddled in the bed, the blanket pulled practically to her chin. "I won't hurt you."

"Not my body, anyway," she mumbled.

Griff sucked in his breath. "What do you mean? Not my leaving?" He couldn't quite accept that idea. After all, she seemed so busy all the time that he doubted she would even miss him. And she hadn't called!

"What do you think?"

He shrugged awkwardly, then decided that honesty was the best policy. "It didn't seem likely."

Her eyes seemed to flicker with unspoken pain for just a second. Then her gaze dropped, and her fingers tightened on the crumpled blanket. "I see," she said woodenly. "Then why did you come back? Who told you?"

"Brendan." He saw her frown and remembered that Brendan had told him that Cassie didn't know he was going to call. "Don't blame Cassie," he said quickly. "She had no idea. But Bren thought I ought to know."

"Why?"

Except in his fantasies, he hadn't thought that this was going to be easy, but damn it, did she have to make it so bloody hard? He hated all this business of questions, all the probing, the tallking. It never led to anything good. Never.

He shoved a hand through his uncombed hair and groped through his fuzzy mind for an answer that would satisfy her and still stop the discussion flat. Lainie waited, her eyes never leaving his, even her puffy right one concentrating on his acute discomfort. He scuffed his toe on the pile of the thick carpet, then shoved his hands into the pockets of the twill pants he had changed into before going to the airport last night. They were rumpled and looked as if he had slept in them. He had.

There was only one answer to her question, and he knew it. He also didn't like giving it, because it left him open, vulnerable, naked. Why hadn't she stayed at the Craigs's where Brendan and Cassie's presence would have inhibited questions like this one?

"Griffin?" Lainie's voice penetrated his mental waffling, and he looked up to meet her gaze, his throat tight.

"Because I love you, damn it," he said gruffly, then turned at once to leave the room. "Get some sleep, all right?"

Before Lainie could open her mouth, he had gone.

"Griff! Griffin Tucker!" She lurched forward on the bed, then groaned and sank back in pain.

Griff, having shut the door when he left, jerked it back open at the sound of her voice in pain. He peered at her, then hurried across the room and bent over her, demanding, "Are you all right?"

She stared up at him, drinking in all the worry and concern in his warm brown eyes, still scarcely daring to believe the words he had spoken before he had bolted from the room. If they were true, she was fine. Wonderful, in fact.

"Are you?" he asked again when she didn't reply. His hand stroked along her arm, and she shivered at the contact.

"I'm okay," she managed. Almost without her realizing it, her left hand stole out from beneath the blanket and touched his fingers, which wrapped convulsively around hers. "Did you mean it, Griffin? What you said?" she asked, still feeling oddly breathless, as though the wind had been knocked right out of her. It was too much like a dream.

"That I love you?" His voice was rough edged, and he didn't look at her, concentrating instead on the patterned quilt on the bed. "Yes, I did." He straightened up abruptly and smoothed the blanket across her. "Now lie down."

She lay, wondering, her mind spinning.

"Sleep a while."

Before she realized it, he leaned over her again and brushed his soft, warm lips gently across hers—a feather-light touch, a promise, nothing more. Then he was crossing the room again.

"Griffin."

He stopped, his hand on the doorknob, and looked back over his shoulder at her. "Sleep," he said again, and his mouth lifted in a hint of his mind-dazzling smile.

"After I sleep, we need to talk," Lainie insisted.

The smile converted instantly into a grimace, followed by a look of resignation. "God help us, yes. If that's what you want."

She looked to see if, by chance, he had his fingers crossed, and she actually thought he might, but she smiled, anyway, convinced that if he had bothered to come back and to tell her that he loved her, she could surely talk him around. "I want," she told him softly but firmly. And this time she didn't mind so much when he pulled the door shut behind him. At least now she didn't feel as though he were shutting her out.

On the contrary, what had just happened was almost better than anything she could have imagined in her wildest dreams. He had walked back into her life totally of his own volition, and he had said that he loved her. Heavens. She settled down against her pillows, smiling all over her face, basking in the warm glow that arose from his declaration of love.

He must, she decided, have realized that he had been wrong to walk out on her in the first place. And he must have been awaiting the first opportunity to come back in such a way that would spare his pride. If he still felt the way he did when he left, he would have wasted no time in telling her, "I told you so." He had innumerable times.

She remembered best the weekend before he left to start work for the regular baseball season. He had been home for two weeks following an early stint in Florida at spring training, and she dragged home late several nights in a row because she was counseling one particular person who was severely depressed. Suicidal, she told Griff.

"How do you know he's not also homicidal?" he asked her, his tone matching the grimness in his face.

"He's not," she said, shaking her head at his ominous voice. "Relax."

But Griff hadn't relaxed. He had paced around their tiny apartment like a tiger in jeans, silently fuming while she ate cold leftover spaghetti that he had made for dinner.

Finally, he had stopped and confronted her. "It's not safe," he said.

"What's not safe?" she has asked, a sinking feeling surrounding the spaghetti in her stomach as she got an idea where the conversation was about to head.

"Your job."

"My job is as safe as yours," she told him.

"Some of the people you deal with are raving maniacs," he went on without stopping.

"So are some ballplayers I know," she countered.

He scowled. "It's not the same thing at all."

And it wasn't, she knew. But why did he have to be so negative?

"You deal with alcoholics, battered wives, abusive husbands!"

"I also deal with pregnant teenagers, the disenfranchised elderly, and even occasionally a banged-up baseball player like Brendan Craig!"

"The exception rather than the rule," he told her sourly. "You ought to quit, Lainie, before you get hurt."

"But I like my—" was as far as she got before he turned and walked out the door and down the steps to go for a long, solitary walk on the beach. It was, she remembered, as far as she ever got in that discussion with him.

And now, thanks to Dick Leary, she had got hurt. But the expected "I told you so" had never materialized. Maybe he had changed!

She snuggled down into the bed, then winced as she shifted her sore right shoulder. Damn Dick Leary, anyway, she thought, then changed her mind. Perhaps she really ought to be blessing him. He had contributed something useful, after all. He was the excuse Griff had used to come back. She gave a little laugh of satisfaction and nuzzled against the pillow, feeling for the first time since Griff had left her a notable peace of mind.

Things would be all right now, she was sure. This time they would make their marriage work! That decided, she closed her eyes, and it wasn't long until she slept.

THE MINUTE he got out of the bedroom for the second time, Griffin Tucker drew a long, shuddering breath and expelled it slowly. He wiped damp palms on the sides of his pants, his fingers trembling. Then he took the few steps to the long navy sofa and sank down. What had she thought when he had said that he loved her. He had almost expected her to laugh in his face, or worse, if that were possible, to look at him pityingly. That was the main reason that he hadn't waited around. Vulnerability was one thing; blatant, outright idiocy was something else.

But he knew there was no point in lying about it. He had been able to conceal a lot behind his poker face, but he knew he couldn't hide his love. The spark between them was too strong—one glimpse of her told him that hadn't changed—and she would only have had to look hard at him to read exactly what he was feeling right there in his eyes.

It would have been easier on his ego to have invented some trivial reason for coming back. It had been, in fact, tempting to blurt out, "I told you so," which, God knew, he had. But he figured she was smart enough to realize for herself that he had been right. Now was not the time to gloat. Besides, the minute he saw her, his concern overcame any desire he felt to be smug.

So, despite his discomfort, he was glad he had been honest with her, even though it made his knees still feel weak. But they were such complete opposites in so many ways that honesty was one of the few things they had going for them. If they were going to make a go of it this time, at least they had to have that.

He let the thudding of his heart slow down before he made a move to get up and make himself a cup of coffee. It was comforting somehow just to be home again. He had missed it, too. His hand strayed over the nubby blue fabric of the sofa, caressing it, since he couldn't, at the moment, caress his wife, and remembering the day they had bought it and the comfortable low-slung contemporary chair that matched it.

Those two pieces of furniture had been the first major purchases that they made together, the first stones, as it were, in the building of their marriage. Griff leaned his head back, smiling as he recalled how Lainie had positively horrified the salesclerk by bouncing up and down on the sofa cushions like a rambunctious child. He could still see her shoulder-length brown hair flipping up and down and the gleeful light in her sparkling hazel eyes. He had tried to sound stern and adult, saying, "Lainie! For heaven's sake!" because her exuberance embarrassed him.

But she had retorted, "This is research, Griff. How else will we know if this furniture will stand up under the onslaught of all of our children?"

Thinking about having children with Lainie had undermined his decorum entirely. Visions of little brown-haired, golden-eyed children made him grin, at first reluctantly. But the next thing he knew he had forgotten every one of his strict parents' instructions about not making a scene in public and succumbed to the temptation to bounce a bit on the sofa, too. The furniture had passed their test, and three days later it had been delivered to their nearly bare South Bay apartment to take up residence with the only other piece of furniture they owned—the double bed Lainie had brought with her from her mother's house in Hawthorne.

The apartment had gradually, and through their loving care, become their own. And looking around it now, Griff was aware of how very much he had been missing it. He loved his job, loved the travel, but he also loved the sense of permanence and support that this place had come to mean to him.

He had never told Lainie, because he thought it sounded maudlin and because he didn't think she would understand, as she came from a loving, warm home herself, but he considered the tiny apartment to be the first real home he had ever had. His parents' house in Santa Barbara, where he had grown up, had been nothing more than the backdrop for their continual battles. But he scarcely mentioned that to Lainie. When she asked about his family home and his childhood, he had told her his one continuing fond memory of the place—its proximity to the beach.

After graduating from high school, Griff had left there permanently, and his residences since then were nothing more than a series of college dorms and impersonal apartments, most recently a beachside apartment he had shared with Chase Whitelaw.

That, too, had meant little more to him than a place to store his things when he wasn't on the road, and it, too, had been close to the beach. But it could have been just another hotel room for all it meant to him. It was Chase's apartment, anyway. Griff just had a bedroom and access to the beach, which was all, until he met Lainie, he thought he wanted.

Lainie, who had shared a cramped three-bedroom tract house with her widowed mother and three single brothers, thought that the place he shared with Chase was wonderful, simply, he supposed, because only two people had to share it. And she was equally delighted when they found for themselves a tiny two-bedroom apartment almost on the beach in the next town up the coast. He had expected that she might want to find something a bit closer to her work— he was indulgent about it before they were married—but she had shaken her head.

"I love the beach, too," she told him. "I spent some of my happiest times there with my family when I was a child. Anyway, it doesn't matter how tiny the rooms are; we can always go outside."

Griff still wasn't totally convinced, but she had pirouetted around the bare rooms with her arms outspread, practically touching the opposite walls, he realized, and had insisted, "It's perfect. I love it." And she had flung her arms around him, her eyes shining with love.

He gave in, though he still couldn't find any more to recommend it than its location only half a block from the beach. He imagined that once they were in, she would see its shortcomings. But it was, in fact, only a few short weeks until he had become convinced that she was right.

Within a few weeks after they had returned from their Hawaiian honeymoon, Lainie had turned a dim, dank, two-bedroom hamster cage into a warm and welcoming home.

She spent Saturdays haunting secondhand shops and junk stores, dragging him in her wake, uncovering old dirty pieces of furniture that his mother would have consigned to the Salvation Army without a second glance.

"It'll look wonderful in front of the sofa," she would say of some long, dark monstrosity, and Griff would try to imagine it sitting there, like an overweight panther crouched in front of their sleekly modern sofa. But her enthusiasm was contagious, and he would let her have her way, figuring that when she tired of trying to turn her ugly-duckling piece of furniture into a swan, it wouldn't be hard to consign it to the trash heap.

But just as with the apartment, she was right, and he was wrong. Over the winter, dressers, commodes, end tables and an incredible variety of dismal-looking pieces evolved into warm, golden oak furniture with undeniable charm and homey character. Over the winter she had transformed the apartment and its furnishings into a welcoming environment that embraced him warmly the moment he stepped through the door.

It was a good thing, too, he reflected grimly now, for he had been there far more than she had over those months. Still, looking around himself now, he was amazed at the transformation that had taken place. She had converted everything—even him—with her enthusiasm. For if he had been reluctant at first, he soon found hinmself offering advice, then elbow grease, and as the months had passed, some of their happiest times were those when they had spent hours up to their eyeballs in paint remover, sanding sealer and tung oil.

The memories made his throat tighten, his eyes sting, and he got up quickly, prowling around the apartment, looking for evidence of what she had been working on since he had left. He sniffed the air for clues, seeking, he supposed, more memories—memories of scents that he hadn't known existed but which quickly became familiar to him and which, when connected with Lainie, were suddenly the most erotic scents in the world. But he could smell nothing now. No turpentine or varnish or anything remotely like it. He felt oddly let down. He looked all around the living room, then explored the spare bedroom thoroughly, but he couldn't find anything new. Odd. But then, he thought with a savagery that surprised him, maybe she hadn't had the time. Maybe her job had consumed her every waking moment. By the time he left, it had certainly been threatening to do that.

Fortunately, the phone rang before he could indulge in the self-pity that was threatening to attack him, and he quickly abandoned the bedroom and grabbed the phone on its second ring, hoping as he did so that it hadn't awakened Lainie.

"How is she?" Brendan asked when Griff answered.

"Okay, I guess. She's asleep right now."

"Is she?" Brendan sounded pleased. "Cassie will be delighted. How are you?" he asked, and Griff heard real concern in his voice when he asked this question, too.

"Surviving," he said. He'd feel a whole lot better when he knew that Lainie had safely quit her job and was staying home, refinishing furniture or, even better, coming along on the road for a while with him. But at least he wasn't plagued with fears of her horribly hurt and lying in the hospital, scenes with which he had become intimately acquainted during his long flight home on the red-eye.

"Good," Brendan said, "because I have a message from the league office for you."

Griff frowned. He had left Brendan's phone number in case of an emergency, figuring that he would be staying there with Lainie, at least the first day. But he also hadn't expected that they'd ever call him. They never had before. "What's up?" he asked.

"Vaughn Clevinger's wife is having her baby right now. He was on the team that was working the game here in town tonight. The closest sub is in Chicago. They want to know if you can cover for him.''

Griff stalled a moment, considering. Then he said, ''Yeah, I guess.'' He didn't really want to, but maybe it wouldn't be such a bad idea, after all. If he hovered over Lainie too much, it might not be smart. And tiptoeing around delicate situations was never his forte. He had always figured, from early childhood on, that absence was the better part of maintaining a good relationship. Besides, Lainie might still be asleep then, and he would be left to pace around the apartment, wondering what would happen when she awoke.

''Give them a call, then,'' Brendan advised. ''And you might try to get a few hours' sleep yourself before the game. You looked beat.''

''Maybe I will,'' Griff replied, though it was highly unlikely that he would. Sleep came to him lately only after sheer and complete physical exhaustion, and he didn't feel exhausted yet. Just tense.

''Hang in there,'' Brendan told him.

''Yes,'' he said, putting down the receiver. That was exactly what he had felt he had been doing for weeks, and still did for that matter. After all, he had flat out told her that he loved her. But she hadn't said anything about loving him.

He rubbed the taut muscles of his neck, trying to ease the increase in tension he felt. But he knew that his hands wouldn't be able to accomplish it. He needed to hear Lainie's words, assuring him of her love. He needed to hear her admit he had been right, that her job was too dangerous, that she was going to quit. He needed her to put him first for once, that was all!

He sagged onto the sofa and stretched out, deciding that Brendan's advice wasn't bad—if he could will himself asleep. He punched a couple of pillows and lay back, closing his eyes.

The phone rang.

"Damn." He jerked around, grabbing it. "H'lo."

A woman's rather whiny, nasal voice asked for Lainie.

"She's not available," he said. He knew that his tone was curt, but he didn't really care. No doubt it was another one of her clients, someone who desperately needed Lainie to hop on her white charger and sally forth to rescue her. Well, she wasn't going to. Not now. Not ever, if he had anything to say about it. Or at least not in the context of her job.

"Tell her Mavis Leary called," the woman told him. "It's important."

Important enough to get beat up for, Griff wanted to ask her. His jaw clenched, and he grunted an ackowledgment of the request. It was not, he decided, an agreement that he would do it. He hung up quickly.

He was damned if he was going to tell Lainie that Mavis Leary had called. He might owe her erstwhile husband, Dick, something for having provided him with a reason to come home, but that was all he owed any of them. And if Lainie owed them anything within the context of her job, well, her purplish eye and obviously painful ribs ought to make that account paid in full.

He was not going to tell her something that would have her grabbing for her car keys and running off out the door. She belonged here right now. He and Lainie needed time together—time without interruptions, without continual demands, without other people. They needed time, he thought as he settled back on the couch to wait for her to wake up, to try their marriage again. This time, he was sure, things would be better.

THERE WAS UTTER SILENCE in the apartment when Lainie awoke. The late-afternoon sun spilled across the quilt, and the bedside clock said five-thirty. She stared at it, surprised. She had only meant to doze, to wrap herself cozily in the dream come true she had experienced for just a little while. She had not meant to sleep away the whole afternoon. Especially not when Griffin was in the other room. Or was he?

Maybe it had been just a dream. Had Dick Leary hit her on the head? Probably. He hadn't missed much, she decided, wincing as she moved. But if it had beem a dream, it was the most vivid one she had ever experienced. She could still smell the lingering scent that she always identified with Griff—a combination of citrus shampoo and after-shave, salt spray and the heady masculine musk she enjoyed whenever she nuzzled against his neck or kissed the base of his throat. A spreading warmth grew within her now as she thought of him, and she struggled to sit up.

If Griffin really was in the other room, what was she doing wasting time in here?

Hauling herself out of bed, she shed the Berkeley T-shirt with some difficulty, then rummaged through her closet to find a scoop-necked blouse in rainbow pastels that she pulled off the hanger with a tiny murmur of satisfaction. She could remember Griff running his fingers along its low lacy neckline, and buttoning it up, her fingers trembled. She pulled on a pair of snug-fitting jeans and assessed the finished product in the beveled glass mirror. Not bad. Her body, womanly curves and full breasts, would be attractive at least. There wasn't much she could do about her face, she thought ruefully as she touched her swollen, discolored eye. Remembering that he had already seen it, she was surprised for the first time that he had made no comment. Maybe he really had been a dream. She ran a brush through her shoulder-length hair, glad that the right-side swath could droop sightly over her eye and artfully disguise some of the damage. She did what she could, half fearing and half wishing that Griff would walk through the door so that she would not have to make an entrance. But even when she dropped the brush accidentally and it clattered on the dresser top, he didn't come. She frowned, realizing that since she had been up, she hadn't heard a sound from the other side of the door.

Impatiently, not caring what she looked like now, she shoved open the door. Griff lay sprawled out, fast asleep, on the couch, his white shirt unbuttoned, his feet bare, his hand dangerously close to knocking a full cup of obviously stone-cold coffee that sat on the coffee table in front of the couch.

For a moment Lainie just stared, drinking in the sight of him. She let her eyes wander greedily over the golden burr of whiskers on his cheeks and along the line of his jaw. Moving downward, her gaze lingered over his partially exposed chest with its mat of curling blond hair; then it traveled past his wide leather belt and along the twill outline of his powerful legs. The physical Griffin was as attractive as ever. It was, she thought with a sigh, the mental and emotional Griffin that she never seemed to completely understand. For a while they would exist in harmony and companionship and yes, love, and then suddenly, without warning, he would withdraw, close up, fence a part of himself off. She never completely understood why, and asking him to explain didn't help. Explaining, she had discovered, wasn't something Griffin did.

But if they did nothing but eat, sleep and make love, what a heavenly relationship they would have, she thought wryly. Limited, no doubt, but heavenly just the same. It was when he opened his eyes and she opened her mouth that the trouble began. Right now, for example, she hadn't the faintest idea what they would say when he woke up and they had to begin to talk things over.

"My God, I'm late!" Griffin said.

Lainie, who had been contemplating his bare feet while she contemplated their relationship, jerked her gaze back up to his face, startled. Griff's eyes were wide open, staring in consternation at the watch on his wrist.

"Late for what?" she asked as he struggled up and lurched to his feet.

"The game. I'm working tonight. Fluornoy's covering for me in Cincinnati, but Bren called and said that Clevinger's wife was having a baby and so they wanted me to cover for him here, and..." These statements, which had begun so matter-of-factly, trailed off slowly as he apparently recollected where he was and why he was there. Yawning behind the back of his hand, he stood flat-footed, his stance wary as he regarded her closely. As if she might attack, Lainie thought.

"I—I see." What she saw was the incredible amount of trouble he had gone to in order to be with her, and the prickling worry that she had entertained since she had awakened that he might not really have meant what he said about loving her vanished. She gave him a blinding smile.

He didn't see it. He had bent over and was rummaging beneath the sofa, looking for his shoes.

"Griff?" She crossed the room and knelt next to him, touching his arm.

He flinched, reaching for his shoe, avoiding her gaze.

"Thanks," she said.

He looked at her then, surprise flickering in the brown depths of his eyes. "Don't mention it," he said gruffly, but he met her smile with a tentative one of his own. It was, she thought, rather as if they were two skaters standing on opposite sides of a thinly iced pond, each wanting to reach the other and neither certain about how much weight the situation could bear.

"I just wanted you to know I appreciate your coming," she explained awkwardly. She moved to perch on the arm of the sofa as if poised for flight. "You must be tired still," she said to his back as he fished out his second shoe.

"Some."

What stunning conversationalists we are, Lainie thought. But she supposed she shouldn't be surprised. A lot of their previous conversation had been nonverbal. There had been such an immediate attraction and rapport between them that they had seemed to be on the same wavelength from the first, barring, of course, his periodic withdrawals. But those had appeared only after their marriage, and especially as spring training had approached, their lines of communication had developed a terrible case of interference. Now she wished they had more practice talking with each other about things that mattered. God knew they needed it.

Griff was stuffing his feet into his socks and shoes. Then he stood up and began to take off his shirt. ''I have to shave,'' he said quickly when he noticed her obvious interest in the proceedings. She hoped he couldn't hear her sigh, or if he did, that he didn't realize it stemmed from disappointment, not relief.

He didn't want to be taking his shirt off to shave. He wanted to take everything off and go to bed with her. He had to hurry away into the bathroom, or very likely he would have done just that. If anyone was capable of undermining his resolve, it was Lainie. But he had promised he would show up tonight. And show up he would. She still might not have said she loved him, but at least she looked interested in him, and that was something, at least.

In fact, he didn't have time to shave. He needed to leave in less than fifteen minutes if he was going to get to the ballpark on time. Damn, he hadn't meant to fall asleep, but the night on the plane and the worry about Lainie, preceded by an entire month of virtual insomnia, had rendered him unconscious shortly after his head hit the pillow.

He ducked his head under the faucet, trying to wake up and get a sense of perspective. The icy water sluiced down over the back of his head, then on over his stubbled cheeks, bringing him back to reality. He lifted his head, letting the water stream down his face as he groped for a towel. Miraculously, it appeared in his hands. He took it without thinking, rubbing his face and hair briskly. Then, realizing who must have handed it to him, he lowered it slightly so that he peered above its lime-colored terry-cloth softness and met the uncertain gaze of his wife.

"Griff?"

"Mmm?"

The smile she offered him was the most hesitant he had ever seen on her face. "I love you, too."

She said it so softly that with the water in his ears he thought he might have imagined it. But the uncertain hope he saw flickering in her eyes convinced him that he had heard right. He shook his head, water drops flying everywhere.

"You do?"

She nodded jerkily. Griff blinked, then swallowed, admiring her courage. He hadn't been able to stand his ground, looking at her with his heart in his eyes, when he had said the same thing to her. A corner of his mouth quirked up in a tiny smile, and he lifted his hand to touch the skin of her cheek just below the bruised eye, doing what he had ached to do ever since the moment he had walked in the door.

"I'm sorry about your eye," he told her softly. "I'm sorry it had to happen. Any of it." His finger traced the barest edge of the purple, and it must have been tender, but she didn't draw away. He dropped his hand and shut his eyes tightly as he clenched his fists. God, he hated the bastard who had done this to her! If he had been here, he would have— He forced open his eyes to meet her curious stare, then drew in a long and very unsteady breath. Maybe it was a good thing he hadn't been here, he thought. And anyway, now she would quit and everything would be all right. His smile, which had vanished, now returned more fully, and he bent his head to kiss her gently on the lips.

The touch of her soft skin against his was almost more than he could take. He had kissed her countless times, but never any that had mattered to him more than this one, never any that made him so aware of her as a woman, as his wife. Shuddering, he drew back. "God, Lainie, I want you so."

Her hands reached up, touching his upper arms, her thumbs brushing against the sensitive skin on the inner sides, making him shiver. "Yes," she murmured. "Me too."

He smiled somewhat raggedly. "We can't. Not now."

Lainie frowned, then remembered. "Ah, yes, the game."

"Uh-huh." He went back into the living room and opened his suitcase, ferreting out a clean shirt and putting it on. Doing so with her watching, the light of desire still lambent in her eyes, was one of the most difficult things he had ever done.

He wanted to ask her to come with him. He wished, in fact, that he had said no to umpiring the game. It seemed insane to leave her now, when they were both at the threshold of finding each other again.

"I'll be back as soon as I can," he promised.

"I'll wait up."

"No, get some rest."

"We'll see," she said, and for an instant he scowled, wishing just once she would do what he said. But then, thinking that it might in fact be nice if she did wait up for him, he turned his frown into a smile.

"Do whatever you want."

And she tried to stay awake; truly she did. She made herself a chicken pot pie for dinner, though the garbage disposal ate more than she did. And then she turned on the radio to listen to the game. It was long and not particularly exciting. She thought Griff's feet would probably hurt by the end of it and entertained herself for a while by fantasizing about a massage she could give him that would begin with his feet and end— Well, she knew exactly where it would end. She decided to wait there for him and got into bed.

She shut the light out and lay back, listening to the game, to the faint roar of the waves, to the steady slap of jogging footfalls and the occasional barking dog that passed beneath her open window. And she was certain that in this historic moment she would lie awake for hours. After all, it wasn't every day that a woman who had nearly lost all hope got her husband back for a second chance.

She rolled over onto her side of the bed, making sure that Griff's side had the covers turned back welcomingly; then she waited impatiently for him to come home and their reconciliation to begin.

She had never had very many kind thoughts about Mavis Leary's husband, Dick, but she spared him a grateful one now. It was, just as she was always telling Mavis, a matter of persistence. Eventually, things worked out.

Chapter Three

For almost two months Griffin had dreamed of waking like this—the morning sun spilling through the sheer lace curtains of their bedroom and he and Lainie held fast in each other's arms. He lifted his head fractionally from the pillow to nuzzle against the softness of her cheek, drawing in the subtle fragrance of soap and roses mixed with the sleepy softness of Lainie herself.

She smiled in her sleep, stretching her limbs, then wincing as if her muscles still ached. Then her eyes flicked open, and she stared at him, first in surprise and then with a gradually dawning welcome.

"Good morning."

Her voice was as soft as her cheek against the roughness of his three day's growth of beard. She raised her hand and brought it up to stroke the side of his face, her palm warm as it caressed him. Her fingers traced the tiny lines at the corner of his eye, then her thumb dropped to brush tantalizingly against his lips. He caught her hand and held it, kissing her thumb and fingers in turn, then planting an extra kiss in her palm. She smiled.

"Good morning, yourself," he growled softly, and rolled onto his back carefully, exercising the utmost caution so that he didn't inadvertently hurt her further. He drew her on top of him so that she stretched almost his length, her toes tickling the tops of his feet, his hips cradling hers, her mouth on a line with the sensitive spot at the base of his throat where she immediately bent her head to press her lips to the edges of the tangle of blond curls that covered most of his chest.

She lifted her head, and her eyes met his, a spark of desire kindling between them. Her hands came up to frame his face, her thumbs outlining his cheekbones with velvet softness, her fingers playing with the hair at his temples, then with the outer shell of his ears. Every inch of him was awakening, becoming instinctively aware of her moves, her touches. Last night, when he had finally got home, she was already asleep, and though he had ached to wake her and love her, he hadn't done it. Somehow he had contained his needs, realizing that rest and sleep were most necessary to her.

But this morning, with her hands working a magic on his body, her eyes entrancing him, he knew the time had come. Quivering beneath her, he longed to be a part of her now, wanted her to be a part of him. It had been so long. Too long. But that was why, in spite of his need, he knew he had to move slowly. This was a loving that needed to be savored, to be shared with infinite patience because they had both waited for it so long.

"Lainie?" He knew his voice shook, betraying his need for her, as if she couldn't feel the readiness of his body beneath hers.

"Griff."

His had been a question, but hers was an answer. She smiled at him, the same warm, loving smile full of promise that she had given him on their wedding day, the same smile that he had fallen in love with the first moment he saw her.

Tensing, he bit down on his lip and clenched his hands at his sides to keep from stripping off her gown and pressing her tightly against him in the wave of unchecked passion that was all too close to inundating him.

Lainie seemed to sense his struggle for control. She rose to her knees above him, her hands leaving his face only to travel seductively down his chest, stroking him gently as her fingers wandered across his ribs, then circled his nipples and moved to the center and then lower.

Griff trembled. Lainie's eyes flamed as he looked into them, and he felt her shudder as she licked her lips, and he knew that she had no more control than he did. Both of them were teetering close to the edge.

He lifted his arms and skimmed the pale yellow gown over her head, marveling at the beauty of her creamy white breasts as his hands moved to cup them. Then, having stroked and circled them as she had done to him, he let his hands drift lower, holding back, making himself go slowly, exploring her body with a thoroughness that belied his need and yet fed the fires of it at the very same time.

Beneath her right breast there were bruises, and he touched them with infinite gentleness, wanting to soothe her and take away her pain. He couldn't, he knew. But perhaps he could share it. He felt an instinctive tightening in his whole body that had nothing to do with passion. It was anger at the man who had done this to her and anger at her being in such a dangerous position. And there was, if he were honest, more than a little anger at himself for not having been able to prevent it. Lainie's hands trapped his fingers and removed them, lacing her fingers with his, leading them away from her pain.

"It's all right," she murmured, and though he shook his head to deny it, she persisted.

"Love me," she urged him, and her hands let go of his, capturing instead that part of him that most yearned for her touch.

He arched off the bed as she drew him inside, surrounding him with her warmth, and suddenly his mind was wiped clean of his worry and her pain.

"Ah, Lainie!" he groaned, twisting on the bed, his heart pounding so violently he thought it would burst right out of his chest. His hands delighted in her, caressing, stroking, bringing her the same joy she brought him. Slowly at first, then with increasing urgency, until waves of release broke over both of them, they moved together. He closed his eyes, totally spent, as Lainie collapsed against his chest, warm and damp, her heart thundering in accompaniment with his own.

"My God," he whispered, shaken, and wondered how he had lived without her so long. With his hand he stroked her dark tangled hair, threading its softness through his fingers, loving it, loving her. "Ah, Lainie, love," he murmured. "I love you so."

She raised her head off his chest, smiling her contented-cat smile. "I never would have guessed."

He grinned. "Skeptic," he pronounced. "Want more proof?"

She laughed, nuzzling her nose against his whiskery cheek, then nipping at his bristled chin. "Are you up to it?" she teased, her eyes roving down his body as she pulled away from him and noted his state of obvious fulfillment.

Griff groaned. "Bad puns will get you nowhere, my love."

"What will?" Lainie asked, using her most seductive voice. It alone had the power to arouse him, and given a few more minutes, he was sure it would arouse him, helped along by the busy involvement of her hands.

The phone rang.

"Don't answer it," he said quickly. He didn't want intrusions now, not when they had just found each other again.

But Lainie sat up, shaking her loose dark hair away from her face and saying apologetically, "I have to. It might be Cassie."

"So what?"

"So if she doesn't get an answer, you can bet she and Brendan will be hotfooting it right on over to see what's wrong."

Griff lifted himself up on one elbow. "She ought to be able to figure out what's right," he argued, but Lainie disagreed. The phone rang again.

"No. If you remember, when she called yesterday, things were not yet all goodness and harmony between us."

Griff scowled. "And you don't think she imagines things will change?" The phone rang.

"I think she'd check," Lainie said honestly, looking at him with one wide innocent eye and one puffy one.

Griff sighed, considering that, remembering yesterday and the assessing looks and not quite trusting tones he had received from Cassie, as well as the promise she had extracted from him before he left her house. "I guess you're right." He shrugged. But he needn't have bothered, because by that time Lainie had made up her mind and was on her way to the living room to answer it. Griff frowned, disliking the intrusion even if it was Cassie Craig. Now, of all times, he wanted his wife to himself.

He was still fuming five minutes later when she came back.

"Cassie?" he asked abruptly. He had got up and was sitting naked on the tousled bed, his arms wrapped around his knees, his blond hair mussed and attractive, and Lainie wanted to throw her arms around him. She also wanted a welcoming smile from him, and she wasn't getting it. Now what was wrong?

"No," she said, snuggling against him on the bed, pushing him back into the covers. "My mother."

If anything, his scowl deepened. "What'd she want?"

"To talk. But I told her you were home and we were busy." She teased his ribs with her fingernails. "We are busy, aren't we?"

For a second she sensed a struggle within him, as if he might reject her, might say no. But her hands didn't let up, nor did she relinquish him from her gaze, and gradually she felt the release of the breath he had been holding and saw his mouth twist into a smile. "Yes," he whispered, and his hands sought her.

This time he wasn't as gentle, but Lainie didn't care. She knew how much his restraint the first time had cost him. He had held back then, giving, sharing, urging her to match his lingering touches until they had both clamored for release together. But this time he needed something else. Affirmation? A proof of her love? Her acceptance?

She didn't know for certain; she was only sure that his need this time was urgent, demanding, possessive. And so she welcomed him, meeting his passion with her own, his cries with hers, until once more they lay, damp and exhausted, among the tangle of covers and she watched the ocean breeze ruffle the sheer lace curtains.

"Griff?" Her hand stroked through his thick blond hair as she wondered at his urgency, at this man who said he loved her—who, she believed, did love her but whom, in many ways, she did not even begin to know.

He raised his head from her breasts, his eyes filled with concern, almost remorse. "Did I hurt you?"

"No," she said softly, her hand still stroking his damp hair. "Not at all."

"I'm sorry," he muttered. "I just needed—" He stopped, clearly groping for some way to explain what he had felt.

She wished desperately that he could find the words, could explain and help her understand what was going on inside his head. But at last he simply shook his head.

"Need you," he finished in a whisper, and he gave an awkward, almost apologetic shrug.

Lainie's hand skimmed down his perspiration-slicked back. "Good," she said in a voice that matched his. "I'm glad." Sometimes she had wondered. Griffin Tucker always seemed so incredibly self-sufficient and independent that it was hard to believe he needed anyone. It made her feel warm and loved, indeed, when he said he needed her.

"What shall we do today?" he asked, rolling over onto his back and looking up at the ceiling. Lainie sensed a momentary tension in him that she didn't understand, but she saw it vanish immediately when she propped herself up carefully on her unsore side and said, "Whatever you want."

Griff raised himself up so that he was leaning back on his elbows and looked at her, a teasing light coming into his eyes. "Horseback riding?" he suggested deadpan.

Lainie laughed. "Trust you!" She touched her ribs and shoulder gingerly. "Almost anything you want, then."

Griff grinned. "Let's have a shower, and then we can decide."

The shower, as it happened, took the better part of the morning, interrupted as it was by Griff's tender caresses and Lainie's minute inspection of every inch of Griff's body.

"Forget what I looked like?" he asked, laughing as she turned him around under the water, running her hands over him, making him hot all over again.

"Never!" Her hands slid down over his belly, then farther. "I remember everything about you." And she proceeded to prove to him that she did.

The rest of the day was touched by the same magic. Griff cooked her a huge breakfast, spoiling her totally by insisting that she prop herself up against the pillows in their bed and wait to be served. Afterward, though, he let her do the dishes.

"I knew you were setting me up!" she complained, smiling as she did so. And he came up behind her and kissed her neck.

"Of course," he said. "Feel like a bike ride? Are you up for that?"

Lainie moved her arms up and down experimentally. "I think so. As long as we go on the walk along the beach. It's smooth. Besides—" she brightened "—you can do all the pedaling."

The bike had been an extravagance when they had bought it last winter. But Griff liked cycling far more than she did, and when he had said, "If you're so lazy, we'll get one built for two, then," she had jumped at it. And the few times they had got to use it had been among her happiest memories. It seemed fitting somehow that they would ride today.

The day was bright, the early-morning overcast having rolled back just far enough offshore to bathe the wide, sandy beach in warm, golden sunlight. Griff hauled the bike out of the garage and met Lainie in front of the apartment.

"You take the front," he said. "If I'm going to do the pedaling, I'd be better off back here. Besides," he added as she got on, "I like the view."

Lainie turned and stuck her tongue out at him, but in fact she felt almost deliriously happy. The more so, she thought, for having felt so miserable before. But she shoved those memories right out of her head. It was enough now that he was here, that he was being supportive, that he had come back.

They rode several miles south, stopping once at a coffee house and record store just off the beach where they drank dark Turkish coffee strong enough to varnish furniture with and poked their way through stacks of old records left over from the fifties and sixties. Then, going farther south, they reached the pier at Redondo. Griff locked the bike in one of the racks and took Lainie's hand. She smiled at the feel of the rough fingers that wrapped around hers, and she squeezed his hand lightly as she walked beside him out onto the pier.

Part of her wanted to talk, to begin to sort out the things that had kept them apart for these weeks. But the afternoon was too lovely to spoil, too heavenly to darken with heavy subjects. If Griff brought it up, she would welcome it. But she wasn't going to force things, not now. Instead, she drew him over to one of the fresh fish markets and peered down into one of the tanks.

"How about lobster for supper?" she asked him.

"Sounds good," he agreed. "Have you ever cooked one?"

She shook her head. "No, have you?"

"Softhearted me?" Griff scoffed. "Throw a poor defenseless creature in a pot of boiling water? You must be kidding."

Lainie blanched, having forgotten that part of the deal. "You don't suppose they would knock it on the head here for us, do you?"

"I doubt it." He grinned at her. "Are you game?"

"Are you?"

They looked at each other helplessly, smiles threatening. Then Lainie said, "How about tuna casserole instead?"

"Fine with me," he said, lifting his arm and putting it around her shoulders gently, carefully, so he wouldn't hurt her. They completed the circle of the pier, stopping to watch a small boy land a fish no bigger than his hand and for Lainie to buy a floppy sun hat that Griff said made her look like his grandmother but which she thought at least masked her still-purplish, puffy eye. Then he glanced at his watch and said they ought to head back.

"I have to be at the ballpark about five-thirty."

He led her back to the bike, unlocked it and held it while she got on. Then he stopped before getting on himself and asked almost hesitantly, "How about coming with me? To the game, I mean."

Lainie tipped her head back and looked up at him from beneath the brim of her new hat.

"Please?" he added when she didn't answer at once.

His smile was tentative, as if he knew he was stepping into dangerous territory. But, Lainie thought, why not? "All right,'' she said, and smiled back at him. "That sounds like a good idea.''

Griff grinned then, his relief evident on his face. "I'm glad,'' he said. "I'm really glad.''

Lainie decided that she was, too. Going with him to the game would be an excellent way to show him that she was ready and willing to work things out, that she would try to do some things his way if he would try to compromise with her. And she had always enjoyed baseball games, even though now she was constrained from rooting for the home team because someone might think her husband was playing favorites, too. She could not understand how Griff could remain so impartial. But he was.

Griff belonged to no one, and nowhere was it more evident than on the baseball field. Unless, she thought, it was in their relationship. But then, she didn't belong to him, either. And he needed to realize that. Today they had had a wonderful experience of simply sharing with each other. Tonight, after the game, maybe they could sit down and actually begin to talk out their differences.

Why was she saying maybe? Of course they could. Talking things out was what she did for a living, wasn't it? She smiled as she pedaled homeward, surging into the wind, with Griff pedaling in rhythm behind her. She grinned over her shoulder at him, feeling far more confident than she had in a long, long time.

SHE SHOULD HAVE KNOWN it wouldn't be as simple as that. Their courtship might have been an exercise in perfect harmony and their winter disturbed by only occasional silences on Griff's part when she was late or when she didn't do what he wanted. But since baseball season had started, nothing in their relationship had seemed to go right at all.

They were just about to leave for the game—in fact, Griff was already getting out the car—when Mavis Leary phoned.

Lainie's first instinct was to hang up, to say, "Sorry, ma'am, you have the wrong number," and bolt out the door before Mavis could check it and ring back again. But she had been in her line of work too long and had too much dedication to do that. Mavis wouldn't call unless she needed to talk to her, so she let Mavis talk.

Not long. Just, she thought with a sinking heart as she went to meet Griff at the car and pretend that nothing had changed, long enough to agree to meet Mavis at the hospital at nine.

"Why so late?" Mavis had demanded, tearful and apprehensive.

"Because I'm going to be tied up until then," Lainie told her, knowing that if Griff had anything to say about it, she wouldn't be meeting Mavis at all. But he wouldn't know. Although one look at the tender smile on his face as she slipped into the car beside him and she felt about two inches high and guilty as hell.

"I'm really glad you're coming along," he told her, and leaned across to brush his lips along her cheek.

Lainie ducked her head miserably, hating herself for her deceit. "Me, too," she mumbled. She couldn't look at him, not without blurting out the truth. And not without precipitating the fight to end all fights right here in the alley in front of God and the neighborhood. "It's a lovely night for a ball game," she went on.

Griff agreed. He was humming, not even perturbed by the freeway snarls that in the past had occasionally driven him nearly to distraction. They would have tonight, too, Lainie thought, if he knew what she was going to do.

Well, thank God, he didn't. And never would, if she could help it. Surely Mavis wouldn't talk too long, probably just enough to get her feelings about Dick into perspective. Then Lainie could get back to the ballpark. It wouldn't take more than half an hour at that time of night. Unless it was the fastest game in history, Griff would never miss her, nor would he ever know unless Cassie or someone else at the hospital mentioned seeing her.

Damn, she hated deceiving him this way. If only he would be reasonable and see Mavis Leary as a person with tremendous needs that had to be met and not just a chore that could be put off until the next time it was convenient to deal with her. She clenched her fists tightly in her lap, and Griff shot her a concerned glance.

"Hey, are you okay? Still hurting?"

"No, no, I'm fine," she fibbed. It was her conscience hurting this time. It shouldn't be, she told herself fiercely. If Griffin were not so stubborn about her job, so sure that he had the only answer, she wouldn't have to resort to things like this. But it didn't help a moment later when he hit a clear enough patch on the freeway that he wasn't constantly shifting gears and was then able to rest his arm along the back of her seat. His fingers trailed tantalizingly along the back of her neck, and she shivered.

"Griff! Watch the road!" she commanded, twitching away from his touch. But he just laughed.

"I am, I am," he assured her. "But I can't just sit here half a foot away from you and not touch you, can I? I've missed you."

"I missed you, too." She ventured a glance at him then, forcibly putting Mavis Leary and all her problems to the very back of her mind and letting herself concentrate on the man she loved. "We still haven't talked," she said softly.

He raised an eyebrow but didn't say anything.

"After the game?" she suggested.

Griff shifted slightly. "If you want," he said offhandedly.

He didn't feel offhand in the least. He wanted to say, "What's to talk about? Quit the damned job and come with me, or at least find a reasonable job that lets you have a life of your own," because they loved each other.

She couldn't have acted the way she had all day if she hadn't loved him; she wouldn't have said she loved him if she didn't. But now, he knew, was not the time to press the issue. It was enough that she had come to the game with him. And if tonight she wanted to talk, well, all right, he would talk. He would tell her politely once and for all exactly what he thought, but the results would be the same.

And then, thank God, they would be together again.

GRIFF WISHED all his problems were as easily solved as that one. But a new visiting team had arrived today to play the Mustangs, and the minute he saw the lineup, he sensed trouble.

LaRue. Disaster in five letters.

He shut his eyes and wondered at God's sense of humor in letting him on a field with Wes LaRue so soon after their last encounter. By rights he would have left Cincinnati and gone to Pittsburg today, and LaRue would have come here. Now here they were, together again. Damn.

Only twenty-two years old, Wes LaRue was in his second season of major league baseball. Last year a runner-up for the Rookie of the Year, he had demonstrated that he had the potential to be one of the finest power hitters in the game— if he settled down. But so far this season, as far as Griff could see, the *if* loomed larger and larger. Always prone to striking out, a not uncommon tendency among power hitters, LaRue seemed to be pressing, trying too hard. And the more he tried, the more he struck out; and the more he struck out, the more irascible he got.

Recently his temper had become both fierce and unpredictable. His mood swings were apparent even on the field. The night before last in Cincinnati, he had come close to decking Griff over a called third strike. And it turned into the fourth time in the relatively young season that Griff had ejected him from the game.

Dan Fletcher, one of the members of Griff's umpiring unit, had jokingly asked him if he "had it in for LaRue." Privately, Griff wondered if it wasn't the other way around.

LaRue seemed almost looking for trouble, and with his generally abusive behavior, he found poker-faced, implacable Griffin Tucker a thorn in his side.

It was good, Griff decided as he walked down the long corridor toward the diamond, that he was on the third-base line tonight. It made the chances of another confrontation less likely. If Lainie hadn't had her run-in with Dick Leary and if Clevinger's wife hadn't had her baby, he would not have had to see LaRue until Chicago just before the all-star break. But he would face LaRue every day of the week, he decided, if it meant getting Lainie back.

He smiled, peering up into the stands behind the dugout, trying to see Lainie in her seat above the first-base line. *Think about the good things,* he counseled himself. For the first time in weeks, things were going the way he thought they ought to. Not even LaRue could bother him now.

Lainie's seat was back about ten rows, halfway between first base and home plate. She could see Griff perfectly, but, she hoped, he couldn't see her because of the rather ample gentleman sitting in front of her. Also, she didn't know anyone seated nearby, which she considered fortunate. She hadn't expected to, but with her luck this could have been the night that Brendan would have brought Keith and Steven to watch his old teammates in action. But happily he was nowhere to be seen, and she would have actually enjoyed the opportunity to watch the game if she had not been so worried about having to leave once it got started. She even found herself examining the cloudless Southern California sky to see if there was a possibility that the game might be canceled because of rain before she would be able to get back.

Griff looked her way more than once, obviously trying to spot her in the stands. She wanted to wave to him. But if she did, what would he think if he looked up here later on and she was gone? So she sat on her hands, deliberately keeping a low profile, counting the minutes until she had to leave to meet Mavis at the hospital.

She almost didn't make it, because in the bottom of the first inning Griff called a player out at a third and the man positively exploded on the spot, screaming so loudly she could hear him even over the roar of the crowd. She immediately lost interest in her digital watch, turning her undivided attention instead to Griff.

Her husband stood his ground, staring at the runner with imperturbable calm. The man stomped and kicked, raging at Griff, doing, Lainie thought with a certain wry amusement, exactly what she sometimes felt like doing herself. Griff refused to respond, turning away instead and motioning for play to resume. Suddenly, without warning, the enraged runner lunged for Griff's back. Clearly startled, Griff stumbled, then regained his balance and shook the man off just as his teammates converged to pull him away.

Griff's thumb traveled a short arc in the air, and no one disputed that, except, of course, the man who had just been ejected. But his teammates prevailed, and they practically dragged him away.

"Good riddance," the man next to her said, biting down on his hotdog.

"Who was it?" she asked him, though she wasn't watching, as was most of the crowd, as he left the field. Her eyes were solely on Griff. He seemed to shake himself slightly, then glanced over toward where she sat as if he wondered what she thought of what happened. Then, calmly, without further ado, he got in a position again, and the game resumed.

"Wes LaRue," the man told her. "Fantastic hitter. Lucky for the Mustangs he's gone."

Lucky for everyone, Lainie would have said. He seemed like a far worse threat to have to face than poor old obnoxious Dick Leary. But she couldn't see herself convincing Griff of that. In fact, that image of Griff, stony and silent in the face of anger, stayed with her all through her hurried drive on the San Diego Freeway toward the hospital. He was such a mystery, such an enigma, her husband. She could no more have remained impassive in the face of a display such as Wes LaRue put on than she could fly to the moon. She would have punched LaRue in the nose; she was sure of it. She certainly hadn't let Dick Leary get in his pokes at her unreciprocated! But Griff had. He had just walked away.

"Like he walked away from you," she mumbled aloud as she flicked on the turn signal, glad that the hospital was looming up on her right. "But he came back," she added firmly in an attempt to convince herself that he had changed his mind, at least regarding his behavior toward her, and that everything would really be all right.

It would be, too, if Mavis didn't come up with some insurmountable problems and she was able to get back before the game ended. She sent up a fervent prayer as she parked her car that there would be lots of foul balls and full counts. A long game and a short problem were what she needed tonight.

Mavis Leary had seen more of life's harsher side in her forty-one years than most people saw in three lifetimes. Dick was only one among many, all of which she loved to regale Lainie with at length. He was not the source of her troubles tonight. Tonight she was distraught about her son, Frankie, who had got picked up for car theft and who was at that moment languishing in jail. Couldn't Lainie get him out, Mavis wanted to know.

Lainie, though she felt sorry for the woman, had an idea that the son took more after his father than her. Even if she could have, she wasn't sure she wanted to.

"I'm afraid it's not possible," she told Mavis gently, giving her a faint smile that connoted more regret than she actually felt.

"But Frankie just got himself a job," Mavis wailed. "He needs that job."

Then he shouldn't have stolen that car, Lainie thought. But the knowledge that Frankie actually had employment made her reconsider. The least she could do was look into it. If he was more victim, like Mavis, than perpetrator, like Dick, perhaps she could vouch for him.

"Let me make a couple of calls," she said, and was rewarded with a watery Mavis Leary smile.

Those calls led to more calls and finally a visit to the jail itself. Frankie was still there, but at least Mavis had got to visit with him, and Lainie was satisfied that job or no job, it was where he ought to be. The Camaro was, it turned out, not the first car he had taken a liking to and driven away in. Still, she had to admit, after she had talked to him at great length, that he didn't seem like a bad kid, just a misguided one. Maybe if she could talk to him when he got out, help him get some good vocational training, he would straighten out. She thought he would. She told Mavis that she would call his court-appointed lawyer in the morning.

"You can help Frankie, can't you?" Mavis asked her as they walked out of the law enforcement center together.

"I'll do my best," Lainie said, and meant it. She certainly didn't want him to turn out like his father.

"You're a good girl," Mavis told her, giving her a pat on the cheek. "I wish my Frankie was a bit older. You'd be just right for each other."

"I'm married," Lainie said automatically, and for the first time since she had walked into her office tonight and found Mavis in tears, she gave a thought to Griff.

Oh, my God. It was well past midnight; the game had to have been long over. What would Griff be thinking? "Heaven help me," she said to Mavis, "I've got to run." She began sprinting toward the parking lot.

Married?

After this she could only hope she was.

HE FELT LIKE A FOOL calling the hospitals, but what else could he do? My God, she had been missing for heaven knew how long. He hadn't seen her for hours. He had looked for her during the game, had guessed more or less where she would be sitting, but he hadn't caught a glimpse of her. He wondered now if she had even got to her seat.

He had expected to find her waiting for him near the umpires' dressing rooms, and when she hadn't been there, he had gone out to where they had left the car. It was gone. Frantic, he had searched, called in ballpark security and made them search, but when the lot emptied, he'd had to accept that she simply wasn't there.

So where was she? He had wondered if she had tired and had gone on home. It didn't seem likely, but he had called home, anyway. There was no answer. And there had been absolutely nothing he could do at the ballpark once he knew she was gone, but he had got into a rare state of agitation as he waited for a taxi to pick him up. But when he arrived, everything was dark. Sick to his stomach, he had slowly climbed the steps and let himself in.

Now, a cold sweat breaking out on his face, he punched out the numbers of all the hospitals he could find in the Los Angeles County phone directories, starting with those closest to the ballpark. None of them had any admissions that night that remotely sounded like Lainie. There were no twenty-eight-year-old women with shoulder-length brown hair, ivory skin and hazel eyes and—he shuddered now just thinking about them—bruises on her face and ribs.

He had stumbled over telling the emergency-room clerks about the bruises, knowing what they were thinking, trembling at the thought himself. Sinking down onto the couch in despair, he wondered if, in fact, they would even tell him if she was there if they thought he was the one who had beaten her.

He glanced at his watch. Past midnight. Where was she? How could she have just walked out on him like that? Had she been abducted? He moaned, then rubbed his hands through his hair and jumped to his feet, pacing the length of the tiny living room, then staring out the window at the silvery moonlit sidewalk, wishing he could see her walking toward him.

He wondered, not for the first time, if he should call the police. But what would he tell them? That his semiestranged wife had gone to a baseball game while he umpired and wasn't there when he finished?

The more he thought about it, the less he thought they would do anything. "Estranged?" they would say, as if that explained everything. And then they would add, "She's an adult, she can do as she pleases."

And what could he say to that? He had no intention of baring his soul to them, either. *But where was she?*

At twelve forty-five he couldn't stand his own imagination any longer. He called Brendan Craig.

"What do you mean, she's missing?" Brendan demanded, obviously fighting his way out of a deep sleep.

"I took her to the game, and when it was over and I came out, she wasn't there." He felt like a first-rate idiot, saying it, but he couldn't bear the worry alone any longer.

"Wasn't there?" Brendan echoed. Griff knew that he was still working himself up to full consciousness.

"Wasn't there," Griff repeated. "Not anywhere."

"Did you fight?"

"No!"

"Don't shout. You have to admit it is not an unheard of possibility."

"We didn't fight." Griff gritted his teeth, trying to moderate his tones and cap the volcano simmering within him. "Things were good, Bren. They really were." For an instant he allowed himself to remember the morning, to recall Lainie's warmth and loving and the sharing and the needs that they had satisfied in their love of each other. But it hurt, and he shoved the thought away.

"I don't know where she is." He felt as if the words were being ripped right out of him.

"Well, I don't know, either," Brendan said, but his tone was conciliatory. "I'll wake Cassie and ask her. She did some surgery this evening at the hospital. Maybe she heard something."

Griff shifted his weight back and forth between one foot and the other, trying not to listen to the soft voices and soothing sounds of Brendan waking his wife, staring instead into the bleak yard below.

"Cassie will call the hospital," Brendan returned to say. "Unless you already have."

"Not where she works, no," Griff said. It wasn't even close to the ballpark. Why would she have gone there? Unless... No. His fingers holding on to the receiver, tightened. She wouldn't go to work tonight. *She wouldn't!*

"Call you back," Brendan promised.

In five minutes that stretched over an eternity, the phone rang.

Griff snatched it up. "Well?"

"She was there," Brendan confirmed.

He sounded pleased, relieved, but Griff, whose heart had been clenched with fear for her safety and anguish over her whereabouts, felt it fall like a stone to his feet.

"She was?" His voice became a monotone, a deathless confirmation of a reality that was in a way worse than anything he had imagined. He shut his eyes, feeling a dull sort of pain—the sort he had become accustomed to living with for the past month—take root and begin to grow again deep inside him.

"One of the orderlies saw her," Brendan went on, oblivious of Griff's pain. "She was with some woman. Cassie says it was probably a client."

"Probably," Griff agreed dully. Undoubtedly, he thought with growing bitterness.

"Anyway, stop worrying. Just tell her not to work so hard," Brendan counseled.

"Mmm, yeah," Griff, managed and hung up.

For a full minute he didn't move, just looked around the living room at the nubby blue couch and chair that they had picked out together, at the record collection beside the stereo that held two of so many albums because their tastes were so similar, at the collection of Mexican pottery on the bookshelves that he had carried back so carefully for her from his winter trip to Mexico and which she was ecstatic over. How could they share so much and be so different? How could she make love with him as she had this morning and then sneak away from his game to go to see a client? Unbidden recollections of his childhood sprang up, taunting him, and he forced them away.

"No," he muttered. "It won't be like that." It won't, he repeated inside his head over and over, clamping down on the anger he felt growing as his fists clenched and his throat tightened.

Fool, he thought harshly. "Fool," he said aloud. She wasn't going to change. Nothing was going to change. It was insane even to have tried. He should have known. Damn. He slammed his fist on the kitchen table.

He strode into the bedroom, snatching his suitcase out of the closet, congratulating himself with a certain bitter irony that at least he hadn't totally bothered to unpack. He picked up the dirty clothes he had tossed into the clothes hamper and stuffed them back into the suitcase along with the clean ones. Then he slammed it and headed for the door. This time he wasn't even bothering to leave her a note. She wasn't stupid, just stubborn. She would know damned well that he had gone—for good.

He was in midstride halfway through the living room when the front doorknob turned.

"I'm sorry," Lainie said the instant she saw him there. There was no question in her mind about what he was doing. She was only glad she wasn't too late. "I—I got a call from Mavis Leary. She needed to talk. Her son Frankie was in jail—"

"I don't care." He stopped long enough to pocket a tiny Mexican pottery owl that he had bought special and tucked it into his pocket. A reminder, he thought, in case he was ever stupid enough to get involved like this again.

"Of course you care, Griff," she said, grabbing his arm as he tried to walk past her. "If you didn't care, you wouldn't be walking out."

His eyes were unfathomable, masking emotions that she couldn't even guess. When he looked like this, she didn't know what to say to him, how to reach him. If he would just look angry, she could understand that. If he would yell or argue, she could handle it. But he never had, and he didn't now.

"I don't care," he said again. And his hand went to cover hers, gently but firmly removing her fingers from his sleeve.

"We have to talk," Lainie insisted.

"No," he said, "we don't. We can't," he added almost desperately. "We don't have anything to say." And he left.

"I said I'm sorry," she called after him, frantic. But he kept on going down the steps. "Griffin! Where can I reach you? Griff, I love you!"

She thought he flinched, but he didn't stop. She scrambled down the stairs after him, not caring what the neighbors thought. After her black eyes she didn't imagine there was much they hadn't thought, anyway. "Griffin!"

"Lainie, for heaven's sake!" He stopped at the door of his car long enough to glare at her. "What will the neighbors say?"

"I don't care what they say! I care what you say!"

"Do you?" His voice was cold, doubting. And even in the dim light from the streetlamp she detected a flicker of pain on his face. "No, Lainie. It isn't going to work." His fists clenched at his sides. "If you want proof, just look at what happened tonight."

"Tonight was an exception," she argued, but as soon as she said it, Griff's face closed. Like the umpire he had been tonight, faced with a screaming ballplayer, he wasn't listening to a word she said.

"Goodbye, Lainie," he said, and she thought if he offered to shake her hand, she would throttle him.

"No," she whispered, a hoarse sound that seemed torn from her.

But Griff had got into the car and was starting the engine, oblivious or uncaring of the fact that she desperately wanted him there, to listen, to work things out.

"Please, Griff," she tried again. But he was looking straight ahead. Then he put the car in gear and drove away.

She stood there until she was shivering, tears streaming down her face. Then she turned and dragged herself up the steps to the apartment, cursing herself and him.

In the window the rainbow sun catcher they brought back from Maui caught her eye and mocked her—a reminder of the promise of a lifetime together. Right now such hopeful dreams seemed a million miles away.

Chapter Four

Lainie took one look at the travel folder she found in her mail that morning, extolling the virtues of a Maui vacation, and speared it with her letter opener, pinning it to the pile of hospital charts in a stack on her desk.

"That sort of day, is it?" Cassie Craig asked, poking her head around the corner of the door but not coming in. Probably wondered if she dared, Lainie thought, knowing her own black look provided no incentive at all. But the last thing she needed was a reminder of her honeymoon and of the tentative plans she and Griff had made last winter to go back to Maui when he took his first week of vacation in late June.

She sighed and wriggled the opener, freeing it. "That sort of week," she corrected heavily. For an optimist, she had had an incredibly difficult time finding anything to feel positive about since Griff had driven out of her life a week ago. For seven days she had been trying to get in touch with him. But he wasn't making it easy. She had had no idea where he went after he left her that night, but once he was back on his regular schedule, she thought it would be a simple matter of calling his hotel room and trying to apologize again and explain. She soon found out it wasn't simple after all.

"Mr. Tucker isn't in," the hotel receptionists would tell her. Or, "Mr. Tucker has asked not to be disturbed," or, "Mr. Tucker isn't taking any calls." It didn't take her long to get to the point, but she kept trying nonetheless. No one was going to say that Lainie Thomas Tucker was a quitter, especially not where her marriage was concerned.

"No word?" Cassie asked sympathetically, finally daring to enter. She gave Lainie an encouraging smile and sank down in the armchair across from Lainie's desk.

"No word." She wasn't actually sure whether to consider that good news or bad. From her own perspective, of course, it was bad. No word meant no communication, and no communication meant no way to settle their problems. But since, at this juncture, she thought Griff's next communication might well be an envelope full of divorce papers, from that standpoint no news was definitely good.

"I am not giving up, though," she told Cassie firmly, tapping the letter opener on her desk. "I know that he loves me."

To her everlasting credit, Cassie did not look surprised. In fact, she asked, "Did you ever doubt it?"

Lainie tipped back in her chair, contemplating the Maui scene on the folder in front of her, remembering the paradise of their honeymoon there and the gradual decline of their relationship afterward. "Yes, I doubted it," she said truthfully. "When Griff left me that first time, I thought it might be because he had decided he didn't love me, after all."

Cassie frowned. "Why would you think he didn't love you?" she demanded, as though that never would have occurred to her. But then Cassie didn't spend her life analyzing things to death, either.

"Because everything started out so perfectly for us. You know what it was like, love at first sight, a whirlwind courtship, a super honeymoon, all pure bliss. But then we came home and settled into a routine, and I went back to work, and I don't know—he just gradually seemed to draw away from me.

"I'd come home after a long day at work and be dying to spend some time with him, and he'd say something about 'if I'd wanted to be with him, I should have been home that day while he went fishing' or some damn thing. And then he'd just get up and walk out, go down on the beach." She swallowed past the growing lump in her throat as she recalled the countless times that she had experienced that form of shutting her out and the rigid set of his shoulders as he walked away.

"It got so I hated that damned beach," she said, shaking her head ruefully, knowing that the beach wasn't the problem but still now knowing exactly what the problem was.

Cassie laughed. "Not me. I love the beach. That's where Brendan and I had our best times." She smiled, her expression one of fond reminiscence. Lainie could imagine quite well what she was thinking about—the beach in Oregon where Brendan had gone to sort out his life and to which Cassie had followed him with single-minded determination. It was there that they had hammered out a compromise between her demanding job as an orthopedic surgeon and his total lack of one now that his baseball career was over. Lainie knew it hadn't been easy. But when they had come back a month later, Cassie cut back on her practice, leaving the full-time work to her three partners, and Brendan had decided to apply to law school the following autumn with the intention of eventually getting a job in contract negotiation for athletes. In the meantime, he was studying on his own and writing detective fiction, some of which was just beginning to be published in magazines.

It seemed like a perfect example of the sort of "working things out" that Lainie thought she could do with Griff. But after he had stormed out of their apartment last week, she had to admit that the possibility was extremely remote.

"You're lucky," she said softly, unable to keep the envy out of her voice.

Cassie nodded. "True." She shifted in her chair, resting her elbow on the armrest and cradling her cheek in her hand while she toyed with the stethoscope that dangled from her neck. "So, if you aren't going to quit like he wants you to, what *are* you going to do?"

Lainie shook her head. "I'm not sure. Wait, I guess. Keep calling. What else can I do?"

"I don't know. You're the expert," Cassie said. She glanced at her watch and then got up quickly. "I've got to be off. I have to meet Gene in surgery in a few minutes. Let us know if you hear from him."

"I will."

Cassie gave her a thumbs-up sign for encouragement. "Meanwhile, keep yourself occupied."

Laine fully intended to. Keeping busy was all that was keeping her sane. She worked even longer hours now than she normally did, scheduling evening appointments frequently because she couldn't bear going home to the empty apartment. It was worse now than it had been before he came back. Whenever she was there, she stared out the window morosely and couldn't think of a thing to do.

For most of her twenty-eight years she had been positively bubbling with projects, whether stitchery or woodworking or, since she and Griff had been married, refinishing old furniture for their apartment. But now she couldn't bring herself to do any of it.

She had been in the midst of working on a three-drawer dresser for the spare bedroom when Griff had walked out the first time. She had tried and tried, but she couldn't make herself finish it. The joy of creating something for their life together had gone. When Griff had left, so had the desire to continue it. After three weeks she gave the dresser to her brother, Mike, who was setting up an apartment of his own.

"Whenever you want it back, speak up," he had told her. But now Lainie couldn't imagine that that day would ever come.

When she got home from work that night, it was nearly eight, and she was starving. She poked a chicken pot pie in the oven to bake and put through her nightly call to Griff. He was in Chicago, which meant he would have been at the game during the day, but when the phone rang in his room, she got no answer. Was he listening to it ring? Had he gone out? Was he alone or with someone? A woman? She wanted to know, and yet she didn't. God, what a refined sort of torture a marriage breakup was!

After hanging up the phone, she went into the bedroom and changed into a pair of white shorts and a pale blue shirt. She forced herself to wear them even though they made her remember the time she had bought them, on Maui. Then, after checking on the pie, she went back downstairs to check the mail. Three bills awaited her, also two sale catalogs, a letter from the local community college and a stark white envelope addressed in bold black letters by Griff.

Hastily, dropping the other mail, she fumbled with the envelope, almost tearing it in half before she got it open. Communication at last.

But all that fell out the envelope was a pale gold check and half a sheet of hotel stationery from the place he stayed in New York. "For expenses," she read aloud, seeing red. He hadn't even signed his name. Furious, she grabbed the check from where it had fluttered to the pavement and ripped it in half.

How dare he? If Griff Tucker thought for one second that she would accept his money while denied his presence, he was wrong!

She gathered up the rest of the mail with trembling fingers, then stomped back up the steps and flung all the mail on the coffee table—except the check, which she consigned to the trash.

Grabbing the receiver, she punched out the number of his Chicago hotel again.

"He's not there," the receptionist told her.

"He damned well is!" Lainie retorted furiously.

"He is not in his room ma'am," the receptionist repeated calmly but coldly.

"I'm sorry," Lainie said, instantly contrite. It wasn't the receptionist's fault, after all. "I know you're just doing your job."

"Would you like to leave a message?" the woman asked cautiously.

Would she ever! But the message she felt like leaving couldn't be passed along a third party; that was for sure. Besides, she had left any number of messages for him to call during the past week, and he had chosen to ignore them all. Well, maybe she should, anyway, just to let him know what she felt about receiving that bloody check!

"Tell him I don't need his money," she snapped. "Tell him I don't need anything of his!"

"And your name, ma'am?" the receptionist asked with total indifference.

"Never mind," Lainie said. "If you give him the message, I'm sure he'll know."

The pot pie was burned by the time she rescued it from the oven. But it couldn't be more scorched than she felt right now.

"He's a jerk," she muttered to herself, stabbing the pie with her fork, watching it ooze out onto her plate. "Forget him."

But that was impossible, and she knew it. Even when he infuriated her, as he had done with the check, he was still too much a part of her for her to shut him out completely. As brief as their marriage had been, it had added a dimension of love to her life, a meaning to her reality, that vanished when he was gone.

If you didn't know about something, you didn't miss it. But just as the fierce island storms and sudden rainbows that she and Griff had discovered during their time together on Maui had made ordinary rainfall seem like a lesser reality somehow, so had life with Griff made anything else pale in comparison.

"So, what are you going to do?" she asked herself, as Cassie had asked her earlier that day. But now, like then, she didn't have any answers. Scraping the rest of the pot pie into the sink and running the garbage disposal, she surveyed the apartment. She and Griff had made it a home, but Griff had taken the heart out of it when he left.

Sighing, she rinsed her plate and then wandered into the spare bedroom, looking at the empty spot where the dresser she had given to Mike was supposed to go. She almost wished she had it there now to work on, not that she really wanted to do something for the apartment, but she had to do something. There was still time to kill before she could go to bed.

Finally, she flicked off the light and went back to the living room, turning on the television so she could pretend she wasn't really alone. Then she washed the dishes, ironed a blouse to wear to work tomorrow and called her mother, trying to sound as if everything was fine.

Mrs. Thomas had no idea that Griff and Lainie were separated. She simply thought he was on the road. And when she said, "Isn't it hard on you?" Lainie didn't have any trouble saying yes. But she had no intention of going into her problems any further with her mother. Lainie's parents' marriage was, by Lainie's reckoning, nothing like hers and Griff's. Her father had been a talkative, jovial man, and he and her mother had argued their way amiably through twenty-four years of marriage before his sudden death of a stroke. When she and Griff first got married, she tried to get him to come with her to her mother's house frequently. Her brothers were enthralled with the idea of an umpire in the family, and her mother loved the idea of a son-in-law to spoil. But Griff had stayed aloof, talked in monosyllables and had let Lainie know in his typically nonverbal fashion that visiting her mother was not his idea of fun. In fact, he seemed to consider it just the opposite. But when she tried to talk to him about it, guess what, she thought wryly now as she washed her hair before heading toward bed—he went for a walk on the beach.

She was blowing her hair dry when she noticed that she still hadn't opened the rest of the mail. The bills were easily enough disposed of, but when she opened the letter from the community college, she almost laughed.

"Me?" she said aloud, drowning out a high-speed car chase on the TV screen across the room. "Teach a course in effective communication in marriage?"

There was an absurdity if there ever was one! Wait until she told Cassie tomorrow! They could both have a good laugh over that one.

Cassie, however, didn't think it was funny at all. "Why not?" she said, propping her chin on her palm and staring at Lainie out of her guileless wide green eyes.

"Oh, come on. What have I got to show for my effective communication?" Lainie asked her. They were dividing a ham and cheese sandwich in Cassie's kitchen after work while Steve and Keith played Ping-Pong outside on the patio and Brendan, sprawled inelegantly on the couch in the den, was burying himself in a law book.

"A caseload that just won't quit," Cassie replied. "You tell me that I'm a workaholic."

"You're not," Brendan chipped in from behind the law book. "Not any longer." He peered at her over the top of his book and gave her a very lascivious wink. A flush rose on Cassie's neck.

"No, but that's just because you're such a wonderful tutor," she said, smiling at him in spite of her embarrassment.

"Lover," Brendan corrected. "Such a wonderful lover."

"That, too," Cassie agreed. "Anyway, maybe Lainie should be a tutor, too. You know, teach the world to communicate."

"Like I've communicated with Griff?" Lainie asked bitterly.

Cassie rolled her eyes. "Quit that. You know that's his fault, not yours."

"Right," Brendan said stoutly, giving her a grin. "You'll just have to teach him how."

"I'd have to catch him first," Lainie replied glumly, taking a bite of ham and cheese.

"Uh-huh. Then tie him down and batter the elements of communication into him." Brendan tossed his law book onto the floor and got up, then sauntered over to the kitchen bar, wrapped his arms around Cassie and filched a bit of her sandwich, popping it into his mouth. "Seriously," he said to Lainie between chews, "you ought to consider it."

"Yeah, sure," Lainie said.

"Well, you have to do something. You're obviously not about to forget him," Cassie argued. "And how much more sitting home and staring at the four walls can you stand?"

"Not much," Lainie confessed. That was what she was doing at the Craigs's right now—avoiding her apartment and the barren wasteland her evenings without Griff had become. "I don't know," she said sighing. "Maybe I ought to take this crazy teaching job. I mean, in theory at least I know what I'm talking about."

"Of course you do," Brendan encouraged her.

"Right," Cassie seconded.

"Besides," Lainie said, "it will get me out of the house at night."

AFTER HE GOT Lainie's cryptic message from a rather astonished desk clerk, Griff tried calling her once or twice. He didn't know exactly what he ought to say. "Keep the money," or possibly, "If you want a divorce, I won't contest it." But he needn't have worried; she wasn't home. Typical, he thought with a mirthless smile. He wasn't surprised, only touched by what he considered justifiable anger. She was never home when he was there. It shouldn't be any big shock that she wasn't home now.

He wished he didn't wonder where she was, who she was with. He wished he didn't think about her at all. Unfortunately, she was the subject of nine of his every ten thoughts.

Right now, for example, en route from Chicago to New York, sitting in the last row of the Cougars' chartered plane, he wasn't at all interested in joining Fletcher and Morelos, two of his fellow umpires, in a game of gin. Nor could he, like Bob Johnson, concentrate on a paperback thriller. Instead, he was staring straight ahead, wondering what Lainie was doing that very minute.

He didn't even notice which ballplayers were moving up and down the aisle past him until one well-remembered voice muttered his last name.

He looked up, instantly wary. He never liked having to ride on a team plane, but sometimes it was the only convenient way to get from one city to another. Generally, though, he tried to have as little to do with the players as possible. Fraternization was not encouraged, and Griff could see why. It would only make his impartiality suspect and his job that much harder. And it was very hard right now when he was confronted with the sour face of Wes LaRue, scowling down at him.

Griff managed a grim smile and a brief nod. Move along, he urged silently, not wanting any conversation and unable to imagine that LaRue would, either. But LaRue stopped cold, leaned back against the seat across the aisle from Griff and stared down at him, his dark eyes narrow and cold.

"Well, look who's here," he said, his tone scornful, and the player who came up behind him elbowed him in the ribs in an obvious attempt to shut him up. It didn't work. "How's your eyesight, Tuck-er?" he went on.

Griff let his eyes slide right past LaRue's. "Perfect," he said tonelessly.

LaRue shook his head. "Pity," he mocked. "I was hopin' you couldn't see any better here than you could on the field."

Griff's knuckles tightened on the armrest.

"Come on, Wes," the ballplayer behind him urged. "Leave it, will ya?"

Griff shot him an almost-grateful look. The Cougars' catcher, a mild-mannered Texan named Tim Huxley, was as unflappable as LaRue was explosive. He put his hand on LaRue's shoulder and gave it a little squeeze. "Come on," he said again. "Stop."

"I will if Tuck-er will," LaRue said in a singsong voice. He gave Griff a smirk that caused Griff to draw in a deep breath.

"He will," Dan Fletcher said easily, folding his hand of cards and saying, "Gin. I'll deal you in this hand, huh, Griff."

Griff didn't say anything. His eyes shifted back to LaRue, probing for an instant, then sizing up the situation in the same dispassionate way he sized up a play, making a decision and acting on it. "All right," he said, and turned away from both players as if he had totally dismissed them. "Deal me in," he told Fletcher.

LaRue didn't move for a moment, apparently unsure whether he had won that round or not. Then, when Huxley prodded with another, "Move it, Wes," he ambled on down the aisle and went into the restroom.

Griff stared at the cards Dan Fletcher dealt him. He wasn't seeing the hand. He wasn't surprised, either, when LaRue came back down the aisle fifteen minutes later, laughing at something another player was shouting, his own response far more jovial and pleasant than his behavior toward Griff had just indicated it ought to be.

Drugs, Griff thought. Pills? Maybe. Cocaine? Also a possibility. But something was very definitely responsible for this almost-instantaneous mellowing of Wes LaRue's behavior. It also went a long way toward explaining his on-again, off-again, erratic moodiness on the baseball diamond.

Griff shut his eyes and wondered what to do now. Then he opened them and followed LaRue's progress down the aisle.

"Gin," Fletcher said again. "You gotta keep your mind on the game, Tucker," he chided. He gave Griff a comradely grin that disappeared when he saw the look on Griff's face and when he followed Griff's gaze.

"He's on something," Griff said slowly.

"Probably." Fletcher shuffled the cards. "He ain't the only one. I didn't see it. Did you see it?"

Griff met Fletcher's eyes evenly and held them. "No," he said grudgingly. "No, I guess not."

Fletcher let out a deep, relieved breath. "Remember that," he advised. "You aren't his keeper. How about another hand?"

Griff shrugged. "Sure. Why not?" After all, there was nothing better to do—only torture himself thinking about Lainie or wonder what the hell he ought to do about Wes LaRue.

He knew damned well that Fletcher had a lot of common sense on his side when he advised, if not explicitly, that Griff mind his own business. Drugs in sports were not uncommon. The smart thing was not to use them yourself and not to get involved with those who did.

Griff wished he had the sort of mentality that would let him not give a damn. The sort, he reflected wryly, that would have let him walk away from his marriage, too, without going back again and again in his mind. Unfortunately, he didn't. Just as he had seen the goodness, the potential, in his marriage and had wanted to come back, to give Lainie another chance to try again, so he also wanted to straighten out Wes LaRue.

It wouldn't matter, he thought, if the potential wasn't there. If LaRue were some no-account jerk whose life couldn't be messed up any further no matter what one did, Griff wouldn't have felt the compulsion to say something. But that wasn't the case at all. Wes LaRue had everything going for him—talent, raw power, quick hands, the ability to know in a given situation exactly what to do. In his rookie year he had had a lot of rough edges, but his immense talent was all too visible even then. All he had needed was experience to hone down the edges and give him the expertise and confidence that came with time and experience.

Griff had found himself watching LaRue in spring training, looking for that eager striving, for the increased knowledge that his second season would bring. And while at first he thought he saw it, more often he saw the hard edge of LaRue's temper, the impatience and the moodiness that went with the increased pressure the young man must feel. Sometimes LaRue was up—higher than a kite—and sometimes he was down. The down times, as far as Griff could see from the times he had been with him on the field, were becoming more frequent.

Drugs. He shook his head wearily, not surprised somehow. Only saddened. Too much pressure on too young a man. Too much money riding on his performance. And what would come of it? A waste. A failed career. And that, like a failed marriage, left a bad taste in his mouth.

He heard LaRue's easy laughter echoing down the aisle of the plane and for a moment wished that he was anywhere else but here. If there had been a commercial flight available, he would never have been as certain that a good part of LaRue's problems was directly attributable to drugs. Ah, hell, what difference did it make? He tried to keep his mind on the hand of cards that Fletcher had dealt him, tried to put both LaRue and Lainie out of his mind.

"Gin," Fletcher said, smiling.

IT WAS A SPUR-OF-THE-MOMENT DECISION when he made it. Jostled along down the tunnel exit from the plane after it landed in New York, Griff found himself shoulder to shoulder with Wes LaRue. Another ballplayer turned to swing his duffel bag over his shoulder and shoved LaRue into Griff. The younger man automatically mumbled, "Sorry," then glanced up and noticed who he had bumped. "Oh, it's you," he said.

Some of the temporary euphoria had obviously drained from his system. His brown eyes were, if not totally cold, at least hard and a little wary. Scared almost, Griff decided. That was when he made up his mind. He kept walking, matching his pace to LaRue's.

"I want to talk to you," he said.

LaRue's eyes narrowed. "So talk."

Griff reached the lounge area and jerked his head, nodding to a corner of the room still unoccupied. He headed for it and wondered if LaRue would follow. For a moment Griff thought he would not. Then, with a backward glance to see who might be noticing them, LaRue came to stand by Griff in front of one of the plate-glass windows overlooking the airfield.

"What do you want?" LaRue stared past him out toward the runway, his tone edged with belligerence.

"I've watched you play ball for two seasons now," Griff said, his hands in the pockets of his gray flannel slacks, his eyes on LaRue's flushed face, noting the rapid blinking of the younger man's eyes and the twitch of the muscle in his jaw. "You've got what it takes."

LaRue snorted. "Am I supposed to say thanks for noticing?"

"Don't bother." Griff refused to be ruffled. "Just don't blow it, either."

LaRue's eyes snapped back to meet his for a split second. "I'm not blowing anything," he denied vehemently.

"You could."

He heard LaRue's teeth grate together in impatient irritation. "You know everything, do you?" LaRue challenged. "Umpire of the universe and all that?"

"I've been around enough to know trouble when I see it. And you're in trouble," Griff said flatly. "There's a lot of pressure on guys in your situation," he went on, trying to moderate his approach.

LaRue leaned against the window, his fingers drumming on the glass. "Tell me about it," he said sarcastically.

"If you need help, get it."

LaRue's fingers abruptly stopped drumming. "Or else?" he demanded tautly.

Griff shrugged slightly. "Or else you'll regret it," he said. It wasn't meant as a threat, just as a statement of fact, but the color in LaRue's face heightened perceptibly, and he spun away.

"Stuff it," he snarled, and sprinted off down the corridor toward the waiting team bus.

Griff leaned back against the window and sighed. *Damn but you're effective,* he chided himself. *First Lainie, now LaRue. That's what trying to tell other people how to help themselves gets you.* He shook his head wearily, feeling the beginning of a headache pounding at his temples. Easing away from the glass, he wandered slowly down the corridor, wondering why it was so damned hard to make other people see where things were going wrong for them.

LaRue was on drugs, and from the look of things, getting in deeper every day. His playing would suffer, his career would suffer, maybe his whole life would be damaged. But did he want to hear about it? No way. No more than Lainie had wanted to hear that her job was dangerous, that she could get hurt, that he wanted her to quit before their whole marriage fell apart because he couldn't handle what her job was doing to them, and if she didn't quit—*Stop it,* he told himself. *Just stop.*

And he did. He always made himself stop before he took that thought to its logical conclusion.

"Are you deaf, Tucker?" Fletcher's voice broke in.

Griff's head jerked up. "What?"

Fletcher scowled. "I said, 'Are you going deaf?' I've been calling you, yelling at you, in fact, for the past five minutes. Johnson is picking up the car. You and Morelos and I are getting the gear. Come on." He practically herded Griff down the crowded corridor. "What were you talking to LaRue about?"

"Nothing," Griff lied. "Nothing at all."

"Good," Fletcher said, and Griff knew exactly what he meant. Well, if LaRue didn't want to solve his problems, that was his business. But now he knew that they weren't going unnoticed. Maybe that would give him the impetus he needed to get help. Griff rubbed his temples, then glanced at his watch, relieved that he would be able to catch a nap before the game that night.

"Head hurt?" Fletcher asked sympathetically.

Griff nodded.

"You could use a break. When's your vacation?"

"In two weeks." The thought of it made his head hurt even more. Trust Dan Fletcher to move from a topic that was bad to the only one that was worse.

"Where are you going?'

"Dunno."

They had been planning a trip back to Maui. "A return to the scene of the honeymoon," Lainie had dubbed it when they discussed the possibility over Christmas. She had been explaining to him why she couldn't take any time off then go skiing with him at Arrowhead or to accompany him on a winter junket to Mexico. "How about Maui in June?" she had tempted him with a Lainie Tucker version of the hula. And Griff, enticed and aroused, had agreed.

Sometimes, when it seemed over the next few months that he rarely saw her, he fantasized about the trip. His memories of their October honeymoon mingled with dreams of their future vacation in his head. Most of January and February had, for him, been filled with the delicious hallucinations of the two of them making love on warm sandy beaches, swimming in clear blue water and walking hand in hand through tropical forests. He thought he had probably been getting high on all the turpentine from the furniture refinishing. Then it hadn't mattered.

Now he hadn't the faintest idea what he was going to do with his week off. "What about you?" he asked Fletcher as they waited for Morelos to show up with their gear. "You go right after I do."

"Going home," Fletcher said. "Best vacation on earth. Me and Margie and the girls."

Griff's head felt like it was going to split. "Yeah, sounds good." Home. Hell, he didn't even have one anymore. He supposed he could fly back to L.A. and get a hotel room or possibly spend a week with Chase in the apartment where he used to live. Maybe by then he would be ready to talk to a lawyer or find out if Lainie had. Hell, he thought, what a super thing to do on your vacation: get a divorce.

But although he might not like the idea, it was better than living out a marriage in a constant state of battle. He had been telling himself that every day, reminding himself that intolerable situations were better left behind. He hoped to God that Lainie wouldn't fight it. It would be best if she would initiate the proceedings herself.

Meanwhile, he wished that Hertz and Avis and all the other rent-a-car firms whose nearly life-size posters of surfers and palm trees surrounded him would start an ad campaign aimed at promoting Paris or Geneva. It was hard enough resolving oneself to a necessary divorce without being plagued by visual reminders of the best days of a love that could be no more.

THE EFFECTIVE COMMUNICATIONS CLASS went well. All the students were eager and responsive. Some were intense and some funny. And all of them thought that Lainie knew what she was talking about. She was particularly heartened to find that Claire and Bob Hudson, whose battle had precipitated Griff's first exit from her life, had signed up for the class.

"We hope we can learn something," Bob told her sheepishly when she smiled at him after class.

"I hope so, too," Lainie said, and actually had great hopes that they might. People who wanted to change often did.

She left the classroom on a psychic high that she hadn't felt since she last heard Griff tell her that he loved her, and when she got home to her very empty apartment, she felt her spirits fall several thousand feet.

What good was theory if it helped everyone else and she still came home to a cold bed and a leftover macaroni and cheese dinner?

"Damn," she muttered as she dumped the macaroni pot into the sink and turned on the faucet to start the dishes.

It would be different, she thought, if Griff didn't love her. The first time he had left her, she hadn't been sure if maybe getting back to his job hadn't unfortunately brought him back to his senses and made him see that he didn't really want to waste his life with her. They had had, after all, an extremely brief and deliriously ecstatic courtship.

But now—now that he had come back—how could she just let him leave her again? Let him leave? That was a laugh. As if she could have stopped him. She swiped at the moisture that fogged her eyes, but her hand was covered with soap bubbles and only made a bigger mess.

"You could have at least let me explain, Griff," she muttered. "At least I said I was sorry."

But there was no answer other than the sloshing of the dishwater and the clinking of the plate against the glass. She sniffed loudly. What did it matter, after all, when he wasn't even there to hear?

She was reminded of a young woman she had been seeing recently, a depressed patient whose own brief marriage was rocky. The girl had gone through a box of tissues in the forty-five minutes she and Lainie had talked. But, Lainie thought wearily, at least the girl was going to be meeting with her again on Thursday night, this time with her husband along. She had better prospects of working things out than Lainie did with Griff.

"You have to be willing to negotiate," she had told the young woman. "Negotiate," she had exhorted her students again earlier this evening. "Communicate! Bargain! Get things out in the open, and then you can begin to work them out."

Hopeful words. Positive words. She pulled the plug and watched the sinkful of dirty dishwater disappear down the drain. She was lucky no one had asked what to do if the person you needed to communicate with just up and walked away. What would she have said? "Tie him down and batter the elements of communication into him," as Brendan had suggested.

Sure, she thought, and flipping off the light, went to get ready for bed.

Four hours later, sleepless at 1:26 A.M. and in the midst of an old Dick Francis novel that was getting her through the night, it didn't sound like such a bad idea.

Griff had a vacation coming up, a whole week that they obviously were not now going to be spending in each other's arms in a cottage on Maui. A whole week. She smiled. Even for Griffin that ought to be enough time.

"YOU WANT ME TO WHAT?" Chase Whitelaw's mouth dropped open exactly as Brendan's had done when she had told him that morning that she was taking him up on his suggestion. He had thought she was just as crazy as Chase obviously did now. But she had convinced Brendan, and she was certain, that when Chase understood, he would be convinced, too.

"I said, 'I want you to help me kidnap Griffin.'"

Chapter Five

"You're not kidding, are you?"

Chase stepped back as Lainie swept past him into the living room of the small beachfront apartment he had once shared with Griff. She smiled hopefully at the tone she heard in his voice. It seemed to be moving from incredulity to resignation.

"No," she told him, sitting primly on his brown leather sofa and looking him squarely in the eyes. "I'm not."

Desperate situations spawned desperate ideas; and Lainie had never felt more desperate in her life. Besides, she had been mulling the idea over for three days now, figuring all the angles, weighing all the possibilities, studying all the circumstances. She had decided that kidnapping Griff was the only viable solution available and Chase was the only logical person to help her. Now she had to convince him.

She just hoped he was as clever and insightful as Griff always gave him credit for being. He was very big on writing terribly vivid and comprehensive articles about the causes he chose to explore. He was, in Griff's word, "committed." She prayed that he would decide that hers was a cause worthy of his commitment.

"Do you want a drink?" he asked her, already busy fixing one for himself, though it was only eleven in the morning.

"No, thank you." Lainie said. "You have one, though, if you think it will help."

"What?" Chase turned to stare at her, bourbon sloshing across his hand.

"I can appreciate your need for fortification." Lainie smiled at him benignly, hoping that a tiny bit of goading might not hurt. Chase had a hard face and narrow, assessing eyes, not the sort that seemed amenable to pleading. She had ruled out that tactic right away.

"Griff is a force to be reckoned with," she went on smoothly.

Chase took a long, deliberate swallow of his drink, and Lainie could almost see him stiffen as it went down. "So are you," he remarked dryly. "Tell me, what is the point in kidnapping Griff? And why are you involving me?"

"The point, as you probably know," Lainie said, "is that we are separated." She looked at him for confirmation, going on when he acknowledged her statement with a brief nod as he settled himself on the arm of the chair across from her. "And we need some time together to work things out. I am involving you because I can't figure out any way to do it myself. He doesn't answer my calls. Besides," she added a bit desperately, "Brendan suggested it."

From the skeptical look on Chase's face, she wondered if her whole journey to see him had been a big mistake. He was, after all, Griff's friend, not hers. Maybe he would think she was out of her mind. But Brendan had seemed to think it was worth a try; although Brendan, since his own marriage was working so splendidly, seemed to think that everyone should have a state of matrimonial bliss comparable to his. Perhaps, then, it was no more than his innate optimism that had prompted him to assure her that he was certain Chase Whitelaw would be willing to help.

"Brendan must be dumber than he looks," Chase said.

He got up from the chair arm and set his drink on the narrow bar that separated the kitchen from the small living room. Then, thrusting his hands into the pockets of his sand-colored corduroy shorts, he rocked back and forth on his heels, considering her carefully. His hawklike eyes examined her with a scrutiny that gave her the urge to wriggle away out of his sight, like a gopher that knows a hungry predator when it sees one. But she guessed enough to know that if Chase were to decide to help her, it wouldn't be because he could intimidate her. He would expect her to fight back.

"Brendan is a brilliant and perceptive man," she countered staunchly. Her tone implied a distinct contrast between him and the man confronting her now.

"Is he?" Chase asked smoothly, refusing to rise to the bait.

He picked up his drink and crossed the room. Sitting down in a walnut-and-canvas director's chair, he rested his elbows on his knees and laced his fingers around the glass in his hands. "All right," he said. "Convince me."

Lainie knew he meant convince him of more than simply Brendan's brilliance. He meant convince him to help her, convince him that this absurd, harebrained scheme wasn't so absurd and harebrained at all.

"I love Griff very much," she began slowly, leaning toward Chase as she talked, letting him see her feelings in her face and hear them in the tone of her voice. "And he loves me."

"How do you know?" Chase cut in quietly.

Like a knife in the ribs, Lainie thought. Or it would have felt that way if he had asked her that same question before Dick Leary had mauled her. For an instant she knew what it would be like to have Chase in his guise as an investigative reporter directing probing queries at her. She thanked God she didn't doubt the answer she was giving him.

"Because he came home to me when he thought I was hurt," she told him. "Because he said so then. Because he wanted to try again."

Chase lifted one dark eyebrow in apparent skepticism, but then he seemed to reconsider. He leaned back in his chair and stretched his bare legs out in front of him, crossing them at the ankle. Then he looked at her through hooded eyes, as if weighing his words before he spoke them.

Finally, he said, "Well, that's worth something. I've never known Griff to say anything he didn't mean."

"He meant it."

"Then why did he leave?"

Lainie sighed and shoved her hair away from her face. "That was my fault," she admitted, and she went on to explain in detail exactly what happened. Chase listened intently, not moving, neither approving nor disapproving. And Lainie didn't know what he was thinking when she finished with the statement "He just doesn't seem to like my job very much."

Then a ghost of a smile flickered across Chase's somber face. "Understatement of the year."

Lainie nodded wearily. "Has he said so to you?" It didn't seem likely somehow; Griff was too private a person to share his feeling in most cases. But he had lived with Chase for quite a while.

"Not really," Chase said easily, taking a sip of his drink. "He just dropped a disparaging remark here and there."

"Ah, yes. Those." Griff's little one-liners that he delivered just before he walked out. She sighed again. Then, just thinking about them, she gained renewed determination. If she could just convince Chase to help her, she could get him where he couldn't walk out on her, and then maybe they would have a chance.

"Anyway," she said softly but firmly, "that's why I wanted to kidnap him. I want to talk to him. I want to explain why I did it. And I want him to talk to me. And the only place I can get him to do that is somewhere that he can't get away from even if he wants to!"

"You don't think he'd just go away with you if you asked him?" Chase queried.

"No. Do you?"

He looked taken aback for a split second; then one corner of his mouth quirked up in wry concession. "No, I guess not."

"Then will you help me?"

Chase didn't reply right away, and Lainie wondered what he was thinking. He certainly wasn't like Brendan and Cassie, willing to jump right in and get involved. She shifted slightly, trying not quite successfully to control her impatience.

"Maybe you're beating a dead horse," Chase said softly. "Maybe even though you say you love each other, you're better off apart. Did you ever consider that?"

Lainie stiffened, crossing her arms across her breasts as if he had attacked her. "No, I did not consider it! I married him, for heaven's sake! I don't want to be apart from him. Not now, not ever! Why would you even think such a thing?"

Chase swirled the bourbon in his glass, making the ice clink as he stared at the carpet just beyond his feet. For a long time Lainie didn't think he was even going to deign to answer her. But at last, as if he had come to some sort of decision, he rubbed one hand through his thick black hair and said, "You're complete opposites."

"So?"

He glanced at her irritably. "My parents were complete opposites," he said to the carpet.

Lainie thought she understood. There was more going on here than just her relationship with Griff. Chase wasn't looking at her, but she could sense that he was waiting for her reaction. He looked relaxed but there was tension coiled throughout his whole frame. His knuckles, wrapped around the glass, were almost white.

"Your parents' marriage didn't work?" she ventured, her voice gentle.

Chase lifted his head fracitonally, his dark eyes shadowed with remembered pain. "Who knows?" he shrugged, his voice curiously tight. "He died before they had a chance to find out."

"But that's just the point," Lainie cried, forgetting his pain momentarily in the sudden sharpness of her own. "Neither of us is dead! We're alive, and we love each other no matter how opposite we are! Don't you think we deserve every possible chance to make things work?"

Chase stared at her silently.

I've lost him, Lainie thought. *Now what?* Would she be able to do it without his help?

Then, just as she was about to get up and go to the door, apologizing stiffly for having bothered him, almost imperceptibly, Chase nodded his head.

Pressing his lips together, he nodded again, and this time there was no doubt. "All right," he said. "When?"

Lainie felt as though the sun just broke through. "We were going to Maui for a week's vacation next Saturday," she told him. "I don't know where he plans to go now, but I do know that he has the time off. I'd like to do it then."

"Sounds good." Chase leaned forward, setting his glass down on the carpet and steepling his fingers. "Where? Maui?"

Lainie shook her head. "I think Maui's too obvious. Besides, I need you to convince him to go somewhere, and I don't think he'd go there with you. He'd know it was a setup."

Chase chewed on his lower lip. "But you want someplace isolated?"

"Yes. The more so the better. Brendan took Cassie to Oregon, but the woman who owns that cabin doesn't even know me, so I can't ask her." She didn't add that even if she did know Susan Rivers, she couldn't have asked her for the loan of her cabin to work out her personal problems with Griff. She could just imagine what her intensely private husband would say if he found out she had spoken to a sports reporter about their troubles!

"I have a place," Chase said, his voice thoughtful. "A family hideaway in southern Colorado. Lots of mountains and trees and damned little else. My sister and her family go skiing there every winter. Other than that, it's not used much. How does that sound?"

Lainie couldn't believe her good fortune. "You think it would be all right?"

"Why not?" Chase spread his hands, as if producing mountain cabins was a common occurrence for him.

"Great." Lainie could hardly believe that finding a suitable place would be so easy. The most she expected from Chase was that he would be able to get Griff wherever she decided to go. She had never dreamed he would come equipped with a cabin in the wilds. She could almost hear Brendan reminding her that everything would work out. Good old Brendan, she thought, and smiled. Then her mind returned to the question at hand.

"But how will we get him there?"

Chase grinned. "I thought that was my job. I can be very persuasive when I want to be."

Looking at him, Lainie could well believe it.

"Just trust me," Chase said. "Get a flight to Durango on Friday or Saturday. Rent a Jeep. I'll give you directions to get to the cabin. You get settled in, and I'll guarantee that Griff and I will arrive sometime on Sunday. Then I'll drive the Jeep back out and come back for you at the end of the week. Suit you?"

"Suit me?" Lainie could have hugged him. "It's brilliant!"

"Of course it is," Chase said laconically. "Perhaps Brendan was right."

Lainie laughed as she got to her feet. "Thank you." He followed her to the door, and she turned and did hug him, asking tremulously, "Do you really think it might work?"

"The guarantee doesn't extend that far," Chase said gently, but she saw real warmth in his dark eyes as he rested his hands on her shoulders. "The rest is up to you, kiddo." Then, as if he were one of her brothers, he chucked her under the chin. "Don't worry," he said.

But Lainie couldn't help but worry. All through the rest of the week she fretted, wishing she could do something constructive besides just getting her ticket, arranging for her Jeep and packing her suitcase. She felt as though she were sitting on a time bomb, waiting to see if it would really go off. Only the minutes went past like hours, and at times she didn't know if she wished they would hurry or not.

Confronting Griff again after all that had happened made her more than a bit nervous. Yet she knew it had to be done. If he wanted a divorce, he would have to tell her so and all the reasons for it. She told her students in effective communication that they should demand communication from their spouses, not just let the silence build like a wall between them. Well, in Colorado she would practice what she had preached.

SHE SHOULD HAVE KNOWN, Lainie thought as she did what must have been her hundredth circle of the living room of Chase's mountain cabin, that nothing could be that easy. Sunday had very nearly come and gone, and there was no sign at all of Chase and Griffin. She hadn't seen a living, breathing human being in almost forty-eight hours.

Probably, she decided, it had been a mistake to arrive on Friday night. It had given her too long to stew, thinking about things she couldn't do anything about. But she had been of no use at all to anyone at the hospital. She had mislaid records, forgotten phone conversations and missed meetings all week. By Thursday she had been sure that the rest of the staff was ready to take up a collection to speed her on her way, so with their blessing she had changed her flight from Saturday to Friday.

By two-thirty Friday afternoon she was in Durango; the rented Jeep was waiting for her. Then, equipped with Chase's directions, she headed east of town, passing through several smaller villages nestled in valleys between the mountains until at last she found the narrow road that led north of the highway toward his cabin. It took her bumping alongside a creek that rushed headlong down the mountain, and just when she thought her teeth would fall out, she turned into a clearing where she found the ranch house belonging to Chase's nearest neighbors.

Complying with his directions, she stopped there and had coffee and cookies with the elderly couple, the Deverels, who lived there. They were the last people she had seen. But now, as the sky grew darker with both the onset of dusk and the approach of thunderclouds from the west, she began to give serious thought to heading back to them. Only the notion that she might be driving down the mountain while Griff and Chase were hiking up it on foot kept her anchored where she was. Chase had told her he wouldn't be coming in by the road.

"There are trails. Dev can show me," he had reassured her. And that made sense, because then Griff wouldn't know he could just drive in from a road not far from the property. It didn't seem possible once you were in; that was for sure. The minute she had parked the Jeep in the garage and had left it, she felt cut off from civilization. The mountain sounds, wild and strange to her urban ears, kept her awake most of Friday night. Saturday she had lugged firewood from the lean-to that was connected to the garage, then wandered down to the stream, enjoying the solitude and envisioning beautiful scenarios of her walking these same paths arm in arm with Griff.

It was thinking about Griff that kept her awake all Saturday night. She realized then quite fully how much she needed him in her life to feel complete. It was true, she thought, some of what he had said about her taking him for granted. Doing so at the ball game had just been the last straw. But she had learned, and she was coming to Colorado to prove it. She was capable of putting their relationship at the top of her priorities. Surely when he saw that she had made all this effort, he would be convinced.

Sunday came, and she felt like a child waiting for Christmas. All day she waited. And waited some more. She busied herself by counting the minutes and exploring in even greater detail Chase's family's cabin.

It was far more elegant than his apartment in California. Expecting a rustic retreat with a wood stove and splintery furniture, Lainie was amazed at what she actually encountered. He should rent it out as a honeymoon retreat, she thought more than once as she walked around it. But of course he didn't need to. Chase's family—his mother's side, at least—had money, lots of it. She had always known that.

Griff had told her, "His grandpa owns a newspaper chain that would make William Randolph Hearst sit up and take notice. Chase had a hell of a time finding a job as a reporter where he wasn't working for the old man."

But he had, apparently. Chase, like Griff, was, she suspected, his own man. Except, thank heavens, he was not above borrowing a bit of the family wealth to aid a good cause. Like donating this split-log work of art for a week to help her save her marriage.

She was now on her one hundred and twenty-fourth lap, and she knew she would enjoy the highly polished floors more if she weren't busy wearing a groove into them. Scattered with authentic Navaho rugs and one huge sheepskin, they picked up the reflection of the fire she had lit in the huge stone fireplace that nearly covered one wall. It was, she thought, an ideal place to bring Griff. If Griff ever showed up. Because there was nowhere—absolutely nowhere—he could go from here. Dense forest surrounded the cabin on three sides, and the small meadow downhill from the house didn't extend very far before it, too, was swallowed up by even more vegetation. Nearly out of sight through the trees, there was the garage, and on the other side, beyond the clearing, were an old shed and an outhouse from the cabin's less high class past. Nowhere, as far as you could see, were there distractions. Surely they could work out their problems here, even though it seemed almost a shame to have to spoil a veritable paradise doing so.

But as it got later and Lainie heard the distant rumble of thunder and felt the stillness in the air, she wondered if they would have a chance to hash out anything at all. She glanced at her watch. It was now nearly nine, almost dark, and as she stared out west across the gloomy meadow, she couldn't see a sign of her husband or his friend.

If they had come in on the same early-afternoon flight to Durango that she had taken, even if they had visited for a while with the Deverals, they would still have had over four hours to hike up to the cabin. So where were they?

Squinting, she tried to conjure them up out of the darkness. No luck. She didn't want to eat dinner alone, she decided, circling the square oak table she had set at eight that morning with the candles, earthware pottery and woven placemats that Chase's sister had obviously stocked for intimate entertaining. Lainie had brought in food for a week, and yesterday she had been ravenous. But today she couldn't eat a thing. She had steaks ready to cook and potatoes and salad prepared. God, why didn't he come?

The first spatters of rain hit the windows, and she hurried to the front door, opening it, straining to hear the sounds of someone coming. But all she heard was the rain on the roof and the swell of thunder moving in.

"Hell," she muttered, and shut the door. Now she didn't know if she ought to wish they were out there in this weather or not. A drenched and disgruntled Griffin was not what she wanted at all. She had been counting on a happy one—one relieved to be off for a week and looking forward to the chance to relax.

"Come on, Griff," she mumbled, feeling like a caged animal, restless and apprehensive. The wind was beginning to pick up. She could hear it thrumming through the trees, louder now, gaining force. The waning midsummer light was obscured totally by the huge rolling clouds. The fire was sputtering, and she debated putting another log on it, then decided she might as well. Soon she had the fire crackling, spitting high, bright flames that reflected in the window, flickering orange lightning to complement the white jagged variety on the outside. A gust of wind threw rain with even greater force against the window, and despite the heat from the fire, Lainie shivered. "Where are you?" she asked aloud, worried.

The thunder rumbled again, and Lainie recalled, without wanting to, the last thunderstorm she had experienced. She and Griff had been together on Maui. A secluded beach. Palm trees whipping. Rolling, storm-tossed surf. The world had seemed topsy-turvy, the wind lashing and lightning flickering against a sheet-metal sky. Then, abruptly, the torrents abated, and after the storm—a rainbow. Griff kissing her, hot and demanding. The kiss had led to a loving more intense than she ever remembered.

"You are my rainbow," he had whispered to her against her cheek as still he kissed her.

And the next day, before they came home, he had gone into a shop and had emerged with a present. The sun catcher still hung in their window at home. A perfect rainbow. A reminder of their love.

Lainie closed her eyes, yet still saw the burst of white light that splashed around her and heard the thunder reverberating against the mountains, rocking her to her soul. Tonight it was dark, and there would be no rainbow. She wondered if they would ever have a chance to see rainbows again.

Standing here now, staring out into the dense forest surrounding her, she could hardly believe that Maui was even on the same planet. It was wholly remote now, both in location and in state of mind.

For the first time she thought that Chase might never have intended to follow through with her plan at all. Maybe the whole thing had simply seemed too crazy and Chase had been too polite to tell her so. Maybe he just thought she needed a week up here by herself to cool off and come to terms with the fact that Griff didn't want her anymore. She felt more than a little sick. Maybe at this very moment Griff was in Maui without her, surfing, swimming and chatting up some pretty wahine who would always do exactly what he said. And here was she, miles and miles from civilization, alone except for five million pine and aspen trees and the occasional mountain lion or deer.

"As rain forests go," Griffin said roughly to Chase's disappearing back as he sloughed after his friend up the increasingly muddy, vanishing track, "this stinks."

"Tell me about it," Chase snarled.

It was the first complete sentence Griff had heard from him in over an hour that was even remotely printable, and Griff shifted the heavy, waterlogged pack on his back and allowed himself a grim smile. *Serves you right,* he thought, *for coming up with this insane scheme in the first place.*

"Fishing? You want me to go *fishing* with you?" he had practically whooped into the receiver when he got Chase's call. "You must be kidding."

But Chase insisted he was not. He went on to wax poetic about trout fishing in southwestern Colorado, laying it on more than a bit thick, and Griff had said so. But Chase had denied it stoutly, maintaining that his grandfather highly recommended it as a good place to "get away from it all," and that that was all there was to it. Still skeptical, Griff had wondered aloud if there wasn't a woman involved. With Chase it was a distinct possibility. There had been a long pause on the other end of the line.

Then his friend had sighed and said, "Yeah, so what?" in such a belligerent tone that Griff hadn't known what to reply. He had only been meaning to kid Chase. God knew he had enough problems in his own life with women—one in particular.

"So, nothing," he had said quickly. Then, considering Chase's offer seriously, he had said, "Yeah, okay. Sounds good. Brendan tell you I've got a week's vacation coming up?"

"Yeah," Chase had said.

Griff knew Chase had heard a bit about his marital problems; it was, he decided, probably why he had made the offer, because he knew Griff wouldn't want to come back to L.A. and hang around. He didn't mention that he and Lainie had been planning to go to Maui. He didn't want to talk about Lainie, didn't want to think about her. And as the week wore on before he was to meet Chase in Denver, he was increasingly grateful for the offer. It was the sort of break he needed, a chance to get used to living like a bachelor again, of living a relatively uninvolved existence, of getting used to life without Lainie.

So here he was now, tramping up the side of some god-forsaken Rocky Mountain, the rain that had been threatening since they had started out from the Deverels' three hours before now beginning to fall in earnest. Maybe this wasn't such a great idea, after all.

Chase had started out from the Deverels' with enthusiasm and a suppressed excitement flickering in the dark depths of his eyes. It was the sort of look he got when he was on a particularly demanding reporting job, and Griff didn't completely understand it. Chase hadn't seemed like the type to get excited about fishing. But at least he had thought then that Chase knew what they were getting into when they set out. Now, as they seemed to have just passed the same tree for the seventh or eighth time, his confidence was eroding as fast as the mountainside beneath his feet.

For all his Indian ancestry, Griff decided, Chase probably hadn't got past tenderfoot in any scout camp in existence. "Do you have any idea at all of where we're going?" he ventured when Chase stopped suddenly just ahead of him and sagged against a tree, shivering.

"Up," Chase said blackly.

"Ah," Griff breathed as if that explained everything.

For a long moment they simply glared at each other. Chase was clearly as confused as he was bedraggled, but Griff, although beginning to get annoyed as he got wetter and colder, was still capable of amusement.

"This up or that up?" he asked, letting his head swivel to take in most of the mountainside, which seemed to ascend in several directions.

"Shut up," Chase answered succinctly. Then, turning his back, he headed determinedly away. "This way, I think," Griff thought he heard Chase mutter.

Sighing and adjusting his pack, mentally counting muscles in his back that he never knew he had before, Griff followed.

They gummed their way upward, exhausted and soaked, for another half hour. The thunder rumbled closer, and the wind picked up. Rainwater trickled down the back of Griff's neck, and he felt a shiver run through him as the water coursed down the length of his spine. A crack of lightning, close this time, stopped him in his tracks, and Chase stumbled, falling to his knees.

"Are you okay?" Griff asked.

"Who knows?" Chase's tone was grim. "Why in hell did I let myself get into this, anyway?"

"It was your idea," Griff reminded him as he hauled Chase to his feet and studied his muddy knees compassionately, guessing how he felt. It wasn't hard. His own jeans clung to him like a second skin, wet and chilly, and the Windbreaker he wore over his lightweight flannel shirt, which had been plenty of protection when they started out, seemed like a wick attracting the rain now.

"That's what you think" Chase muttered ominously. But then he straightened up, shifted his pack and plunged ahead. "It can't be much farther now," he said, and Griff hoped he was only imagining the second "I think."

Chase was right. The muddy track eventually gave way to a clearing, and beyond the clearing in the dim light provided by periodic cracks of lightning, Griff saw the cabin. And—for a moment his eyes seemed to be playing tricks on him—in the cabin there was a fire.

"Someone there?" he queried, catching up with Chase, whose breath was coming in ragged gasps.

"Yeah. Uh, yeah..." the other man's voice trailed off vaguely.

"I thought it was just us," Griff said, momentarily annoyed.

"I asked a buddy to come if he got the chance," Chase replied. "A guy I knew at Harvard. I ran into him last week and mentioned it. He needed a break, too, but he didn't think he was gonna get time off."

Griff wiped a wet hand across his face, brushing drops of water from his eyelashes, reconsidering. He knew the feeling—needing a break. He could hardly begrudge the guy that. Besides, at least he had made a fire. "Come on," he said to Chase. "Let's get warmed up." He started across the clearing, a burst of energy coming from somewhere.

Chase didn't move.

"Hey, what's wrong?"

Chase shook his head. "Nothing. I'll stop at the shed." He jerked his head to the left where Griff could scarcely make out a building through the trees. "If I haul up a log now, I won't have to come down later."

"You sure?" Griff asked. But Chase was already on his way toward the shed without a backward glance. A gust of rain caught Griff across the face, and he bent his head. The hell with it. Going out later and taking a turn hauling wood couldn't be as bad as going now. If Chase wanted to play martyr, let him. Griff shrugged and lifted the pack strap that was cutting into his shoulder. Then he began to slough through the high wet grass of the field, his eyes trained on the beckoning light of the cabin.

Reaching the porch, he stamped heavily on the steps shaking the water off his jacket and backpack like a hunting dog fresh from the lake. His heart hammered from the exertion and the thin mountain air, his ears rang with the throb of blood in his veins. But even exhausted, he felt strangely exhilarated. It was good to be physically tired, to feel the strain on his muscles, the ache of his feet. It was, he decided, exactly what he had been needing. Physical demands, solitude, rest and the quiet company of a nondemanding friend.

Turning the knob of the door, he went in. The entire room basked in the golden glow of the fire, and the scent of wood smoke and the warmth of the blaze enveloped him. He stood motionless by the door, acclimating himself, adjusting his eyes to the increased light, soothed by the sense of homecoming he felt. Then, dropping his pack to the floor, he called out, "Anybody home?"

From out of the corner of the long leather couch, hiding in the shadows beyond the firelight, a woman rose. Silhouetted against the flames, she moved toward him, and he blinked, disbelieving. He shook his head, trying to clear it. It was the altitude, he thought, breathing deeply, trembling. She came closer, a half smile on her face as she looked up at him. He swallowed, his throat suddenly parched and aching.

Dear God, no, it couldn't be.

"Hello, Griffin," she said softly in a voice that had plagued him in his dreams for weeks and weeks.

He shut his eyes. "Lainie."

Chapter Six

An incredible variety of emotions surged over him. Anger.
Hope. Fear. Disbelief. Despair. Joy. Anger.

Whatever else he felt, it began and ended with that tremendous sense of anger. Like a tiny spark that suddenly
caught on dry forest tinder, it was a conflagration before he
knew it. *Damn it, no,* he wanted to scream. His gaze flew
from her to the door and back again as, just for a second,
he contemplated turning around and walking right back out
the way he had come in.

A friend from Harvard? Sure. Fishing in Colorado?
Yeah, right. *You sucker,* he berated himself. *You gullible
fool.* Hearing the faint sound of a car's engine over the noise
of rain on the roof, he took three quick steps to the door and
jerked it open, peering out into the black of night. Through
the trees he could just barely make out a pair of headlights
moving steadily away back down the mountain. He felt ill.

"You set me up."

It wasn't a question.

"You're shivering, Griff," Lainie said quickly. "You
must be freezing. Come on in and get out of those wet
clothes." She started to pluck at his sleeve, but he shook her
off.

"I'm all right," he muttered. But he didn't feel all right.
He felt betrayed, sold out. Damn Chase Whitelaw.

"Please, Griff," she urged, golden eyes beseeching. "At least shut the door."

He shut it. Slammed it, actually. Then stood against it, glaring at her, his sodden clothes dripping on Whitelaw's glossy wood floor. "You've gone to a hell of a lot of trouble just to serve me with divorce papers."

"I didn't bring any divorce papers."

"No?" He had been afraid of that. "What's all this about, then?"

"You're soaking wet. We can talk about it later. We've got all week."

Griff blanched. He'd worked himself to death getting in the frame of mind where divorce and leaving her behind seemed the right thing to do. He was damned if he was going to be stuck here with her a whole week!

"Like hell," he said roughly. "I'll leave in the morning."

"You can't. Chase won't be back till Friday."

"I walked in. I can walk back out."

"You can't!"

"Want to bet on it?"

She didn't. The way Griff looked now, if he'd said he could fly, she'd have been tempted to believe him. His normally warm brown eyes were stony and dark with barely suppressed fury. This wasn't the way things were supposed to go at all. She almost wished Chase hadn't left them alone. But he had, and now she had to make the best of things.

"We can talk about that in the morning," she offered. "It's too late tonight to even think about such things."

Griff didn't move. He didn't speak, either. And she was caught once more in the web of frustration she had so often experienced during their marriage. Every time she offered to talk, he withdrew. Every time she advanced, he retreated. His expression became shuttered and remote, and she hadn't any idea what he thought.

He was thinking she was beautiful, and he wanted her, and he hated her for it. She looked like an angel, but the temptation she provided was sheer hell. He had to get away from her now. When she urged him again to take a hot bath, he grabbed at the suggestion.

It wasn't the bath he wanted so much, although warmth of any sort wouldn't be amiss at the moment; it was really the privacy he needed, the space. Being with her again after having been without her was having a devastating effect on him. He needed to regroup, rethink and mostly to remove himself at once.

Lainie heard the door to the bathroom bang shut with a tremble of relief. *Idiot,* she chastised herself. *You wanted him here.* But she knew at once that she couldn't do anything about them and their relationship until she improved his frame of mind.

"Pick your spots," she had counseled her class. "Don't attack your spouse with problems the minute he or she walks in the door." And the advice was good, she decided, whether he was coming in from work or from sloughing up the mountainside in a rainstorm. He had to mellow a bit before they could talk. The bath would help; so would a hot drink and dinner. A full and warm Griffin would be a more amenable Griffin, she was sure. All the books said so. Besides, cooking and sharing meals were things they had always enjoyed, and she was counting on a familiar welcoming situation to help her get a foothold here. She opened the refrigerator and got out the steaks.

As THE WATER LAPPED against his chest, soothing the cold out of his bones if not the worry out of his mind, Griff lay back and contemplated what the hell he was going to do now.

Walking out in the morning seemed the only real possibility. He didn't know what scheme Lainie had cooked up, but if it wasn't to serve him with divorce papers, it was very likely that she had stranded them out here so they could talk and "sort things out." It was a move that, to him, seemed fraught with possibilities for disaster, but he could imagine that Lainie would have decided it was a great idea. It went with the sort of job she did, and she had tried similar things any number of times before. He wished she hadn't bothered. Both then and now.

Talking things out wouldn't work.

He sighed, rippling the water with his hand, making tiny waves, watching them get bigger as his hand moved faster. Lainie had always come home to him as if he were her safe harbor in the storm of life. Well, God knew he had tried to be, but it hadn't been easy. In fact, he knew it wasn't really even possible. But she had no idea of the undertows he faced himself, and he wouldn't—couldn't—tell her. The growing waves could only destroy them both if he waited around. The "talking" would turn to harsh accusations, the accusations would become shouts, the shouts would turn to threats, and— His fist clenched and thudded angrily against the side of the tub.

Damn it, why hadn't she just let well enough alone?

It wasn't fair. He closed his eyes, trying to forget the vision of her, all golden and ethereal in the firelight. Why couldn't he stop wanting her when all it would bring was pain? She wasn't going to change. She only wanted him to. But he couldn't. He was what he was.

"Griff?"

The door opened a crack, and he scowled discouragingly at her as she peeked in at him. Did she have to follow him even in here?

"What do you want?" He knew his voice sounded cold and angry, and the hurt look she gave him when she opened the door caused him a twinge of guilt. But it was better this way, he reasoned. Better for both of them.

"I—I brought you a hot buttered rum." She set it on the counter so he could reach it.

He steeled himself against breathing in the subtle scent of her perfume, staring straight ahead at the tips of his toes that poked out of the soapy water.

"I thought you might want to warm up your insides, as well," she added. Then she seemed to realize that there was more than one way to interpret that remark, for she suddenly flustered as she tacked on quickly, "I didn't mean—"

"Thank you," he said abruptly, because her presence alone was doing all that was needed to warm him. The hot buttered rum was entirely superfluous. *Leave,* he pleaded silently. *Please leave.*

"Dinner will be ready soon."

"I'm not hungry."

He was starving. But he wasn't going to sit down to a meal with her. He hated her for putting him in a position where it would be all too easy to be seduced into believing that they had a chance of making a go of their marriage, that loving each other was enough. It wasn't. They had proved that over and over. And if she tried to provoke a discussion—his fist tightened again, and he consciously made himself open it and reach for the rum, taking a swallow and feeling it course through him—and he couldn't make an exit, he was afraid what might happen. He couldn't risk it; he didn't dare.

Deliberately, he began to soap his chest, ignoring her, knowing she was probably wondering what he was thinking and absolutely incapable of telling her. After a moment's silence, Lainie shrugged and left.

The smell of the steaks cooking made his stomach growl, accusing him of treason. It had been hours since he and Chase had eaten a late lunch at the Deverels', and the long hike up the mountain had left him weak and ravenous. But he promised his stomach an apple and a granola bar from his pack later. In the meantime, he was staying right where he was.

"NOT HUNGRY, HUH?" Lainie sniffed when she opened the door to the bedroom just a crack three hours later. The room was dark, for she had banked the fire in the living room and had shut off all the rest of the lights, but she could still make out the three apple cores and the granola bar wrappers on the nightstand by the bed.

Tiptoeing over to where Griff lay sprawled out under the comforter, she peered down at him, wondering if he was really asleep or only pretending. She wouldn't have put it past him to fake it. He had cheated himself out of a perfectly delicious T-bone steak, a hot fluffy baked potato and a scrumptious green salad earlier in an attempt to avoid her. Successfully, too, she had to admit.

But he wasn't going to be able to avoid her now. Not unless he was the one who wanted to go sleep in the cold loft on an unmade bed without any blankets. She certainly had no intention of doing so.

Griff shifted his position slightly, mumbling something inaudible and groping for the pillow, which he looped his arm over in a sort of sleepy hug.

"Looking for me?" she whispered, sending up a prayer that he was. He seemed so worn and almost fragile looking asleep, his exhaustion clearly apparent. Griff sighed and began breathing deeply again. The temptation simply to stand and look at him was almost overwhelming. She loved him so much, and she had been alone so long. But there were certain things she had to do first.

Kneeling down quickly beside the bed, she patted the floor furtively until she found what she was looking for, then crept stealthily out of the room again. Fortunately, it had stopped raining, so her trip to the shed near the outhouse was accomplished with a minimum of water and mud. Once back, she changed quickly into a long flannel granny gown and slid into the bed, hoping that Griff was sleeping soundly enough that her movements wouldn't awaken him. The hard, muscular length of him was like a magnet, and she tried to resist. If her cold feet touched him, there was no telling what he would do, but she was willing to bet it wouldn't be to wrap her in his arms and warm her up.

Shivering, she huddled into a little ball on the edge of the bed, rubbing her hands together, trying to heat them, wishing she dared move closer to the human warmth just inches away. And then the warmth moved closer to her.

Griff rolled onto his side, and his chest pressed up against her back; then his strong thighs curved around beneath her bottom. She tensed, wondering if he was awake, but then his breathing settled into a smooth, even pattern again. His hand had come to rest on her hip, and when it didn't move away, she dared to reach around to touch it. It felt hard and warm against the cool softness of her palm, the hairs slightly rough on the tips of her fingers as first they skimmed over the top, then settled and cupped around his knuckles. It was a taste of heaven, lying there. A profound sense of coming home.

She wanted to turn in his arms and kiss him awake, loving him and murmuring to him that she was sorry, that their stupid misunderstanding had been all her fault. Because she knew it had been. But she also knew that now was not the time to tell him so. Now they needed closeness and touch, some tiny thread to link them. The rest would come.

He hadn't meant to fall asleep. He had intended to lie awake till the first light of morning, then creep out without waking her and make his way back down the mountainside. But he hadn't counted on his exhaustion. The red-eye flight from the east coast to L.A. to pick up his things, then the flight from L.A. to Denver and the short hop back to Durango, followed by that marathon hike up the mountain had done him in. He had got into bed, nibbling on an apple, wrapped in the gentle warmth of a soft, lightweight down comforter, perfect for the cool June night, and against his better judgment, he relaxed, lulled by the sounds of domesticity, relieved that Lainie hadn't tried to push things yet.

He lay back, listening to the sounds of knife and fork on plate, then the washing up, then soft music—romantic music—soothing music—and then...

"Yes," she was murmuring. "Yes...yes...yes" and Griff's eyes first struggled open, aware that the aching need in his dream was pressed again the soft, yielding warmth of reality.

"Yes...yes..." Tree branches scratched their encouragement against the window, and the body pressed to his own moved slowly, enticingly, in instinctive rhythm with his.

"No," he moaned, and sanity returning, he went to draw away from her, to loosen her from the embrace in which he held her.

But the dream wouldn't vanish, merging instead with reality, and Lainie's hands closed over his, small but surprisingly strong. "Shh, Griff," she whispered, her voice a lullaby. "Shh." She laced her fingers through his, holding them in front of her breasts so his hands could feel the smooth, warm fullness of her flesh beneath the nightgown.

He was torn with wanting her, needing her, yet telling himself he shouldn't. "Lainie, we can't."

She turned in his arms, loosing her hold on his hands, only to wrap her arms around his waist and draw him against her. Her lips brushed his stubbled chin, trailing a line of kisses along his jaw, and one of her legs slid between his. "Why can't we? You love me."

Yes, his mind cried out, and his body echoed, arching against her. "Yes," he murmured.

"And I love you," she went on. She nuzzled beneath his ear, driving him mad with gentle nips and soft feathery kisses.

"Oh, Lainie."

It was a moan of surrender and a plea for mercy at the same time. God knew his body was betraying him; now his mind was deserting him, too. *Why not,* it asked him. *She's right. You do love her.* And the future was going to be long, lonely and unutterably cold without her. Why not store up memories for the barren days ahead? Why not have one last taste of shared ecstasy to remember in the bleak and love-less years ahead? Especially when Lainie wanted it, too.

His hands fumbled with her nightgown, drawing it up past her thighs, then smoothing over her narrow waist. His fingers trembled, stroking her breasts, cupping the warm globes, kneading them, teasing the already-taut nipples un-til she sighed and dug her fingernails into his back as she murmured his name again and again.

No other woman could do this to him, make him feel whole, cherished, loved. Only Lainie, whose soft endear-ments aroused him so that his hands tugged the gown over her head, then swooped down to caress her curves and gentle warmth, ever brought him to this pitch of excitement. How would he be able to live without her? How?

From the moment of her waking, Lainie had sensed the struggle going on in him. How their loving had begun, she didn't even know. She had fallen asleep, wrapped in Griff's arms, confident that somehow—despite his initial negativ-ism—things would work out. She felt grateful just to be with him and glad to share this closeness, which, in his uncon-scious state, he wasn't even aware of. Then later—several hours later—she had been awakened by the urgent press of his masculinity, the insistent stroking of his hand cupped around her breast. Her own body moved in response. It was right, she thought with as much coherence as she was cap-able of at that moment. It was only another way of show-ing him she loved him. Maybe, right now, it was the only way.

But once Griff was aware of what was happening be-tween them, he fought it. Lainie felt his whole body tens-ing, withdrawing from her in the same way his mind with-drew at times, and she knew she couldn't let him. With his need, even if it had begun before he was awake enough to disguise it, a wall had started to crack between them. If she let him retreat now, he would have it firmly cemented shut again by morning.

And so she turned, wrapping her arms around him, drawing him against her, insinuating her knee between his thighs, needing him, too. He had argued, protested, and she had kissed him, loved him. And at last, thank God, she had felt him respond, mind as well as body.

Once persuaded, Griff was almost feverish in his need of her. Hot, eager lips fastened on hers, his tongue teasing at hers, then plunging on, eliciting her response. She gave it to him, meeting him with equal fervor, trying to show him physically, if she couldn't any other way, the depth of her love for him.

He turned her so that she lay beneath him, then drew back away from her far enough to gaze down upon her face in the darkness. The storm had passed, though clouds still obscured the moon except for brief glimpses of its silvery crescent. And just now there was enough of the pewter-colored light for her to see the expression on his face, the strain of passion and need, as yet unfulfilled, that raged within him. And something more—a searing, wondering look that made her feel as if he were cataloging every feature, memorizing her for all time. He settled back, kneeling, resting against his heels, as his hands skimmed over her body, starting at her neck, brushing across the width of her shoulders and gliding down her arms, then shaping against her waist and moving back up her sides. His light touch made her shiver with pleasure. The tremulous touch of his fingertips taught her blood to sing beneath her flesh.

"Beautiful," he murmured, and bent to press kisses against her breasts. And she remembered that on Maui he had called her that. "Beautiful," he had said, "Oh, yes, my beauty." And now, as she threaded her fingers in his silky blond hair as it brushed across her throat, her breasts, she reiterated that sentiment.

"Yours, Griff," she promised. "Yours."

He lifted his head, aching eyes meeting hers in the shadows, piercing her with the naked longing she saw in them. It made her want to cry for him, for both of them. He started to shake his head, to deny it, but she clasped her hands around the back of his neck and drew him down again, meeting his lips with hers, sealing her promise, praying—for both their sakes—that her promise would come true.

He was lost. Sanity, noble motives, rational behavior, all deserted him. He knew only that he loved her, needed her, had to possess her and to be possessed by her one last time.

One last time...

The realization lanced through him, making him rough, desperate. His hands, which had been trembling, now shook noticeably. He wanted to make the experience beautiful for her, to bring her slowly and lovingly to the brink of ecstasy, but his control snapped.

She seemed to realize it, for she moved to welcome him willingly. Her hands urged him down to her until he felt himself sheathed in her warmth and let out a long sigh. For just a moment he didn't move. He simply savored their oneness, resting in the peace of their shared being, loving her.

Time faded into eternity as he began to move and she to move with him. He watched her face, the slow half smile of passion and desire that she saved only for him, the heavy-lidded eyes that caressed his face just as her body caressed his. Past, present and future melded into one instant. Minds, hearts and bodies became one.

And then they were two again.

Lainie knew she was crying. She pressed her wet face into Griff's damp shoulder and prayed he would think that the moistness was a product of their sweat-slicked bodies and not the emotional overflow of her heart. For at this moment she couldn't explain her tears. She, who was so skilled at using words to get at feelings, knew only that words for once didn't begin to express the love she felt for him, the joy she experienced in becoming part of him and the hope she felt for having been permitted once more into his life. He wouldn't understand these tears, for they were born not of sadness but of promise. And it was a promise she didn't think he was ready yet to accept.

But she didn't want to talk about it now; she didn't want to spoil things. There would be time enough to talk in the morning. She smoothed her palms down his back, kissing him gently.

Don't say anything, he pleaded with her silently. *Please, don't talk. Give me these memories. They're all I'm going to have of you.* His breathing came in ragged gasps, and he swallowed hard, squeezing his eyes shut against the tears he could not suppress. Something close to a sob wrenched through him, and he wondered how it was possible to feel both fulfilled and empty at the same time.

For that was how he felt—beloved and bereft simultaneously. Lainie shifted slightly beneath him, and he eased away somewhat to allow her to move, but he couldn't stop touching her, couldn't let her go just yet. He rolled onto his side and guided her so that she turned, too, nestling back against his chest, cocooned in the comforter with him. He heard her sigh and held his breath, waiting for her to break the mood. But she only edged closer, and he let his breath out slowly when she drew his hand to her lips and kissed his fingers but didn't speak.

He lay his cheek against her hair, savoring the scent of her, storing up impressions. Lainie's breathing deepened and slowed; her fingers loosened but still held his hand against her breast. Griff synchronized his breathing with hers and thanked God for these stolen moments. He knew he shouldn't have taken them. It hadn't been fair to offer her love, to offer hope where he knew none could survive. But he wasn't strong enough to tell her so. And maybe, when she remembered him, she would think of their loving this night and not hate him too much for what he was about to do.

SUNLIGHT REFLECTING off the brass bedpost threw a shaft of clear golden light across Lainie's hair. It gave her the look of an angel, all pure, untarnished innocence, and if Griff had stopped to look at her, he might have been inclined to store up the sight with his other memories.

He couldn't take the time. He didn't dare. It was already past six in morning, and the birds had long since raised the sun on their chorus of song. A lone woodpecker was tapping out a staccato rhythm designed to wake the dead. Griff knew he should have started down the mountain ages ago.

Except, he grumbled inwardly for the twentieth time as he crawled around the bedroom floor on his hands and knees, peering under the bed, under the armoire and the dresser and the nightstand, he couldn't find his shoes.

"Hell," he muttered almost inaudibly. "Bloody, bloody hell."

He could not remember what he had done with them. Last night he had been so exhausted and shell-shocked when he arrived, only to be confronted by the last person he needed or expected to see just then, that he was scarcely coherent. He remembered a chilling anger, an aching hunger, a hot bath and bed; after that, nothing. Except, of course, making love with Lainie in the middle of the night. But now, he reminded himself, was definitely not the time to be thinking of that.

He heard her sigh and shift in the bed, and he froze where he knelt. Even his breathing was suspended as he prayed silently that she would continue to sleep. He had to get away before she woke. He couldn't talk to her, not after what they had shared. He needed to leave with his memories intact.

Lainie settled once more, and Griff straightened up, grinding his teeth in frustration. Where the hell were they?

He damned well wasn't going to make much headway trying to go down the mountain without them.

Getting stealthily to his feet, he padded out to the pine-paneled living room again, scowling at his pack, which he had leaned against the door. They weren't in his pack. He had unpacked it clear to the bottom and packed it again. No shoes. Had he stuck them out on the porch because they were so wet? Had Lainie?

That last thought made his frown deepen. He eased the door open, grimacing at the squeak it made and glancing furtively over his shoulder toward the open door of the bedroom. But Lainie didn't stir. His gaze scanned the porch. No shoes. A stack of logs lay at the far end, and he walked down to examine them, annoyed as he remembered Chase's subterfuge about going for logs. Obviously Lainie had taken care of the matter before they arrived. She seemed to have had things very well in hand.

Had she taken his shoes in hand, too? Somehow it didn't seem unlikely.

"So, what're you going to do?" he asked himself. "Wake her up and ask her?" Yeah, sure. "Damn her, anyway." There was grudging admiration mixed with anger in his tone.

Now what was he going to do? Look for them, of course. She might think she was clever, but he doubted she could hide his shoes any place he couldn't find them. There weren't that many places around.

He strode quickly back into the house, his bare feet slapping softly on the cool polished wood. Now that he was virtually certain that it wasn't his own forgetfulness but her concerted effort that he was up against, things would go quickly enough.

Sleep on, he told her silently, a grim smile lifting the corners of his mouth as he looked in on her. *Give me a few minutes and I'll be gone.*

He was wrong. In a few minutes he had ransacked all the logical places. In an hour all he had done was fray his temper and put holes in his athletic socks. He had systematically searched every nook and cranny of the cabin, even going so far as to search the vegetable bin in the refrigerator, though he couldn't believe she'd actually have put them in there. She hadn't. But he didn't know where she had.

So, irritated, he had sloughed though the muddy field to the garage and searched there. But he still hadn't found them. It was past seven when he admitted defeat, contemplating instead a trip back down the mountain without them. But the ground was uneven and the pine needles were sharp. Infuriated, he stomped back to the house through the wet grass of the meadow, stubbing his toe on a rock. "Damn!"

He felt like committing mayhem. For a man who prided himself on his ironclad control, he was perilously close to losing it now. "Damn!" he said again. He wanted to wake her up and shake her, shout at her, demand she give him the shoes. But emotion—particularly anger—was the one thing right now he needed to avoid.

So his consternation was enormous when he jerked open the front door and was greeted by the smell of frying bacon, the scent of maple syrup, and the sight of Lainie still clad in her fuzzy red bathrobe, heaping a pile of delectable pancakes onto a plate.

She smiled at him. "Good morning."

He stopped dead in the doorway, shoving his fists in the pockets of his jeans and drawing in a long, necessary breath. "Where are they?"

She moved with easy grace around the side of the table and sat down, forking two pancakes onto her plate and cutting off a wedge of butter with her knife. "Where are what?"

"My shoes."

"Ah." She took a bite of pancake.

"Lainie."

"Hmm?"

"Give them to me."

"No."

A pause. *"Lainie."*

"No."

It was a miracle she could sound as cool and collected as she did. Inside she felt a mass of frayed nerves and twisting panic. The moment she had awakened to find herself alone in bed, she knew the worst had happened. He had got up early, hoping to sneak off without a confrontation. It was precisely what she had feared he might do, which was why she had hidden his shoes before she went to bed the night before, but being clairvoyant was damned little comfort now. Why, oh, why couldn't he just have stayed in bed until she had awakened so they could talk things out reasonably in an atmosphere of love instead of having to confront each other like this?

For a confrontation was what it was—there was no other way to describe it. And for once Griff wasn't going to be able to walk away. Her having tucked his shoes neatly away in the shed by the outhouse had seen to that. With great concentration she dissected a pancake, taking a bite and allowing herself an oblique glance at Griff to see how he was taking her refusal.

He wasn't taking it well. His fists clenched, unclenched, then clenched again in the pockets of his jeans. The movements drew the material taut across his thighs, emphasizing his masculinity and recalling for her the feel of the hard evidence of his arousal that had awakened her from her dreams the night before. Deliberately, she shoved the memory aside, needing for the time being to concentrate on more important things.

"Would you like some pancakes?" she offered, hoping that she could establish some sort of aura of cordiality before they really got into it.

"No." The color was high in his cheeks, and his lips were thin with suppressed anger. It was as fierce as she could ever remember seeing in him, and it wasn't a sight she particularly relished until she recalled that it was far better than seeing the back of him walking away.

"Then have some coffee with me. I'm not going to let you walk out of here until I've apologized to you for what happened at the ball game."

Griff made an impatient gesture. "Apology accepted. Now can I have my shoes?"

Lainie sighed, exasperated. "No." She pushed back her chair and got up, walking toward him. "Griff, why won't you talk to me? For a marriage to work, the people have to communicate. You can't just keep walking out. I need to hear your feelings."

He scowled. "I don't want to talk about my feelings," he said tightly.

"Why?"

"Because I don't."

She just looked up at him in silent entreaty. Finally, he shoved a hand through his hair and backed away.

"It doesn't do any good," he said bitterly.

"You never know unless you try," she said more lightly than she felt. She offered him an encouraging smile, which he ignored. He turned and stalked away from her, placing himself in front of the fireplace, where he turned and confronted her.

"I know," he said flatly.

"How?"

"I just do." His jaw tightened.

Lainie shook her head. "Now you sound like Dick Leary," she complained, hoping to get him to smile at the absurdity of the comparison. Big, burly, loud-mouthed Dick was as far from Griff as chalk from cheese. But instead of a smile, she saw Griff turn absolutely white. "What's wrong?" she demanded. "I was kidding," she went on hurriedly. "You're not like him, Griff. It's just that he said the very same thing the first time I—"

"How do you know I'm not?"

Lainie stared at him, speechless.

"I said, 'How do you know I'm not like Dick Leary?'" Griff's voice was deadly quiet, the cords of his neck taut with tension.

"Well, I mean, you—you're nothing like him. He's a chronic—he's..." Her voice trailed off as she saw Griff nodding.

"He's a chronic what?" he prodded. "Say it."

She looked at him warily. "A chronic wife beater."

"And how do you suppose he got that way?" he asked. When she didn't immediately answer, he urged her. "Come on. You must have some social theory that will explain it." His tone was sarcastic and underscored with a pain she didn't understand.

"It was all he knew," she told him bluntly. "All Dick Leary ever saw was his father taking out frustration on his mother. Beating her."

"That's what I saw, too."

"What?" She stared, not believing what she heard.

But Griff's eyes dared her to. Stunned, she started toward him, but he brushed her off, striding away, the words he had dammed up so long now spilling out so fast she could hardly keep up with him.

"Is that what you wanted to hear?" he demanded bitterly. "Here you were, thinking I was the safe haven you could come home to at the end of the day, and I'm just as bad, if not worse, than everyone else."

"What are you talking about?" Lainie cried, confused.

"All those times you came home exhausted, worn out dealing with the problems of the world! That's what I'm talking about. Expecting me to be the harbor in the storm!"

"I—I didn't want you to be a—a haven," she protested, at the same time realizing that perhaps she had.

"You could have fooled me," Griff snapped, his eyes flashing. "Well, damn it, I tried. I tried to be what you wanted. And then I tried to get you to leave the damned job because I couldn't be! I also tried to get you to see that there were people you were counseling that wouldn't change any more than my father changed. I told you to get out of there—"

"But you didn't tell me why," she said quietly.

"Why! Why?" He gave her a look of sheer anguish as he paced the room. "You wanted me to tell you that every argument, every discussion, my parents ever had turned into a full-scale battle? You wanted to hear that my father gave my mother three broken ribs? That I left home at eighteen and never went back because I couldn't stand the way they treated each other?" He gave her a scathing stare. "Yeah, sure."

"I would have understood."

"You would have pitied me. You would have dragged out all your damned theories and psychoanalyzed me. You would have counseled me, not married me! And I love you, damn it!"

"And I love you. That's why we should share—"

"Share?" He snorted. "Do you know what happened when my parents decided to 'share' their views on things, like how to raise kids or whether my mother ought to spend time volunteering places or even how much they ought to spend on someone's wedding present?"

Lainie didn't but she could guess. "They fought?"

"They fought." He sighed and rubbed the back of his neck. "He pushed her down the stairs. I was fourteen, and I saw it happen. Usually I got the hell out of the house the minute I sensed a fight brewing. But this time it was my fault. I was arguing with my mother about something. Curfew—I don't know. Something like that." He shrugged his shoulders awkwardly. "And my dad came home. I was going to drop the subject, but he heard what I was saying.

Something about her not understanding me. Kid stuff, you know?" He looked at her beseechingly, seeking understanding.

She nodded.

"Anyway, he got into it. They started yelling. Not much at first. It never started out bad. Just a 'discussion,' you know?" His emphasis on the word made Lainie wince as she remembered the times she had said she only wanted to discuss something with him. "Well, as usual, the discussion escalated. She slapped him. He shoved her against the wall in the upstairs hall. I started to step between them, but he pushed me out, shouted at me, told me he was on my side and what the hell was I doing. Then he pushed her down the stairs." He took a long, tortured breath and shut his eyes as if he could see the whole ghastly scene in his mind.

Lainie hovered close to him, wanting to touch him, wanting to share his pain, understanding it at last, yet knowing instinctively that he would flinch away if she so much as reached out her hand.

"I went down to help her," he went on in a low, pain-choked voice. "I bent over her, and she wouldn't let me touch her. She said, 'Get away from me. You're just like your father. Get away.'"

And then there was silence.

Lainie would have given anything to be able to fill it, to wash away his pain and memories with words of love and hope, but she was beyond that. He was beyond it. Nothing could touch him now. Nothing but the memories he had tried to forget.

"I am just like him, Lainie," he said slowly, not looking at her, concentrating instead on the wall of rock where the fireplace was. "He had a terrific temper. So do I. He wanted his own way. So do I. But I learned something he never has. I learned that I can't always have it my way. So I also learned to walk away." He shrugged. A smile that flickered like a ghost on his lips was both painful and rueful. "I'm sorry, Lainie. I didn't want for it to end like this. I would have liked to let you keep a few illusions about me. But it didn't work. I can't stay here. I won't. I could hurt you, don't you see?'' He looked at her helplessly.

''No, Griff. We can—''

''We can't. We tried. I can't do it your way. You can't do it mine. So it's better that we stop now.'' He paused, and his voice broke. ''I wish it could have.''

Then, as if he couldn't help himself, he reached out a hand and touched her cheek for a brief moment. The woodpecker attacked the dead aspen with renewed vigor. Griff's hand dropped, he blinked, and once more the smile flickered. Then he turned and strode out the door.

Lainie didn't know how long she stood, unmoving, after he had gone. Nothing she thought made any sense; nothing she did, once she moved, had any purpose. She was simply buffeted about the hours by rampant emotions. His. Hers. She didn't even know if he intended to come back. He couldn't go far, she remembered, without his shoes. Well, she thought ruefully, she had certainly got her confrontation.

And nothing—not one single thing—had gone as she had thought. She ought to stop playing God. At least she ought to stop trying to pretend she knew what was good for Griff. Obviously she had no idea what was good for either of them. She swiped at her tear-stained cheeks, almost surprised to find them damp. How long had she been crying? *Please come back,* she begged silently. *Please.*

She trudged across the field and through the trees to the shed, her mind seeing his pain-ravaged face as she retrieved his shoes and carried them back to the cabin. *God, Griff, I'm sorry. I didn't mean to hurt you, to give you pain. I only wanted to help. Please come back.* She lay the shoes on the floor next to his pack. There was nothing more she could do. God knew she had done enough already.

She didn't see him for the rest of the day. And that night she fell asleep in the living room, the door to the cabin open so she might be able to hear his footsteps if he came back again.

But in the morning when she awoke with a crick in her neck, the door was closed securely, and Griff's shoes and his pack were gone.

Chapter Seven

Chase was sorry; Cassie was philosophical; and Brendan, the only person to whom Lainie confided the whole unvarnished truth, was aghast.

The two of them sat in the den of Brendan and Cassie's rambling home on the Sunday immediately following Lainie's disastrous kidnapping attempt, and while Cassie attended to the victims of a highway disaster, they discussed a disaster of their own.

Brendan sprawled comfortably on the couch, stirring a glass of iced tea, keeping one ear cocked for the sounds of the boys playing in the yard and listening to Lainie with the other. She sat huddled in the armchair opposite him and hauled the whole messy experience up sentence by sentence. He merely nodded now and then, allowing her to stumble through it uninterrupted until she reached the part where she told him about Griff's parents.

"His father did what?" Brendan sat up abruptly, his bare feet hitting the floor with a pronounced thump.

Lainie repeated what Griff had told her in a low monotone, almost as reluctant to share what he had told her as he had been.

"My God," Brendan said.

"Yes," Lainie concurred. "And the worst of it is, Bren, I didn't have any idea. He never ever said a word, never told me about his parents at all. I had no notion of it. I just assumed he was being obtuse and stubborn when he wanted his own way. Why didn't I realize?'' The last was almost a wail.

"You?" Brendan shook his head incredulously. "I've known him for twenty years, and I never knew!"

Lainie lifted her eyes and stared. She assumed that Brendan must have had some idea. How could Griff have kept such a thing from his best friend?

"Oh, I knew they had problems," Brendan said, obviously reading the question in her eyes. "Sometimes when we were kids he would show up on my doorstep at odd hours and wouldn't seem inclined to go home. But sometimes I felt that way, too. And he never said why, so I never asked. It wasn't the sort of thing we talked about." He shrugged helplessly.

"What did you talk about?" Lainie wanted to know. Being a person who dissected everything good or bad that had ever happened to her, she couldn't imagine being the sort of person who didn't talk about what bothered him.

"Oh, we talked about girls," Brendan said, smiling at his memories. "And the surf and girls and jobs and girls and colleges and—"

"Girls," Lainie finished in duet with him, smiling in spite of herself at the vision of Griff and Brendan as teenagers. But with the smile came a renewed pain as she found herself wishing she had known him then, when all this was happening to him. Maybe if she had, some of what they were going through now could have been avoided.

"It wasn't a bad life," Brendan went on nostalgically, then added, "but I reckon it must have been hell at times for Griff. God, to think I never even knew."

Lainie smiled ruefully. "He wouldn't appreciate you knowing now."

"I won't say anything."

"Not even to Cassie?"

"Not if you don't want me to."

"I don't. I wouldn't have even told you, but I needed to talk to someone about what happened. And about what to do now."

"What *are* you going to do now?" Brendan lifted a quizzical dark brow.

She shrugged and spread her hands. It was the question she had been plaguing herself with ever since Griff had left. She had, at first, been tempted to go after him down the mountain. But then she had thought better of it.

Always impulsive and always certain she knew how to deal with whatever came along, she had forced herself to stop and reconsider, forced herself for once to see things his way. And it hadn't been easy admitting that she hadn't always tried to do that. But when she had got up to find his pack and shoes gone, there was only one conclusion possible. She had thought she knew how to deal with him, and she had been wrong.

She had taken her chance, and she had failed.

To go after him, to plead with him, to mouth all those wonderful, understanding platitudes about how terrible his life must have been while he was growing up, would only have driven him farther from her. She had to face the fact that she had just made things worse, that she had completely misunderstood the situation and that she had no right to ask him to come back. She didn't like it, but she made herself accept it. And she made herself live with the knowledge all week, going about daily chores, hiking in the woods, fishing in the stream and thinking—always thinking—about Griff.

It hadn't been easy. Every day she was tempted to leave, to hike back down the narrow gravel road to the Deverels' and to escape into the rigors of civilization, which would help her forget what a mess she had made of everything. But every time she was tempted, she fought it down, staying on at the cabin, coming to terms with how Griff must have perceived their marriage and acknowledging that it was far different from her own perception.

It was penance of sorts, she supposed. And she used the time to recognize that talking things over might not always be the answer and that there were no easy solutions to make some relationships right. At the end of the week, when she left the mountain with Chase, she had no idea of what she should do at all. Griff, though, had a very definite idea, which she learned when she got home.

"There was a letter waiting for me," she told Brendan softly, lacing her fingers together.

"And?"

"He sent me the name of a lawyer," she said heavily. "He said that he was sure, now that I understood, I would want to get a divorce."

Brendan took a slow swallow of iced tea, looking at her over his glass. "And do you?" he asked gently.

"He wants me to," Lainie said, dropping her gaze.

"Yes, but are you going to?"

"I don't know." She had been asking herself that question, too. Flustered, she jumped to her feet and began pacing up and down the room. "I don't want to, God knows. All my instincts tell me to refuse. But as we know, my instincts where Griff is concerned have not been notably reliable."

"I'm not sure that's true," Brendan protested.

"I am. Look at the way I badgered him. And I manipulated him into coming to Colorado. I thought I knew exactly how to make him open up to me."

"You were right," he reminded her.

Lainie snorted. "What good is right when you see where it got me. We're farther apart now than we ever were. Sometimes I wish I'd never found out."

"You don't mean that."

"No." She sighed, tugging at a lock of hair. "I suppose I don't. But it was so awful—like making a terrible remark about someone and discovering that they were listening. Here I was, pontificating to Griff all about counseling these people, telling him how they ought to be able to work through their problems and thanking God we didn't have similar ones—and then finding out we do!'' She felt the heat grow in her cheeks just thinking about it. "He must have wanted to die, listening to me. And whenever he said anything, I didn't understand.''

"I can relate to that," Brendan told her, a rueful grin on his face. And she remembered that he had had trouble making Cassie see how he was feeling at times, too. But Brendan's insecurities involved his career and what would become of him after an injury that destroyed his future in baseball. Griff's insecurities went far deeper than that. His were rooted not in career identity but in the very person he was. And he felt he couldn't change.

"You don't really think he's like his father, do you?" Lainie asked, tilting her head in appeal.

"It doesn't matter what I think," Brendan replied. "What does he think?"

"That he is." She told him what Griff had said about his mother, about what she had said to him.

Brendan didn't reply at once. He seemed to be weighing her words, comparing them to his own memories as he stared out the window, watching his own boys as if reflecting on the effects parents have on their children. Then he drew a long breath. "It's possible, I suppose, that he could feel that way. Certainly there is a physical resemblance between Griff and his dad. And his father was always intense. Driven, I guess you could say. He had to be the best at whatever he did. He sold insurance, I think. But whatever it was, I remember him having sales awards around the house. Little gold plaques attesting to his greatness. And I know Griff could never argue with him. Not even about stuff that didn't matter, like which baseball team was better. Now, my dad, being a theologian, would argue about anything." He grinned.

Lainie smiled at the comparison but then zeroed in on Griff again. "So in some ways you think Griff is like him?"

"On a superficial level maybe."

She frowned. "Damn."

"Why? It's not genetic or something, is it? Wife beating?" Brendan asked.

"No, of course not. But it is a learned behavior, one you can learn from you parents. And Griff knows that. That's the main reason I think he's telling me to get the divorce. He thinks he's protecting me."

"Maybe he is," Brendan said reasonably.

Lainie shook her head vehemently. "No, I can't believe he's like his father. Not in that way."

"Why not? You said yourself he could have learned it at home."

"Yes, but he never has let himself be dragged into an argument—unless you count that last one up at the cabin. And that just proves my point. He does know another way to handle his anger. If things get out of hand or if he thinks he won't be able to control them, he just walks away, like he did with our marriage. It may not solve anything—" she gave a short, mirthless laugh "—but by God it works! You can't argue with it the way his parents did; that's for sure."

"So?"

"So as long as it works for him, he has no incentive to try something else." She shook her head and dropped into the chair again, tasting defeat. "And I sure as heck can't convince him. I've tried. It's certainly a lot easier to make other people's marriage work than it is my own."

Brendan gave her a sympathetic grin. "So what about this lawyer person?"

"I don't know. I can't call him yet. Maybe I ought to, but it doesn't feel right. Lord knows, my way of trying to make things work wasn't successful. But I'm not sure that letting

Griff do things his way is a good idea, either. It feels like a cop-out to me."

"Stalemate, then?" Brendan asked.

"Stalemate," Lainie agreed, and closed her eyes. "Stay tuned for the next installment." She opened her eyes then and gave him a grateful smile, thinking how blessed she was to have him and Cassie for friends. How many other people would have the patience to listen to her try to sort out her life?

"What's new with you two, then?" she asked, trying to put things on a lighter plane for a while. "Or," she corrected as she heard the whoops and shouts of the boys in the garden, "should I say, you four?"

Brendan rubbed his hand against the back of his neck as though his shirt collar were suddenly too tight. "It's odd that you should ask," he said. "Talking of the effects of parents on kids and all has made me wonder, but—" he paused, then shrugged "—it's too late now. Cassie's going to have a baby."

"A baby?" Lainie couldn't completely hide her envy.

Brendan lifted his shoulders comfortably. "We'd been talking about having one and—"

"I know," Lainie said softly. "I'm happy for you, really." She was, although she felt a lump growing in her throat and memories of how she used to plan to have Griff's babies assailed her. She swallowed hard.

Brendan stretched out his legs. "Maybe I shouldn't say this, but in some ways I reckon I owe this kid to you and Griff."

"How so?"

He pinched his nose at the bridge as if debating his choice of words. "I guess because Cassie has been affected by all this hassle the two of you have had. She came home one night and told me how bad it made her feel, how she hoped everything would work out for you and how happy she was for what we had. Next thing you know, we were having a baby,'' He spread his hands and grinned sheepishly at her. ''So thanks, Lainie, for what it's worth.''

Lainie didn't know whether to laugh or cry. She stood up and fetched her purse from the table where she had left it and headed for the door, pausing to give Brendan a sisterly peck on the cheek.

''It's always nice to be an inspiration, Bren,'' she told him lightly as she left. She just wished it didn't hurt so bad.

''BUSTED?''

''*Who?*''

''When?''

''Cocaine?''

''Who?''

''LaRue, man. Wes LaRue.''

Griff felt the bottom of his stomach drop out. No one noticed him at all. The other two umpires were staring at Jack Morelos, who had just delivered the news. Griff himself was staring, but at his plate, not at Jack. The midday breakfast that he was having trouble eating anyway, suddenly loomed insurmountable on his plate. Sucking in a deep breath, he lifted his eyes as Jack sat down at the table across from him. Dan Fletcher and Bob Johnson had asked all the questions so far, but they weren't the only ones who wanted to know the answers.

''I ran into Bray when I was getting out of the elevator,'' Jack said after giving the waitress his order. Bray was a columnist for the local metropolitan daily. If anyone knew, Griff supposed that he would. ''He said they busted LaRue last night at the airport.''

Fletcher's eyes widened, and he shot Griff a questioning look. Griff ignored it, deliberately forking up a bite of sausage and chewing with great concentration.

''I'm not surprised,'' Johnson said, echoing Griff's own thought. ''You only had to look at him lately. Higher than a kite half the time.''

Jack nodded. "It's too bad, though. Heck of a waste of talent."

"Yeah," Fletcher said, still studying Griff. "Well, I reckon he won't be giving you fits any more for a while, huh, Tucker?"

Griff grunted. His mouth was full. He made sure it stayed that way, working his way through his meal with diligence even though he felt less like eating now than he had when he started. He didn't want to talk about LaRue, didn't want to discuss it. It made him sick. Finally, he couldn't eat another bite and laid down his fork, pushed his chair back and stood up.

"Leaving?" Fletcher asked.

"Think I'll take a walk."

"Me, too." Fletcher said, taking a last swallow of his coffee and getting to his feet. "See you two later," he said to Johnson and Morelos, then followed Griff quickly out of the restaurant into the hotel lobby.

"You were talking to LaRue a few days ago, weren't you?" Fletcher began without preamble as he caught Griff up.

Griff let out a long breath. "Yeah." He kept walking.

Fletcher kept pace, looking at him expectantly. Griff headed for the main doors of the hotel. "I am going for a walk," he said pointedly. "Are you coming or not?" He gave Fletcher a stony stare that said better than words that he had no intention of talking further about LaRue or about his conversation with him in the airport in New York. Obviously it had been in vain, and he had no desire to hash it over. Fletcher, on the other hand, was fond of dissecting disasters. Rather like Lainie, Griff remembered grimly. Another subject he wanted to avoid. His reluctance must have been more than obvious, for Fletcher backed off and shook his head, saying, "No, thanks. I think I'll take a swim. See you later."

"Yeah."

Shoving his hands into his pockets, Griff walked through the open doors and into the bustle of midmorning downtown Montreal. He didn't see any of it. His mind was a total blank until he reached the waterfront of the St. Lawrence River and stood there, overlooking the traffic on the river. It wasn't the same as walking by the ocean, but it helped.

There was something inherently settling about great bodies of water, he thought. Even the St. Lawrence, studded though it was with boats of all sizes and descriptions, was no exception. It gave him a sense of space, a sense of perspective. After he had left Lainie, he had flown back to L.A. and had driven north to camp along Big Sur for the rest of the week, never more than a quarter mile from the ocean as he sorted out his feelings and got a grip on himself. And hearing the news about LaRue had prompted him to do the same thing. In the café he had felt as if he were suffocating. Here he could walk, breathe, think.

What he thought about was getting involved in other people's lives. And what he decided was that it didn't work. Before Lainie, he had never even been tempted. Given his particular set of parents, it had never seemed a good idea. So his relationships were casual at best. Even Brendan, whom he had considered his best friend for years, could only be called a pal, never a confidant.

Griff had never confided in anyone, and he had never got close enough to allow anyone to confide in him. It was, he had decided long ago, the safest and sanest way to live. And he had never had any trouble doing it until Lainie had whirled into his life like a miniature tornado, upsetting and enchanting him simultaneously.

He, who had never given love more than a passing thought, suddenly found himself head over heels. And though he had thought initially it was a lark, he soon discovered otherwise. After he met her, road trips seemed interminable. Being alone was intolerable. It was as though he had found his other half. And Lainie seemed to agree.

Though they had little time together, she was always ready to fall in with whatever he suggested, do whatever he wanted. It was too good to be true, he feared. But he couldn't imagine life without her once he had lived life with her, and so he had proposed. And they had married.

And, then, in short order, he discovered that his fears had been justified. Day-in and day-out living together didn't work. Lainie, who had always seemed so amenable before, now had more obligations than he could count. And when he had tried to talk her out of them and out of her job, things had only got worse. She hadn't changed, and neither had he. He couldn't. And, he decided as he watched a heavily loaded boat chug upriver, maybe she couldn't, either. It was probably too much to ask. He should have known better than to hope. He ought to have learned from his parents' marriage that he wasn't cut out for that sort of life. He ought to have stayed uninvolved. It would have been better for both of them.

It probably would have been better for LaRue, too. He sighed and kicked a rusty tin can toward the water. He hadn't had any more success with LaRue than he had with Lainie. So much for getting involved in other peoples' lives. Hell of a lot of good it did.

He turned and started walking slowly back toward the church of Notre Dame de Bonsecour, aware all at once of crowded streets and sidewalks, of people talking, laughing, sharing. A polyglot of French, English, Portuguese, Yiddish, Greek and Italian surrounded him, and he felt suddenly alone. But that was stupid, he told himself. If he had wanted company, Fletcher would have been glad to oblige. It had been his choice. Maybe if he hurried, Fletch would still be in the pool when he got back. They could swim a few laps, have a beer, talk about Fletcher's passion for skeet shooting. He began to walk more quickly, threading his way through the groups of people ambling along. Yes, swimming sounded good right now. Take his mind off other things. Thinking about relationships was too complicated and did damn little good. The next thing you knew, he thought with a smile, he would be asking himself about a batter's frame of mind before he called him out on a perfect third strike.

No way. Life was complicated enough without that. The best thing to do was simply to move full speed ahead and forget about people. Lainie was a part of his past; he had to keep her there. And Wes LaRue had made a mess of his life on his own. If he ignored Griff's advice, so be it. It certainly wasn't a problem for Griffin.

OR HE DIDN'T THINK it was until that night after the game when he was coming toward the dressing room, his mind on a cool shower and getting off his feet.

"Tucker?" a voice from behind him called out, detaining him.

Griff turned to see Bill Bray heading his way, notebook in hand. Odd. Bray ought to have been in the players' locker room. There had bee a grand-slam home run that night as well as a four-hit shutout. And Griff, the third-base umpire, hadn't made more than two calls.

"Yeah?" He leaned against the wall until Bray caught up.

"Got a rumor I want to check out," Bray said, pushing his horn-rimmed glasses up on his beaky nose.

Griff shifted his weight from one tired foot to the other. "Mmm-hmm."

"Wes LaRue is saying you're his supplier."

Griff stared, nonplussed. "What?"

Bray smiled cagily. "Is that a no comment?"

Griff shook his head, scowling. "It's not anything. I don't know what the hell you're talking about."

Bray shrugged. "It's only what I heard, y'know."

"You heard wrong," Griff told him flatly, and turned on his heel and stalked into the dressing room, banging the door shut behind him. *What the hell?*

"Was that Bray?" Morelos asked as he stripped off his sweat-soaked shirt and tossed it aside. "What'd he want?"

"Nothing," Griff said vaguely, his mind spinning. "He made a mistake."

He had to have made a mistake. LaRue couldn't be a big enough idiot to expect that anyone would believe a story like that, could he? The whole thing was patently absurd. Griff shook his head again, as if he could shake Bray's words right out of it. No, it was insane. Who would ever believe a story like that?

"THE COMMISSIONER?"

Griff's voice was fuzzy with sleep. He pried one eye open and squinted at the clock on the bedside table. It was 9:23, and the phone book said Montreal, so he wasn't dreaming. But surely he hadn't heard right. Maybe the late-night drink on the Rue St. Denis that he had shared with Morelos and Johnson had fogged his brain.

"The commissioner, did you say?" he mumbled, struggling to sit up in the tangle of sheets on the bed.

"That's right," the brisk female voice on the other end of the line told him. "He's sent two men to Montreal. Their plane arrives in less than an hour. They'll be at your hotel by eleven. Wait for their call."

"Wha—"

But the line had gone dead.

He sat there, stunned, the receiver dangling from his fingers, not quite believing what he had heard. The commissioner of baseball was sending two men to talk to him? Why? Not because— No. His mind rejected that out of hand. It couldn't be because of that ridiculous rumor he had heard from Bray last night. Nobody in his right mind could think that Griffin Tucker, the straightest man in the universe, could actually be supplying Wes LaRue with cocaine. He dropped the receiver onto the bed and rubbed a hand along the coarse stubble of his cheek. Of course it was crazy. Wasn't it?

"Of course, we can't ignore the accusation. Not that we think it will come to anything at all," someone was saying in a tone of voice that implied he had no doubt it was true. Griff's eyes shifted around the hotel room, trying to pick out which of the men in three-piece suits was speaking. But his mind was reeling, gone almost out of control after the last half hour of interrogation. At this point it was all he could do to sit in the chair and keep breathing.

"You do see that we're in a bind here," another one of the men said. There were four or five of them. Men he had rarely seen before. "Staff," they had explained to him. "Lawyers and such." He had blanched at that, but there had been an umpire's representative there, too, who didn't seem surprised to hear it. Griff himself was amazed. He thought it couldn't be happening. But it was.

"Integrity is of paramount importance for an umpire," the man droned on, like a fly caught in the curtains. "Surely you agree, Mr. Tucker."

"Yes, but—" His words seemed made of ashes. He could scarcely get them past his teeth.

"And an investigation is, naturally, in order. The police who arrested Mr. LaRue have assured us that they intend to look into the matter."

"What about charges?" the umpire's rep asked. "Are they filing charges?"

"No. Pending the results of the investigation, no charges will be filed."

"Well, then—"

"But the news is out. Mr. Tucker here, no matter how fine an umpire he might be, is under grave suspicion."

Five pairs of eyes seemed to bore into him. He felt a sort of primitive, raw anger begin to flame within him as he wondered why, if they claimed to think he was so fine and full of integrity, their eyes condemned him even before he was charged.

"I didn't do it," he said. It was the first full sentence he had got out since he had come into the room. Everything else had been one- or two-word responses to their questioning. And he knew as soon as he spoke that he might as well not have bothered. The man who had been doing most of the questioning flipped his leather notebook shut.

"Whether you did or not, Mr. Tucker, it doesn't matter."

Didn't matter? Bloody hell, of course it mattered!

"So I'm confident that you'll understand our position here. You will, of course, continue to be paid unless the police deem it necessary to file charges. But in the meantime, throughout the course of their investigation of Mr. La-Rue's charges against you, we will be relieving you of your duties."

"What?" He wanted to protest, to explode, to say they were wrong, that they should let him continue working. He wanted to say that it would make him look guilty if he stopped. But somewhere down in the small reservoir of sanity that he had left to him this morning, he knew they were right.

"See sense, Mr. Tucker," one of the other men chimed in. "You certainly can't do a good job under suspicion. The press, the fans and most of all the players would be wondering about you. Concentrating on the umpire, not on the game."

They all looked at him expectantly.

It isn't fair, he wanted to shout. *God in heaven, it isn't fair!* But he stared at them mutely, a lifetime of masking his feelings standing him in good stead now. The rep reached over and patted his arm sympathetically, saying, "I think they might be right, Griff." He offered a commiserating smile. "Do you agree?"

Everyone waited, breath drawn.

Back to the wall, Griff agreed. But a jerky nod of his head was all he could manage. He still couldn't believe it was happening, that his career, the one thing over which he had always had supreme control even when the rest of his life was falling apart, was now crashing down around his ears, too.

The commissioner's men all smiled and stood up, coming across the room like wind-up soldiers, lining up to shake his hand. "We have great confidence in you," one of them said.

"It's only a matter of time," another one told him.

"Think of it as a vacation," the third added. "Your replacement will be here this afternoon. You can get a flight home as soon as you like."

Home? Griff thought suddenly, feeling as though he'd been hit. Home? Hell, he didn't even have a home. First his wife and home gone, now his job. White-faced, he gave the commissioner's minions a bleak smile and let them shake his hand. He would rather have strangled someone. First them, then, slowly, Wes LaRue. Home? The word caught in his throat, and he swallowed the pain and blinked back the stinging wetness in his eyes. Then he turned and headed blindly for the door.

The rep caught his arm. "Don't worry," he told Griff, giving him a look that would have been better reserved for a wake. "I'll be in touch."

"Yeah," Griff mumbled, shell-shocked and seething. "Sure." No Lainie. No home. No job. What next?

The barrage of flashbulbs caught him the second he opened the door.

"Hey!" He threw up his hands as a shield. "What the hell?"

"Any comment, Tucker?" one reporter yelled.

"Are you out?"

"You've thrown LaRue out of games six times this season. Any comment?"

"Are the police filing charges?"

"Hey, Tucker, where you goin'?"

"Tucker?"

"Tucker!"

He plowed right through them all. Head down, arms against his chest, he simply drove through the whole crowd, fending off questions, turning his head away from cameras, knocking a tape recorder inadvertently from someone's hand. *Leeches.* He sprinted down the hall, bypassing the elevator, heading for the stairs. *Bastards.*

He ran down three flights, one below the floor his own room was on, then ducked into the corridor and slumped against the wall, trembling, his breath coming in gasps, not from exertion but anger. It didn't help that he knew they were only doing their job. Not when he had just got his ripped right out from under him on false pretenses. He tasted bitterness just thinking about it. His heart pounded as loudly as his head. *Stop it,* he told himself. *Get a grip on yourself. Calm down. Think straight. Make sense.*

It wasn't easy. He needed to walk. He started out down the corridor, then went down a flight of stairs, then another corridor, then down again. He walked them all, up and down, then did it again, seething, aching. It was mindless, aimless and absolutely necessary. It was the only way he could cope without doing what his father had always done. Bashing reporters' heads together wouldn't solve anything at all. He clenched his fists and walked on.

He didn't know how long he walked or how far. He only knew he couldn't go back to his room. The press would be there; they would call on the phone. They would want comments, discussion, and he had nothing to say.

"I didn't do it" didn't sound very convincing somehow. And even if he said it, what would it prove? They would just ask more questions. And the last thing he wanted was the press or anyone else poking around in his life. His privacy was just about the only thing he had left. He certainly had no intention of giving it up. Especially not because of a bastard like Wes LaRue!

God, all he needed was for them to contact Lainie. The very thought made him stop in his tracks. Cripes, no, they wouldn't do that—would they?

He sighed and ran a hand through his already-disheveled hair. *Stupid, stupid question, Tucker,* he chastised himself. *You know damned well that's exactly what they'll do.*

Chapter Eight

The light on Lainie's desk phone had been flashing on and off for the past five minutes. She watched it distractedly, most of her attention still focused on Bob and Claire Hudson, who were seated across from her. They were finally getting somewhere. Between private counseling and going to her course on effective communication, they were beginning to make progress in their relationship, in believing that it had a future, and she didn't want to interrupt. She knew, she thought wryly, better than anyone just how precious understanding was and how hard won.

But the light kept on flashing. Pam, the office secretary, must have forgotten it. No one waited on a phone this long to talk to her. Maybe, she thought, glancing surreptitiously at her watch and noticing that it was already far past the lunch hour, Pam was using this means to get her to wind things up. Ever since she had got back from Colorado, Pam had been harping at her about working too hard. Little did the secretary know, Lainie thought, that it was work that was keeping her sane. If she couldn't help her own marriage, she could at least help someone else's.

The light continued to flash. Lainie scowled at it. Bob and Claire were talking to each other now, ignoring her. The way it ought to be, she thought, a rare feeling of satisfaction stealing over her. It was times like these that made everything else worthwhile. Her stomach growled. Well, maybe Pam had a point. She was certainly being persistent enough.

She waited until she heard a pause in Claire's low-toned comments, and then she eased her way into the conversation. "It sounds as if you have found a real basis for further sharing," she said, giving them a smile of encouragement, which they both returned. "Do you think you can continue on your own now for a while? We can work a bit more in class next week."

Suddenly conscious of both Lainie and the time, Bob flushed, a sheepish but happy grin lighting his face. "Yeah, I think so, Ms Tucker." He got to his feet and offered a hand to his wife, drawing her up to stand beside him. "Thanks."

"I'll see you in class, then?" Lainie asked as she walked them to the door.

"You sure will," Claire said. She gave Lainie a heartfelt smile as Bob opened the door for her. "I can't tell you how much you've helped. You're really wonderful."

Lainie stood in the door and watched them walk down the hall, pleased and aching at the same time. "Really wonderful," she observed, shaking her head. "Yeah, sure."

She went back into her office and punched the phone button down. "It's me," she said to Pam. "Was all that flashing a hint that it's lunchtime?"

"Something like that," the harried secretary replied. "There's a man here to see you. He's a bit insistent. In fact, he's on his way down—"

"Man?" Lainie's heart leaped unbidden.

A dark head poked around her door. "Not Griff, just me," he said, obviously aware from the expression on her face where her thoughts were.

"Chase!"

She hadn't seen him since he had brought her back down the mountain. After that fiasco there hadn't been much to say, and Griff was their only point of reference. So what, unless it was Griff, could he be doing here now?

"What are you doing here?" she asked. "What's going on?"

"Lunch." He plucked her jacket from the hanger on the back of the door and tossed it to her. "Come on."

She went. She told herself she needed to eat, but in fact she was curious. And Chase didn't look as if he were going to take no for an answer. He hustled her down the corridor of the hospital, his eyes darting right and left. Then, with a brisk nod to Pam, he whisked her out the door and into his waiting sports car. The radio blared as he switched on the engine. It was tuned to an all-news station, and he promptly shut it off.

"I don't mind it," Lainie said. "I rarely get a chance to listen."

"You're not missing much," he told her, and he didn't turn it back on. He drove to a coffee shop about ten minutes from the hospital, glancing around the parking lot as if he were in a detective movie and was trying to spot the car following them. Lainie wondered if being an investigative reporter made him worry about things like that. She hoped not. Anyway, she hadn't noticed him behaving oddly any other time she had been around him.

"Have you heard from Griff, then?" she asked, hoping to discover the reason for their lunch date.

"No."

He led her into the restaurant, shaking his head when the waitress led them to a table next to the window, and indicated instead a booth in the back. Then he sat so that she was facing the wall and he could see all the people who came in. Strange.

"Is there a hit man after you?" she asked him with a smile.

"No," he said as she picked up the menu. "After you."

"What?"

"Relax." He put out a hand and covered her suddenly trembling ones. His palm was warm and comforting, help-

ing to assuage the sudden chill she had felt at his words.
"The press is going to be wanting to talk to you," he went
on.

"What for?" The chill came back with arctic sudden-
ness. "Has something happened to Griff?"

Chase's face was grave. "He's okay," he reassured her.
"He's just in a bit of a mess."

"What sort of a mess?"

She couldn't have guessed what he told her next if she had
had a million years.

"They think Griff sold Wes LaRue drugs?" If it weren't
for the obvious seriousness of Chase's expression, she would
have laughed.

"LaRue said so himself."

"But that's ridiculous."

"You and I know that because we know Griff. It isn't so
obvious, I'm afraid, to everyone else. Several players have
commented on a certain friction between them all year. And
I heard that one of the umpries he works with has admitted
that he saw Griff and LaRue together in the airport in New
York." Chase spread his hands as if to say, "Look at the
evidence."

Lainie did, but she still couldn't fathom it. Griffin Tucker
was the most moral man alive. If anyone was holier than
thou, it was Griff. "It's so circumstantial," she said plain-
tively. "They don't have any evidence. Not really."

"Doesn't matter," Chase said. "It's enough in his
profession to have had suspicion cast on him."

"So what happens now? Where is he?"

Chase shrugged. "He's on what might euphemistically be
called a 'leave of absence' until the police investigation is
completed. Then they either file charges or they don't."

"They can't."

Chase scratched his nose as if he weren't quite so sure, but
as least he didn't say so.

"And until then?"

"I don't know." He shook his head. "I don't even know where Griff is right now. But I expect he'll be flying home from Montreal. I'm not really sure."

Neither was Lainie. She wasn't even sure he considered this his home anymore. She had serious doubts that he would be winging his way back to her.

"What can I do?" she asked.

Chase waited until the waitress had returned, taken their order and departed again before saying, "It's up to you, I suppose. I doubt that Griff expects you to do anything. Though he'd probably be grateful for a 'no comment.'"

Lainie snorted. That was probably all he would expect, the idiot. He would just stonewall it out the way he did everything else, never looking for help from anyone. Well, damn it, whether he wanted her or not, he needed her now even if he didn't know it.

"I want to help him," she told Chase firmly. "He needs me."

Chase regarded her levelly over his water glass. In his eyes she read the skepticism that he never gave voice to as well as some of the questions that he tactfully had not asked her when he had driven her, shaken and miserable, back down that Colorado mountainside. No doubt he was recalling her last disastrous attempt to do something for Griff and wondering if his friend really needed that sort of complication in his life right now.

But Lainie had no intention of being a complication. She had given Griff a lot of thought since then and had realized how little actual support she had offered him. She had never thought he needed it before, even when he had. But now the need was obvious. If his integrity was being questioned, he needed a wife who would stand by him, and she was going to see that he got it.

She felt as if she were settling in, putting down roots. All her airy hypotheses about what made a marriage work had been blown away, replaced by a steadfast understanding that now there was really something she could do—something she had to do for him. If he would let her.

She didn't want to think about that.

"Are you sure?" Chase asked.

"Yes."

He pressed his lips together and drew in a deep breath, then he gave her an almost-relieved smile, as if her response had been what he was hoping for. "Good."

The waitress reappeared and slapped sandwiches in front of them both. Chase immediately bit into his, while Lainie nibbled on a French fry, thinking of Griff. She didn't know where he was or what he was doing, but she was sure he was hurting. A lot.

"Do you think he'll be back in L.A. soon?" she asked.

Chase's mouth was full, but he nodded his head. "You know Susan Rivers?"

"The sportswriter?" She was a friend of Brendan Craig's, but Lainie had only met her.

"Yeah. She's the one who called me. She was clued in by a writer she knows in Montreal. She's keeping tabs on things. So am I. As soon as we know where he is and what he's doing, I'll be in touch."

"Bless you," Lainie said, and meant it.

The corner of Chase's mouth lifted. "I wonder if you'll be saying that in a few days. This 'stand by your man' stuff isn't going to be easy, you know. I hate to say it when I'm one of them, but the press isn't going to just walk away from a story like this."

"Nothing in my marriage has been easy," Lainie reminded him, not self-pityingly but just stating a fact.

"No," Chase agreed around a bite of his hamburger. "That's true enough." He glanced at his watch. "Eat up, love. We've got to get going. I want to check with some contacts before I go to a meeting at three."

Lainie pushed away her plate, her French dip sandwich almost untouched.

Chase's eyebrow lifted. "Not hungry?"

Lainie shook her head.

A speculative look surfaced in his eyes. "May I?"

"Be my guest."

She watched him eat, almost amused by his voracious attack on her sandwich. Sipping her coffee, which was the only thing she felt she could manage with her stomach in turmoil, she recalled the comforting feelings she had had when she watched Griff tuck into a meal. It had been a long time. Far too long. Could it be true that she would be seeing it again soon? Would he really be coming home?

Granted that the circumstances for his homecoming weren't what she would have wished, she still couldn't help feeling something akin to happiness as Chase paid the check and they walked back to the car. It was a little like being granted a death-row reprieve—the miracle she had been praying for. Now all she had to do was pray she didn't blow it again.

"I'll be waiting to hear from you," she promised Chase when he let her out of his car at the door to the hospital.

He flashed her one of his stunning grins, a slash of white against his dark face. "I hope it won't be too long."

"Me, too," Lainie said softly to herself as she watched him drive away. "Oh, God, me too."

It was ironic that the call came when it did. Lainie was in the midst of an interminable session with Mavis Leary, one that had stretched far past her dinner hour, and her stomach was protesting the fact that she had given Chase her sandwich at lunch. As she listened to Mavis rave on and on about Dick's latest transgressions, some of which had obviously been provoked by Mavis herself, she watched the sun glint off the roofs of the cars in the parking lot and wondered if she ought to take the time to stop for fish and chips on her way home. Presuming, of course, that Mavis stopped talking before breakfast.

Ordinarily, Lainie didn't mind how long a conference took. As long as it was accomplishing something, she could see a point in continuing it. But tonight she couldn't see that point. In fact, Mavis seemed bent on eliciting sympathy, not help, and Lainie's mind kept drifting to thoughts of Griff. Every time the phone had rung that afternoon, she had jumped to answer it. But Chase had never called. She was beginning to worry. Maybe Griff wasn't even going to come to L.A.

When the phone rang this time, she answered more out of the relief that it would provide from Mavis than any hope that it was Chase.

"Are you still at work?" he demanded when she said hello.

"Chase?" Her abrupt tone shut Mavis's monologue off in midsyllable. "Have you heard?"

"Yes. Just. He's on his way now."

"When does he get in?"

"About an hour. Can you meet me at the airport?"

"Yes, if I leave right now." She was already standing up and cranking shut the open window, lifting her brows at Mavis in the hope that the other woman would take the hint and leave. Mavis's mouth was open in astonishment at Lainie's aberrant behavior, but she was sitting tight.

"Good." Chase told her the airline and gate number. "Brendan will be there, too," he added.

"Brendan? Why?'"

"To run interference."

"Oh." Lainie wasn't sure what he meant and opened her mouth to ask, but he had hung up.

"He's no good, Dick isn't," Mavis went on. "I told my sister that, and—"

"I have to leave now," Lainie said. It was the first time in fifteen months she had cut Mavis off. It was the first time in her career, in fact, that she had ever cut off anyone. But Mavis and Dick had had problems for years. Even if they talked all night, Lainie knew they weren't going to be able to solve them. It was quite possible, she had begun to admit, that Mavis didn't even want to solve them, that she only wanted to talk about them. But whatever the truth was, Lainie did want to solve her own problems with Griff. That was the top priority in her life now. She wasn't going to make that mistake again. "I'll be in the office tomorrow," she told Mavis. "Could we continue then?"

Mavis looked a bit miffed, but Lainie was opening the door. "Yes, I guess," she said gruffly. "I'll call you."

"All right," Lainie agreed. But she was down the corridor and into the parking lot before Mavis could button up her sweater and follow.

Once on the freeway, she spared Mavis no thoughts at all. Her mind was entirely consumed with Griff. What would he say to her? Would he tell her to get lost? Was he still angry that she had tricked him into going to Colorado? They hadn't exactly parted on amicable terms. And what did Chase mean about having Brendan along to run interference?

The minute she walked into the airport's waiting area, she knew. Two television cameras were already set up, and the place was humming with people, some of them quite obviously reporters. Confused, feeling a bit like bolting herself, she looked around for Chase. He was standing behind a potted palm, trying to appear invisible. He was alone, and she guessed that Brendan hadn't arrived yet. But she understood quite clearly now what they would need him for. Were all these people here just to interview Griff?

She smiled a bit grimly as she reflected on just how much Griff would like that. It gave her a renewed surge of confidence that she had done the right thing in coming along.

Chase hadn't seen her, and she started to cross the waiting room to go to stand with him when suddenly a man swooped down on her, pencil poised, asking, "You're Mrs. Tucker, aren't you?"

"Yes, I am," Lainie replied, still heading toward Chase. He saw her just then, but his smile turned to a scowl when he also spied the man talking with her, and he dodged around a crowd of people to make his way toward them.

"Could you please comment on the accusations against your husband?" the man pressed.

"They're absurd," Lainie said flatly.

"You don't have to talk to him," Chase told her, coming up alongside and slipping a protective arm around her.

"I'm sure she doesn't want the accusations to go unanswered," the other reporter countered smoothly.

Chase's frown deepened. "That's what the investigation is for, Dunston."

"You have some special interest in this, Whitelaw?" the other man asked, eyebrows lifting speculatively.

"I'm a friend."

"Ah."

Lainie didn't need to be a mind reader to see the construction Dunston was putting on that remark. "Of my husband's," she inserted bluntly.

"Uh, yes," Dunston agreed, his smile was still skeptical. He was joined quickly by several other reporters who had apparently figured out who Lainie was. They were all starting to bombard her with questions, and she wished that Brendan were there to run interference for her.

"Did he do it, ma'am?" one of them asked baldly.

Chase shot him a pained look, as if wondering how any self-respecting journalist could ask such a question.

"Of course not," Lainie said. "My husband would never do a dishonest thing. He has more integrity and a greater sense of right and wrong than anyone else I know." She glared at them as if daring them to contradict her. Thankfully, none of them did. They all scribbled dutifully, and one of the cameramen moved in to film her. At that moment the loudspeaker announced the arrival of Griff's flight, and as the reporters all turned and headed en masse for the passengers' exit, Brendan puffed up to them, out of breath.

"Cutting it a bit close, weren't you?" Chase asked mildly, but Lainie felt the grip on her arm tighten and knew he was annoyed.

"Couldn't find a place to park," Brendan panted. "As it is, I'm gonna get a ticket." He brushed windblown hair off his forehead and shrugged, a faint grin on his face.

"All for a good cause," Chase assured him.

"I know." Brendan turned and offered Lainie an encouraging smile. "How are you doing?"

She managed a wan one in return, her thoughts more concerned with Griff now than with how she felt. The crush of reporters had unnerved her; she could just imagine what they would do to Griff.

Brendan looked as if he might have said something else, but Chase cut in. "He's coming," he announced, and Lainie, who had been watching other passengers disembarking, now saw the reporters surge forward and the camera begin to flash as Griff came through the door.

The noise level grew. One of the television reporters thrust a microphone in Griff's face, and the others shouted questions at him. Other passengers, obviously curious about who this unrecognizable celebrity in their midst was, stopped walking and turned to gawk. Griff froze where he stood.

"Come on," Lainie said, and hurried toward him, with Chase and Brendan following in her wake. It didn't matter that there were easily fifty people between them; she only knew she had to get to Griff.

She was aghast at how gaunt he looked. Since he had left her in Colorado, she had only tortured herself three times watching games that he umpired. And now she discovered that it was true what people said about television adding pounds. Griff had never looked this thin on the screen. He was pale and exhausted; his normally tanned skin, contrasted with his fair hair, had taken on a sallow pallor that shocked her. Though clean-shaven, he had the beginnings of shadow on his jaw, and that made the contrast only more obvious. But the most noticeable thing of all was the totally vacant expression on his face.

It was as if he were somewhere else entirely, as if only the shell of Griffin Tucker was standing in the airport lounge, being bombarded with questions. The man himself wasn't there at all.

One instant she was separated from him by three hulking male bodies, and the next Chase had taken the initiative and had hauled her past them so that suddenly she was looking up directly into Griff's eyes. They looked right at her, but she didn't know if he was seeing her or not. He didn't even blink. She touched his hand and found it icy. Wrapping his nerveless fingers in her own, she reached up and brushed a kiss against his tightly pressed lips.

Then he blinked.

It was as if the kiss had brought him to life again and he seemed to see her for the first time.

"Mr. Tucker has been asked not to comment on the case," she heard Brendan saying to the reporters, who turned and gaped at the sound of his voice. "However," he went on with the same genial grin that had endeared him to reporters during his baseball career and would undoubtedly charm them when he became a lawyer, "I don't mind if I do."

"Let's go," Chase urged, and while Brendan launched into an extemporaneous but highly informed monologue on drugs in sports, he practically stampeded Lainie and Griff out of the lounge. Looking over her shoulder, Lainie marveled as the reporters hung on Brendan's every word.

Chase slanted her a grim smile. "It's called a red herring," he said. "And Brendan, because he's still got a big name with them, is the perfect one to pull it off."

"Thank heavens," Lainie said. "And thank you."

She glanced at Griff, who was being borne right along with her. He was staring straight ahead, not saying anything at all. The only response she had had from him was the grip of his fingers, which had almost automatically curved around hers and now held a death grip on her hand.

Chase hustled them down the escalator and through the baggage reclamation area to the parking lot. "I'll come back for your luggage," he said to Griff.

Griff didn't reply.

"What about my car? We can take it," Lainie began.

Chase shook his head no. "We'll come back and pick it up. Let's just get out of here. Unless—" he looked over the top of his sports car at Griff's pale, vacant face "—you want to hang around and talk to them."

"No," Griff said, his voice raw.

It was all he was capable of saying. In the hours that had intervened since he had met with the commissioner's staff that morning, he had been walking around in a daze. He felt like a wounded animal, trapped in a box canyon. No matter where he looked, there was no way out. And it didn't matter what he said; no one was prepared to believe him.

If he had been thinking more clearly, he might have come up with better plans than he did. As it was, he had simply headed for the airport and bought a ticket on the first plane to L.A. If everything else in his life was going to fall apart, at least he would have familiar surroundings.

He had no idea what he would do when he got there. He wasn't able, at that point, to think beyond getting on the plane in Montreal and getting off at the other end. All he felt when he did think was sheer, mind-numbing rage, so he chose not to think at all.

He didn't hurry to get off the plane. There was no point when he didn't know what he was going to do when he did get off. He heard whispers about television cameras filtering back through the crowds of disembarking passengers, and he prayed it was for someone in first class, some celebrity he didn't know anything about. But having dodged reporters at the Montreal airport, he was realistic enough to steel himself in case it wasn't. When the cameras began flashing and the microphones grazed his lips, he wasn't surprised.

What surprised him was seeing Lainie.

What in God's name was she doing there? After what had happened in Colorado, he would have expected her to be running like fury in the other direction as fast as she could. Yet she came through those reporters like Moses parting the Red Sea, and he knew it wasn't a mirage the second he felt her lips on his.

At their touch he breathed again. The ice that had bound him since early that morning began almost imperceptibly to melt. He felt her fingers encircle his, their warmth giving him new life. And if, intellectually, he didn't believe that she ought to be there, he was powerless to send her away. His hand wrapped around hers and clung.

They walked briskly together, fingers entwined, hips touching, past the crowds of milling people. They went down the escalator, then along the seemingly endless mosaic-tiled corridor toward the parking lot, with Chase hovering about, cutting in and out like a well-trained sheepdog.

Griff heard him say something about luggage, but he didn't respond. His luggage had never left Montreal. He hadn't gone back to his hotel room after the meeting with the commissioner's staff. He knew he would just run into more reporters if he did, and he was afraid he might do something he would regret. Anyway, Fletcher would send it along to him. That was the least of his worries. By the time he had got to L.A., he had talked himself into a stoic uncommunicativeness, and he had made up his mind that whatever happened, nothing would faze him now. Nothing at all.

He hadn't counted on Lainie.

For perhaps the fiftieth time he wondered why she had come. She hadn't said one word to him, and that, for sure, was not like Lainie.

He looked at her now out of the corner of his eye as she scrambled none too gracefully into the tiny back compartment of Chase's silver sports car. It was odd that she was here, so real, so vivid, just when he was getting himself convinced that he might never see her again. He got in the front seat beside Chase and settled back against the curving leather bucket seat. Lainie's hand came up to rest on his shoulder, light but steadying, and in spite of himself, he was grateful for its presence.

Chase whipped the car out of its parking place and out of the lot with all the finesse of a bullfighter. Then, once on Sepulveda Boulevard, he mopped his brow and said, "God, I hate that place. I always wonder if I'll get out alive."

This time, more than ever before, Griff could empathize with that. He managed a faint smile. "Thanks. How'd you know I would be on that flight?"

"Connections," Chase answered cryptically.

Griff turned his head and looked at Lainie, expecting a response from her, too, but she was strangely silent. She gave him a gentle smile that was impossible to interpret in his present befuddled state, and her eyes were wide with an emotion he couldn't quite put a name to. At the best of times he wasn't good at deciphering the subtler feelings. He had always needed full-blown anger or rapturous joy, he thought grimly, or chances were he would guess wrong. He certainly felt out of his depth now.

"I can't believe Brendan," he said now, still marveling at his friend's easy control over a situation that had him floundering. "He could talk them into believing anything, I think."

"I hope," Chase said. "From what I've heard, you need all the help you can get."

Griff felt his stomach muscles tighten. "What are they saying?"

"A load of rubbish. Sometimes I'm ashamed to be a journalist." Chase slapped his palms on the steering wheel.

"That bad?"

Chase merely grunted in response, leaving Griff to think what he chose.

Griff thought he understood then why Lainie was there. He had become another of her "causes"—one of the poor unfortunates that she dedicated her life to helping. He stiffened, needing suddenly to withdraw from her touch. He managed a surreptitious glance back at her again and noted for the first time what she was wearing. A tailored lilac-colored cotton skirt and matching jacket over a prim white blouse. Work clothes. He clenched his teeth. It was almost dark, damned near nine o'clock at night, and she had obviously come to the airport right from work.

Lainie's fingers, which had been resting on his shoulder, reacted at once to the sudden tension she felt in him. They went right to his neck and began a slow by steady kneading caress. He swallowed hard, wanting to pull away, yet somehow healed by her rhythmic touch.

Neither of them said a word throughout the drive to the apartment. Only when Chase stopped the car in the alley behind their place did Griff manage to speak.

"I don't have to stay with..." His voice faltered, but he nodded toward the apartment, and both Chase and Lainie knew exactly what he meant.

"Come on," Lainie said. They were the first words she had spoken directly to him. And despite the tremulousness of her looks, the words came out strong and clear.

Chase looked at him, too, obviously waiting for him to make a move. He stalled for a moment, weighing matters, then realized that as far as he was concerned, matters were so far out of control that he couldn't make a rational decision if he tried. Defeated, he got out.

Lainie crawled out of the back to stand in the alley, shaking her arms and legs to get the cramped kinks out. Then, shutting the car door, she bent down and spoke to Chase through the open window.

"You've been a real friend," she told him. "Thanks."

Chase slanted her a smile. "Don't mention it." He winked at her, and Griff felt a twinge of disapproval. Then, looking at Griff, Chase gave a slight wave of his hand.

"Don't worry," he told Griff, just as the umpire's rep had. But then he added, "I'll get to the bottom of this," and from his expression Griff knew that he meant it.

One corner of Griff's mouth lifted. "Right," he said.

"Talk to you tomorrow," Chase promised, and drove off.

Griff stood and watched him leave, not moving an inch, waiting with dread for what he knew must come next. This was the moment in which Lainie would launch into her social-work babble, encouraging him to share his feelings with her, to express his inner self. He gritted his teeth.

"Come on," she said easily, touching his hand for a brief moment. I'll bet you're starved."

Chapter Nine

Off balanced by her brisk matter-of-factness, Griff stayed where he was. But then she turned and beckoned him, offering him a genuine smile. "Come on," she said again, and he pushed the hair back off his forehead and followed her around the corner of the building and up the steps to the apartment.

It was odd how his wariness turned to relief the moment he walked in the front door. In spite of himself, he felt a sense of coming home. He had the urge to walk around the touch everything—the shell Lainie had brought back from Hawaii, the rainbow sun catcher in the window, the embroidered seascape her mother had made them for Christmas, the dainty fronds of the asparagus fern that seemed so much fuller now than he remembered. They were all part of a simpler time, a paradise lost, and he ached for them. But he willed himself to stop and stand still just inside the door. This wasn't his home any longer, no matter what he felt. He didn't belong here anymore; he was just a guest.

"There're only leftovers," Lainie was saying as she rooted through the refrigerator. "Some spaghetti from when Mom came over on Sunday, a little pastrami and—" She stopped, then opened the freezer compartment and pounced on a small packet with triumphant sound. "Shrimp," she crowed. "How about some curry?" She turned and gave him a victorious smile, waving the package as if she were a hunter bringing home a deer.

Griff's mouth curved into a reluctant grin. "Sounds fine."

"I'll just get changed a minute first," Lainie said. "Then I'll get started." Her tone changed from bright to slightly strained as she noted that he hadn't moved away from the door. "Griff, are you all right?" she asked suddenly. "Why don't you sit down?"

He shouldn't, and he knew it. It was insanity to be here. The temptation was too great. "Really, Lainie," he protested, "I shouldn't stay."

"Why not?" She looked perplexed.

"We're getting a divorce."

She felt her heart sink a little. So time and space hadn't done anything to change his mind. Damn. Well, she shouldn't be surprised, she supposed. "Not right now, surely," she protested in turn.

"What do you mean?"

"I mean, what's the press going to think if we get a divorce right now?"

"What does the press have to do with it?"

"Ordinarily not a thing. But right now you're news."

Griff grimaced and raked his fingers through his hair, giving it the appearance of a wind-blown haystack. "So what?" he growled.

"So it's going to make you look even more likely to be guilty if we separate now. You know, WIFE LEAVES HUSBAND ACCUSED OF DRUG DEALING. There are definite 'rat leaving sinking ship' overtones."

"That's crazy."

"Maybe so. But that's the way people think. You know it is!"

Griff sighed. "So what do you propose?" He walked over and sank down on the couch, feeling rather as if he were going under for the third time.

"Simply that you stay here while the investigation is going on," she said, hoping he didn't hear the tension in her voice.

"Make it look like everything is beautiful between us, you mean?" He lifted an eyebrow in sardonic amusement.

"Yes, if you like."

"Aren't you afraid to?"

"You mean, am I afraid you're going to beat me?"

Griff flinched, but when he forced himself to look at her, she was meeting his gaze square on. "Yes," he said curtly. He expected her to spew forth with a load of psychobabble then and was amazed when she simply shook her head.

"No, I'm not." She wanted to tell him that she didn't think he was at all like his father, that they had every chance in the world of making their marriage work even if he did come from a background like that. But she couldn't. She had sworn to herself that she would not do her marriage-counselor number on him this time. And she knew by now that with Griff there was no such thing as talking him around. He had to see the truth for himself. And if he didn't, she asked herself.

Well, if he didn't, she'd lose. They both would.

Griff wasn't saying anything. He sat perfectly still on the couch, his elbows resting on his knees, his fingers laced together, his head bowed. She hadn't the faintest idea what he was thinking, but whatever he thought, he didn't seem convinced that he should stay, so she tried another shot.

"Listen, Griff." She crossed the room and planted herself directly in front of him. "Chase Whitelaw has been working his tail off for you ever since he found out about this charge. He and Susan Rivers plan to interrogate everyone from the batboy to the league presidents. Brendan would do anything to help you, and he probably will. They are your friends, and they care about you." *Just as I do,* she wanted to add. But she didn't think it would aid her argument, so she left it out. "You owe it to them to give it your best shot possible. And you owe it to everyone in baseball, too. You didn't do it. Why give them the slightest reason to think you did? I'm sorry if you're finding living here with me so distasteful, but—''

''I don't!'' Griff exclaimed, looking up at her, astonished, but before he could continue, she had turned and fled, the bedroom door slamming shut against her echoing words.

When she reemerged, clothes changed, five minutes later, she was surprised so see him still sitting there. Griff was surprised, too. The temptation to bolt had been almost overwhelming. Her angry tone had set off his warning system, and that, combined with the sound of the surf and the seductive smell of salt and sea that beckoned him, very nearly made him give in. But what Lainie had said had touched the inner core of his being.

It was true that Chase had put himself out for him. Obviously, so had Susan Rivers and Brendan, even when he hadn't expected anything at all. They were clearly prepared to do even more. And so, he knew, was Lainie. But why? Just because he was a cause? Or did she— He shook his head, feeling muddled, tired, hungry and confused. Nothing made sense right now. The harder he tried to grasp the implications of the situation, the more easily they eluded him. He sighed and closed his eyes.

The smell of sautéing onions and celery reached him, tantalizing his senses, disarming him. He sank back into the soft cushions of the sofa, unresisting, letting himself enjoy momentarily the quiet domestic sounds of silverware clattering against frying pan, of running water and the swish of rice poured into the blue enamel pot. He expected Lainie would pick up the thread of the argument she had been advancing when she had suddenly left, but she didn't. Clad now in jeans that hugged her curves and a scoop-necked T-shirt of bright blue, she hummed her way around the kitchen, doing things that, in his mind's eye, he had always associated with married bliss.

He stiffened. He couldn't let himself think things like that.

"You have time for a shower before dinner if you feel like it," she said now, sparing him a brief glance as she rinsed the shrimp off in a colander under the running water.

He was almost too tired to move. If this hadn't been the longest day of his life, it certainly came close. But she was probably right. A shower sounded good. He might revive, get his act together, make sense. He hauled himself to his feet and headed toward the bathroom, then paused. "All my clothes are in Montreal," he said, "except the ones I've got stored with my car." After he had left her, he had put the car in storage, and all his worldly possessions with it.

"You left the pair of jeans and the shirt you painted in," Lainie told him tautly, not turning around. "They're in your dresser drawer." She didn't mention that she periodically opened that drawer just to reassure herself that they were still there. She had found them hanging, stiff and turpentine soaked, on the back porch after he had left. She had washed them with a care all out of proportion to their ragged state and had put them in his drawer. They were there still.

She didn't turn around until she heard him shut the door to the bathroom and start the shower. Then she dropped the spoon with which she had been stirring the onions and celery and pressed hot hands to her flushed face. How she was going to survive this—tiptoeing around him, loving him as she did, yet keeping her distance—was something she hadn't really considered until now.

In a way she was glad she hadn't. If she had realized how difficult it was going to be, she might never have suggested to Chase that she get involved. It was going to take every ounce of willpower she possessed to curb her tongue, mind her hands and stay a respectable distance from him. Please God this investigation would be settled and Griff cleared before she lost her mind completely. Living with a man who believed that divorcing you was the best thing he could do for you—especially when you were desperately in love with him—was not conducive to anyone's emotional well-being. Certainly not hers!

Griff took his time in the shower, giving Lainie plenty of opportunity to get herself together, so that when he emerged, looking tired but still terribly attractive in his snug, paint-spattered jeans and blue chambray shirt, she was able to keep a calm facade even though her heart pumped like a bellows in her chest.

"Good, just in time," she managed, not looking at him as she set the bowl of curry on the table. Her mouth felt suddenly dry, and she took a long swallow of the wine she had poured for herself, then offered a glass to Griff.

He took it, and their fingers brushed. The brief touch was all it took to ignite the spark between them that both had been trying to smother. For an instant their eyes connected, searching. Then, as if to break the spell, Griff lifted his glass to his lips and swallowed. Finding her breath again, Lainie cleared her throat and said, "If we don't eat now, it will get cold."

The meal was more of a strain than he thought it would be. Having anticipated that she would probe his psyche, he was disconcerted when she didn't ask him anything at all. She didn't even mention their last disastrous meeting in Colorado. She simply sat and ate. She smiled at him, almost self-consciously now and then, and Griff felt himself fumbling for things to say.

"It's delicious," he mumbled around a mouthful.

"Thank you." She ducked her head like a shy adolescent, and he felt his heartbeat speed up. Again he was struck by how unreal sitting here across the table from her seemed, and he paused in his eating just to let himself look at her. It was a mistake.

All he could think was how he wanted her, how they had loved each other that last night in Colorado. He grew hot just thinking about it, and the heat owed nothing to the spiciness of the curry. She raised her eyes almost surreptitiously to look at him, and finding him staring at her, immediately averted her gaze.

"Do you want some more rice?" she asked. "Or curry?"

Griff did. It surprised him how hungry he felt all of a sudden. *It's that you can't satisfy your other hunger,* he told himself wryly, and he knew quite well that it was true.

Lainie filled his plate again, heaping rice, curry and condiments on it, and he dug into his second helping without pause. Finally, replete, he leaned back in his chair, holding his wineglass against his lips as he contemplated Lainie over the top of it. She had got up and was rinsing her plate in the sink, her attention distracted for the moment, and so he allowed himself the brief luxury—and agony—of simply looking at her.

She was thinner than he remembered. Her figure, which he had always considered nicely rounded and feminine, now seemed almost boyish in her jeans and T-shirt. The overhead light made her look tired, too—more tired than she used to. There were dark shadows under her eyes and a pale cast to her normally healthy, tanned face. She probably was more tired than ever, he thought grimly. She worked hard enough. He felt a prickling return of tension at the thought of one of their most serious bones of contention. But before it could develop, Lainie lifted her head and looked at him, brandishing the wine bottle as she did so.

"More?" she asked.

He shook his head. "No. I'll fall asleep in my plate if I do."

She looked at him assessingly. "Sleep might not be a bad idea. You've had a rough day."

Griff rubbed his hand between his neck and his shirt collar. "Not yet," he said. And whether it should be here or not, he didn't know, either. He kept telling himself that things between them couldn't work, that they were over—

finished. And yet she had been at the airport. And he still wanted her; there was no doubt about that. He shut his eyes wearily. Damn, he wished his mind were not quite so fuzzed by wine, worry and exhaustion.

"I think I'll take a walk," he said. Pushing back his chair, he got up and carried his dishes to the sink. "Don't bother with the dishes," he said to her. "I'll finish them when I get back. You made dinner, after all." He gave her a brief smile that he hoped masked his confused state of mind and headed for the door.

"Hang on," Lainie said. "I'm coming, too."

Before Griff could open his mouth to protest, she followed him out the door and locked it behind them. "Where to?" she asked brightly. "The beach?"

Griff shoved his fists into his jeans pockets and shrugged, feeling totally outmaneuvered. "Why not?"

Lainie walked by his side down the sidewalk, careful not to touch him on purpose or by accident. Just inviting herself along on one of his solitary excursions had been daring enough. It had been a spur-of-the-moment decision, but as they walked down the broad walkway toward the beach, she became increasingly convinced it had been the right one.

Going for a walk had always been Griff's way of excluding her in the past, his way of avoiding what she could see now had been occasions when he might have been experiencing anger, might have feared he would lash out at her. Whenever that had happened in the past, he would state his case, then walk away, and she would stand fuming in his wake. Well, as of now, that pattern was going to be broken. New patterns were going to be established—for both of them.

She hadn't argued with him, tried to make him talk, see reason or any of the other things she had been wont to try in the past. She had only stated objective reasons for him to stay. Now she was crossing her fingers, praying that he would decide they made sense. And she was walking with him for as long as he walked. If she could keep up, she thought, increasing her stride as they reached the beach. Griff's long legs weren't making it easy.

Until they reached the high-tide line, neither of them spoke. Griff had no intention of it; he never did when he walked. In part, of course, because he always walked alone. But also because he walked to think things out, to put distance between himself and what was bothering him. He was trying to do that now. With minimal success, because one of the things that was bothering him was walking right by his side. He couldn't even begin to focus his mind on LaRue and his job and all that mess when Lainie was six inches away.

He glanced down at her, watching the wind whip her hair across her face, making her smile. She brushed it back, then dropped her hand again, and for an instant her fingers grazed his. He wanted to touch them, to touch her. She had touched him earlier, at the airport. She had given him life again through her touch. He wanted to feel it now. But she was swinging her arms, a slight smile on her face as she stared straight ahead, and he couldn't, didn't dare. He didn't know what to do.

He knew what he wanted to do. He wanted to stay. But did he dare? Could he live with her on borrowed time? Her arguments made sense, of course, but he was honest enough with himself to admit that if he stayed it wasn't her arguments that had convinced him. It was his own overpowering need to be with her, in spite of his better judgment, for as long as he dared.

Lainie began talking softly then, telling him about catching sand crabs when she was a child, about moonstones and riptides and memories of her parents taking her to the beach. He listened, drawn to her, imagining what she must have looked like then. He murmured responses, smiling, relaxing his guard.

"I love the beach at night," she told him, and then, without warning, she darted on ahead of him, running for all she was worth, her arms outspread, the breeze lifting her hair and rippling her T-shirt against her back. Griff couldn't help it; he was enchanted. This was the Lainie he had fallen in love with. This was the woman he had married. He couldn't leave. Simply couldn't. Now now. He loved her too much.

Lainie was more than a block ahead of him, her figure etched in the silver moonlight. Quickening his pace, he moved to catch up. By the time he reached her, she had sunk down and was sitting on the cool sand, her arms wrapped around her drawn-up knees. She looked up at his approach, her exuberance replaced by a gentle, almost beatific smile. His heartbeat quickened, but he tried not to show any sign of it, kneeling carefully on the sand and leaving a couple of feet of space between them.

"I've decided that you're right," he told her.

She gave him an inquiring look.

"About staying with you. If you're sure you don't mind," he added.

"It's fine."

"It would look better," he went on, reiterating her earlier arguments as if he now needed to convince her. "And if looks aren't everything," he said, giving her a rueful smile, "they do seem to count."

"Yes."

"But I won't get in your way," he promised. "And I'll leave as soon as I can."

Her lashes dropped to cover her eyes, and he couldn't read her expression. Was she glad he was staying or not? He had no idea at all. She certainly didn't seem willing to pursue her earlier attempts to patch up their marriage. In fact, she hadn't even mentioned it. And while she denied being afraid of him, he wasn't sure she meant it. He was afraid of himself, after all. He felt oddly let down, even though he told himself that he hadn't expected she had wanted him there because she still loved him. No, it was obviously her do-gooder mentality. She was helping him out because he was in need, and that was all. The minute it was no longer necessary to show support, she would be only too glad to say goodbye, he was sure.

God, what a mess his life was. He didn't know what to think anymore. In a single fluid movement he rose to his feet and tossed the hair back out of his eyes. "I'm going back," he said.

Without a word, Lainie scrambled to her feet and followed him.

He didn't stop, but unlike before, he did slow his pace, allowing her to match it easily. Once the soft chambray of his shirt brushed against the bare flesh of her arm, and she felt an almost inexorable temptation to reach out and catch hold of his hand or to wrap her arm around his waist. But while she had touched him at the airport, when the reporters had made such displays of affection necessary, and in the car, when he had simply seemed to need a lifeline to hold on to, now, when she desperately wanted to touch him, she knew she couldn't. He had allowed her to walk with him, he had agreed to stay at the apartment, but she could sense from some indefinable aura surrounding him that he would not be able to handle her touch.

So she matched her stride to his and thought that if anyone had told her this morning that she would be walking on the beach with Griffin tonight, she would have had them committed to Mental Health. She was still unsure of what she ought to be doing, but at least he wasn't walking away. She crossed her fingers and sent a prayer winging to heaven. So far, so good.

One day at a time was the philosophy Brendan had been preaching to her. It had, he told her, stood him in good stead when he was trying to get himself together after his base-ball career had gone down the drain. Well, all right, she thought. She had tried everything else with Griff to no avail at all. Now that she knew for sure he needed her presence, she would give him that. One day at a time for as long a he would let her.

She supposed that in a way she ought to be grateful to that obnoxious Wes LaRue. He had managed to send Griff home to her when she had had no other hopes. But she certainly wasn't going to say that to Griff. If or when he wanted to share his feelings with her about Wes LaRue or baseball or their marriage or anything else, she would listen. Until then, she had learned her lesson: she would not push.

Still, they were going to have to do something together over the next few days or weeks, especially if they didn't soul-search. She looked up and caught sight of a perfectly breaking wave, its white foam brilliant in the moonlight.

"Remember when you promised to teach me to surf?" she asked him suddenly.

Griff glanced down at her, his expression wary. "Uh-huh." He sounded reluctant.

"You could now," she told him, wondering as she did so if her suggestion was overstepping the limits.

He shrugged, his gaze going toward the ocean, though she suspected that what he was seeing was the Maui coastline where he had first made that vow. "Maybe," he allowed cautiously. "If you have the time."

He didn't sound sarcastic, but she couldn't help believing that there was real bitterness in his voice. Before, she hadn't ever had the time. Or, she thought with more honesty, she hadn't made the time because she had thought that other people—clients—had always needed her far more than Griff.

Well, there was no question in her mind that he needed her now, that he always had. "I'll make the time," she promised.

He turned back to look at her for a long moment. He had stopped walking and stood very still, the wind lifting his hair as he studied her. She felt like squirming beneath his gaze but strove to control it, forcing herself to stand still under his scrutiny, meeting his eyes guilelessly.

"Then you let me know when you can," he said evenly as he started back up the beach toward the apartment.

It was a challenge, and she knew it.

"I will," she vowed.

He woke up at 4:00 a.m., sweating and scared, and he couldn't remember where he was or why he was here. Sitting up, he stared, disoriented, his mind groping. Then he remembered.

Trembling, he sank back down against the damp pillowcase, willing his heart to stop pounding, concentrating on steadying his galloping pulse. He couldn't remember what he had dreamed, only that it had been awful. And waking up in the narrow bed in the spare bedroom of the apartment was a relief.

Until he remembered, too, that Lainie was sleeping right on the other side of the wall.

He punched the pillow into a more comfortable shape, then rolled onto his side, willing himself into oblivion again.

But his mind would not comply. It entertained him with images of LaRue's florid face, the gray-suited underlings from the commissioner's office, the snap and pop of flashbulbs at the airports here and in Montreal. He flipped over, shifting to find a comfortable spot. But staring at the wall only brought him thoughts of Lainie.

He sighed, turning onto his back, his restlessness now augmented by a persistent throbbing in his loins. It must be some damnably subtle form of torture that God had devised for him that he had ended up back in her life now, when he had told her about all the horrors of his past, when things were definitely over between them and she was only being kind in letting him stay.

He had headed straight for the spare bedroom after he had helped her with the dishes, making it quite clear that he didn't expect her to share her bed with him. Now, while he applauded his common sense, he ached like a sex-starved adolescent. And he wondered how long he could stand living with her and not being her husband anymore.

God willing, the investigation would soon be over.

Chapter Ten

If God had any intention of cooperating, it wasn't immediately obvious.

The first thing Lainie did the following morning when her alarm went off at six-thirty was to grope her way out to the living room and call Chase. He wasn't any more coherent than she was at that hour, besides being less than pleased at being dragged out of a sound sleep. But she did manage to understand from his mumbled response that as far as he knew, nothing had changed. LaRue was still sticking to his story, the police hadn't cracked it, and no real culprit had emerged.

"I'll call you later," Chase promised blearily, "when I wake up."

"Thanks," Lainie whispered. She hung up and tiptoed to the door of the spare bedroom, debating whether to open it. It wasn't a long debate. She eased open the door and peeked in, praying that Griff was still asleep. He was.

Sprawled on his back amid tumbled sheets and blankets, he lay with one arm hugging the pillow against his bare chest. Something deep within Lainie tightened as she looked at him, loving the shadowed jawline and sharply defined nose, the tousled wheat-colored hair. She desperately wanted to erase the lines of strain and exhaustion that were still apparent, even in sleep, on his face.

Griff muttered something and scowled, then rolled onto his side, still clutching the pillow, and Lainie wanted to take away the pillow and replace it with herself. But things were too tentative, too fragile. She didn't want to do anything to jeopardize the truce they had. But her good intentions didn't stop her from blowing him a kiss before she pulled the door shut behind her and went to get dressed for work.

Ordinarily, and especially lately, work was the be-all and end-all of her existence. The minute she walked into the hospital, she didn't think about anything beyond her clients and her work until the halls were dark and the lights dim at night. But today was different. Today she couldn't keep her mind off Griff.

She sat through a staff meeting and was only faintly aware of what was being discussed. Her mind was preoccupied with her husband. Just knowing that he was home and she was not, that he might need her and she wasn't with him, preyed on her constantly. It was illogical, it was stupid, it was a lot of things. But most of all, it was true. She spent the rest of the morning with several elderly patients, one of whom was terminally ill and two of whom had no future other than a nursing home staring them in the face. But none of them wanted to moan about the future. They talked instead about the past. And Lainie listened, relating it to her own.

No matter what any of them said, everything seemed to come back to the memories they had of time spent with people they loved. And Lainie loved Griff. She sat in Mrs. Carmody's room, her eyes brimming with tears as the old lady talked of her dear Dermot, with whom she had spent fifty-four years—hard years, lean years, but loving years. And Lainie thought of Griff.

What was he doing? Was he awake yet? Was he worried about the investigation? Was he thinking of her? Did he miss her as she missed him? She glanced at the clock on her way back to the office. It was almost noon. If Griff was at home, she could call him and ask if he wanted to drive over and have lunch with her. The way things were going, they weren't even going to have a year together, much less fifty-four. But at least, she thought as she picked up the phone, they could have this.

She had never called him at home before during the day except on rare occasions when she had found time to call and let him know she would be late. He sounded astonished when he heard her voice on the phone.

"Are you all right?" she asked him, and knew it sounded inane the moment she said it.

"Yes."

Dead end there.

"I was, um, wondering if, um, you'd like to have lunch with me?"

"Lunch?"

"I mean, if you don't want to, it's okay. I know it's short notice and—"

"No, no. That's fine. I—I'd like to. Where?"

"Could you come here? I have one more person to see before I can leave."

"Sure. When?"

"I can be ready by twelve-fifteen," she said, relieved that he had agreed.

"I'll be there."

He hung up before she could say goodbye. Her heart was still pounding in her chest when she set the receiver down. *Shape up,* she told herself. *All you've done is invite your husband to lunch.* But even so, she felt strangely exhilarated. Pushing down the intercom buzzer, she told Pam, "Send Cathy in."

HE SHOULD HAVE SAID NO. He should have said he was busy. But then, when had he ever shown good sense with Lainie except when he had sent her the name of his lawyer? He wondered now, as he dressed in a pair of casual cotton slacks and a navy-and-green striped polo shirt that he had retrieved when he had got his car out of storage that morning, if she had ever contacted Fred. He supposed he ought to call the lawyer and ask him. Or maybe he should just ask Lainie. Yes, why not do that, he thought as he brushed his fair hair back off his forehead. Maybe that was why she had asked him to have lunch with her, because she had had second thoughts about letting him stay here. Maybe the lawyer advised against it. Maybe she wanted him to leave. He set the brush down on the dresser, feeling more apprehensive than ever. Maybe he wouldn't ask her, after all.

It only took him twenty minutes to get to the hospital. In the middle of the day the freeway was uncrowded, and he arrived a few minutes early. That gave him time enough to think—exactly what he didn't want to do. Once, during the early weeks of their marriage, he had decided to drive over and meet her after work. That was the only other time he had been to the hosptial since their marriage.

That night she had been running more than an hour late. And even after he had arrived, she had spent another hour and a half with the family of a chronic alcoholic while Griff had cooled his heels and fanned the flames of his temper in the waiting room. He had known then that it was rotten of him to resent it, but he had just the same. He had waited that time until nearly seven-thirty before he had left without her. He hadn't been back since. And he wished that he hadn't remembered that occasion now as he sat in the car with the engine still running.

There were other memories, too—even more deeply buried—memories of other sterile counselor's offices, other waiting rooms with color-coordinated office furniture and walls filled with diplomas, of his mother's hysterical voice going on and on, his father's rough baritone. Griff snapped off the engine and got out of the car, slamming the door with a barely controlled ferocity. Damn, he didn't want to think about that now. He drew a deep breath, letting it out slowly as he willed himself back in control of his feelings. Otherwise, he would never be able to face her.

Her secretary smiled at him. "Hi, you must be Griff. I recognize you from your picture. I'll let Lainie know you're here."

Griff's eyebrows lifted in surprise as the woman buzzed Lainie and got an answer at once. He had expected to be left standing until she finally disposed or whatever of whomever she was with at the moment. But barely a minute passed before the door at the end of the long narrow hall opened and a sulky teenaged girl padded out, followed by Lainie, whose eyes met Griff's with a smile.

"I'll see you tomorrow," she was saying to the girl, who didn't appear to be listening. She was walking along in a sort of dazed fog and nearly tripped over Griff's feet. A nurse met the girl at the door of the social services section and escorted her out while Lainie told the secretary when to set up another appointment. That done, she turned her full attention on Griff.

"I'm ready. Shall we go?"

"Sure."

He felt tongue-tied and awkward, like an adolescent taking a girl out on a first date. He didn't know what to talk about or where to put his hands or feet. "Where do you want to go?" he asked finally, when he had settled himself beside her in the car and found her looking at him expectantly.

"How about something Mexican? I know a good place nearby."

"Sure. That's fine."

She directed him to a restaurant, not far from the hospital, that catered to the professional crowd. The luncheon rush was thinning out a bit by the time they got there, and the waitress seated them with almost no waiting. It only seemed to take an eternity, Griff knew, because every second that he was in her presence and didn't know what to say seemed more like a hundred years.

He couldn't decide at first if it was a comfort or not that Lainie seemed to feel the same way he did. She scarcely said a word in the car once she had given him directions, asked how he slept and commented on his having his car back. He wondered if perhaps she was just waiting for the right moment to tell him that she had changed her mind and wanted him to move out. Why else would she have called him to have lunch with her? He didn't know if he should say something that would give her an opening or not. He only knew he didn't want to.

They ordered and sat sipping margaritas, avoiding each other's eyes, until Lainie said, "It's hot today."

He replied, "Yes," and then they sat in silence some more.

The waitress brought Lainie her taco salad and him a plate of enchiladas, and then, at least, they had something to occupy their hands and mouths. Griff remembered times when they had gone out to eat before when the food would grow cold because Lainie was telling him something and couldn't be bothered to eat. His eyes flickered upward to catch a glimpse of her now. She was eating with total concentration. Damn.

"Have you heard from Chase?" she asked him then, and he shook his head.

"No."

"You must be anxious."

"Yes." But not just about that, he wanted to say. About us. About this business of living together again and what it all meant. He wanted to ask her why she was offering. He wanted to know if it was only out of the kindness of her heart, as he feared.

"I hope you hear soon," she said, giving him a tentative smile.

He managed a wan one in return. "Yes."

She lowered her eyes and concentrated on her salad again.

Griff shoved the enchilada around his plate, picking at it, not sure what he was feeling except dissatisfaction. What did he expect, after all? That she would throw her arms around him and tell him she loved him and believed in him? Hardly. Well, then? He sighed and pinched the bridge of his nose between his fingers.

Lainie cleared her throat. "I really ought to be getting back." She looked at him apologetically.

Griff shrugged. "All right." He pushed back his chair and stood up, then waited for her while she took one last swallow of her margarita. She followed him silently out of the restaurant and back to the car, and he wondered again why she had bothered to call him. She hadn't said a word—or nothing that mattered, anyway.

"You didn't have to call me, you know," he said a bit roughly as they drove swiftly back to the hospital.

Lainie sighed and shoved a hand through her hair. "I know," she said in a low voice. "But I wanted to."

She didn't say anything else, even when he dropped her off, just gave him another half smile and fleetingly touched his arm as she got out of the car.

Why did you want to? Why? he asked her silently as he watched her walk up the broad steps. Then he drove away, still wondering. He hadn't come up with a satisfactory answer by the time he reached home.

LAINIE WAS DISGUSTED. With Griffin. With herself. "But then, what did you expect, idiot?" she fumed as she walked down the corridor to the social service office. It wasn't what she was expecting exactly, it was what she was hoping for— that break in the wall that separated them, that spark that always flared between them no matter what their differences. But it hadn't been there today. Today she had felt nothing but awkwardness. And obviously Griff had felt the same.

She certainly hadn't had any idea what to say to him. She had thought, when she first got the idea of asking him to come, that conversation would take care of itself. Where she was concerned, it usually did. But she hadn't realized then that every avenue of conversation would be literally fraught with mine fields. They couldn't talk about his job or her job; they couldn't talk about their relationship, their marriage. And if you took away all the big things, you couldn't handle the little ones, either. She knew as sure as she knew her own name that she could not have been coherent even discussing the weather.

For the rest of the afternoon she brooded about what she should have said, what she could have done. But none of it helped her decide what to do when she got home that night. And after their lunch together she had no idea what to expect at all.

He might, she thought, be gone. It wouldn't have been out of character, and she knew it. She tried to steel herself in case he was, and her relief was extraordinary when she pulled into the garage to find his Toyota still there. She hurriedly grabbed her purse and walked briskly around the side of the apartment and up the steps, then stopped, astonished, at the decided aroma of garlic and oregano in the air.

The front door was open, the stereo was playing, and Griff was sitting on the floor, clad only in a pair of oyster-colored corduroy shorts, playing solitaire on the coffee table. He looked up when her shadow darkened the doorway, and at least his expression wasn't forbidding. Lainie felt weak with relief.

She smiled and sniffed the air appreciatively. "You didn't have to do this," she said, waving her arm in the direction of the oven from where the wonderful smells obviously came.

"I didn't." Griff rose lithely to his feet so that she was even more aware of him. "Your mother brought it."

"My mother?" Lainie felt a tiny frisson of unease. And how had Griff taken that? He had never said much about her mother and brothers, but she knew he had never been at ease around them. Until she had experienced his Colorado blowup, she hadn't been able to guess why. Now she knew. Griff and families were not compatible. He always kept waiting for the ax to drop.

Oddly enough now, though, he had a faint smile on his face, and he was shaking his head bemusedly. "She just dropped by this afternoon and said she knew I like lasagna and she wanted to cheer me up."

"Oh?" Lainie's voice reflected her caution.

He nodded. "She's nice, your mother," he said reflectively, as though he didn't quite believe that mothers could be. Then he went on. "I wasn't quite sure when you'd get home, but I put it in when she told me to." He was looking at her with a question in his eyes born, she was sure, of the doubt he had developed that she would ever get home on time.

But today she had. Had he but known, wild horses could not have kept her at the hospital. She had waded through her afternoon's appointments with one eye on the clock and half her thoughts on Griff. She knew she had been particularly short with Mavis Leary, but she was finally realizing that Mavis, perhaps like Griff's mother, didn't know when to quit. For a long time now she had allowed Mavis to sponge up as much time as Mavis thought she needed. But things with Dick had not improved noticeably, nor, Lainie was beginning to think, would they ever. Mavis, she suspected, rather liked the soap-opera quality of her life. But today Lainie had scarcely given her time to reiterate her latest installment. She had soap opera enough of her own now with Griff.

"Well, whoever made it," Lainie said now, tossing her purse into the corner of the couch, "it smells fabulous. And I'm starved."

Neither of them referred to a possible reason for her hunger—the less than satisfactory lunch they had shared. But by some mutual, unspoken pact they seemed resolved to do better over dinner. Perhaps, Lainie thought, because sharing dinner wasn't an entirely foreign experience to them. Even if she had frequently been late, they did have several together to fall back on.

Griff put himself out, telling her about an article he had read on antiques in the paper that morning, and Lainie listened, interested, not only because he was the one telling her about it but because she really did enjoy life more when she had a bit of furniture restripping going on. She hadn't done any since he had left the first time. All the joy had gone. But now she found herself saying, "Maybe we could look for a rocking chair for the spare bedroom."

The moment she said it, she realized that she was thinking again in terms of a future for them and their marriage, and she hastily took another bite of lasagna and avoided his eyes.

But if Griff noticed, he made no remark. "Sounds like a good idea" was the only thing he said. And if she heard caution in his tone of voice, she kenw it was only understandable. Besides, she wouldn't have been surprised if he had outrightily refused. Why would he bother looking for a rocking chair with her when ultimately they were going to be getting a divorce? She took a bit bite of garlic bread and directed her thoughts as far away from that possibility as she could.

"How about giving me one of those surfing lessong after dinner?" she asked. There, that was a change of topic!

He looked up, his fork arrested halfway to his mouth. "Are you serious?"

"Yes."

He considered her unblinkingly, and she gave him a hopeful smile. When he still didn't answer, she tried a nonchalant shrug, though inside she was hurt. "Well, it was just an idea."

"Okay, then," he said, as if making up his mind. "If you want."

What I want is a little enthusiasm, she thought irritably. When he had first suggested teaching her on Maui, he had laughed, absolutely delighted with the idea. Now he looked as if he would have to grit his teeth to go in the same ocean with her.

Did she have any idea what she was doing to him, he wondered, gritting his teeth as he balanced the surfboard on his head and followed her bikini-clad, lissome body down across the wide sandy beach toward the breaking waves. Simply her walk was driving him mad. He felt the hot press of desire against the material of his swim trunks and turned his gaze on the incoming surf, trying to concentrate on the chill of the water and not the sway of his wife's walk as she preceded him.

God, why had he ever agreed?

Lainie dropped her towel on the rise just above the damp sand at the high-tide line and turned to watch Griff approach. With one quick movement he dropped the board from his head and wrapped his arm around it, holding it like a shield across the telltale evidence of his body.

"You remember how to bodysurf, don't you?" he asked.

"Sure."

"Well, then, I'm certain you'll have the hang of it in no time." He dropped the towel he had slung around his neck with his free hand and started briskly toward the water. "Come on. Time's wasting."

It was the cool water against his overheated body that he was longing for, he told himself. It was definitely not the feel of Lainie's flesh against his own.

But within minutes he had both. He had swum with the board out beyond the breakers, leaving her to swim out on her own, which she did easily, paddling alongside him, her nearness temptation enough. But once they were out there, then the real challenge began.

"Here, you get on," he said, and slipped off the board, holding it at the end so she could clamber on.

She did, stretching out so that her face was only inches from his own, and he dangled, treading water in front of her. "Now what?"

"Huh?" Mesmerized by the sparkling hazel fire of her eyes, he hardly heard what she had said.

Lainie grinned. "What do I do now?" she asked patiently, enunciating every word.

"Oh." He made an effort to get his mind off her and on to the mechanics of riding a surfboard. When he had first proposed teaching her, he had been thinking how he would love to share the confines of a surfboard with her. And while he still might, nothing was the same now. Now he had damned well better keep his hands off! "Well," he told her in a slightly strangled voice, "you have to get into position. That's just like bodysurfing. Here, paddle in a little. Then just ride it, lying down once or twice to get the hang of it."

"Right." Lainie glanced over her shoulder, then paddled somewhat awkwardly into position. The next thing Griff knew, she was shooting away from him, borne shoreward on a wave. Then the board went one way, and Lainie went the other, and he saw her bob to the surface, a sheepish grin on her face.

"I forgot to hang on!" she yelled at him, grinning through the water that sluiced down her face.

"Practice!" he yelled back.

Lainie practiced. And practiced. He was amazed at her stick-to-itiveness. Whatever he suggested, she was willing to try. If one thing didn't work, she tried another. And with such an enthusiastic pupil, he went on suggesting things for a long while until his teeth began to chatter in the cool chill of the sunset over the water.

"You're getting the hang of it," he praised her when she came paddling back out to him once again, her wet hair straggling down past her ears and clinging to her shoulder, making her look like a mermaid. "Maybe next time you'll stay up."

"You come with me," Lainie said.

Griff frowned. So far he had kept his distance, and things had gone quite well. He had tamped down his desire and was simply enjoying being with her. But if he surfed with her, if he touched her— "Please," Lainie cajoled. "It always looked like such fun."

Griff shook his head in exasperation. "When did you ever see anyone ride tandem?" It certainly wasn't common. He didn't even know if he could do it, and he said so.

"Of course you can," Lainie scoffed. "They're always doing it in the movies."

"What movies?"

"Oh, you know. *Gidget, Beach Blanket Bingo,* those movies."

Griff rolled his eyes.

Lainie grinned. "Oh, come on. What can James Darren do that you can't?"

Put like that, how could he refuse? "Move up," he commanded.

The simple logistics of putting two bodies in balance horizontally on one surfboard were difficult enough. Combine them with moving water and an attempt to rearrange the bodies to a vertical position while in motion and something very close to drowning could occur. The tangle of arms, legs, bodies and board churned, twisted and ultimately ground to an ignominious halt in about eighteen inches of water.

"Any more bright ideas?" Griff spit the words out with a mouthful of saltwater, checking Lainie over for bruises at the same time.

She shook her head, laughing and wiping hair out of her mouth with one hand while she made sure she still had both halves of her bathing suit with the other. "I wonder how they did it," she marveled. "It looked so simple. Like standing in a bathtub."

"That's probably where they did it," Griff muttered, hauling himself to his feet and stumbling after the board, which was being towed back out to sea in the backwash.

Lainie struggled to her feet and followed him. "We could try that," she said.

Griff stopped where he was and looked at her over his shoulder. The grin that she had been wearing slowly faded from her face. It was, he thought, a moment rather like that in the Garden of Eden right after both Adam and Eve had had several bites of the apple.

"No," he said, and from the look on her face, he knew she had come to the same conclusion.

"You're right," she said softly.

"I think you've had enough for today." *I've had enough,* he meant.

"Yes." She turned and walked back up the beach to the spot where they had dropped their towels. "Thanks, Griff. I enjoyed it."

"Me, too." *Enjoyed? So what's wrong with enjoying it,* he asked himself savagely. What more did he want?

They didn't linger on the beach. The breeze was cool, the sun low in the sky, burnishing their bodies a dark copper color and setting Griff's fair hair on fire. Lainie purposely lagged behind as he strode back toward the apartment, watching him, admiring the economy of his movements, the smooth flex of his muscles as he walked through the deep sand. It was the first time she had allowed herself to appreciate the beauty of him since they had come down to the beach that evening. She had made herself concentrate wholly on the surfing and the suggestions he made, just wanting to show him that they could still have a good time together without putting their relationship in jeopardy. And she hadn't done too badly, even though she might have messed things up a bit at the end with her crazy suggestion that they try tandem surfing and that remark about trying it in the bathtub at the end.

That had brought back memories of an earlier time—to Griff, obviously, as well as to her—and those memories and where they might lead were something that right now neither of them was willing to discuss. She could tell that at once by his cool withdrawal and the stiff set of his shoulders as he walked.

Well, maybe by the time they had reached the apartment, the strain between them would have disappeared. Silence seemed to be the way Griff healed rifts. All right, silence it would be, then, she vowed, thankful to have learned that anything she might have said in such circumstances would only have got her in deeper and deeper.

Griff waited for her where the sidewalk met the beach, and while he wasn't smiling, he didn't seem as tense anymore, either. She was just about to congratulate herself on handling the situation right for once when Griff looked up toward the apartment and said, "Hey, isn't that Chase?"

Lainie lifted her eyes to look where he was pointing. A man and a woman were walking back up the hill toward a sports car parked in the alley. "Sure is," she said, remembering that Chase had promised to call. Had he found out something already? She didn't know whether to hope he had or not.

"Chase!" Griff shouted, and let forth a piercing whistle. The dark-haired man stopped and turned around, then said something to the woman with him, and they both turned and walked back down the sidewalk to meet Griff and Lainie in front of their picket fence.

"You remember Susan," Chase said to Lainie as he nodded at the tall, raven-haired woman with him.

Lainie did. Susan Rivers was even more beautiful than she had remembered. It was hard to conceive of a woman that lovely spending her life writing about sweaty jocks, but Brendan Craig said she was one of the best. And even Cassie, now that she had controlled her jealousy, had only praises to sing of Susan Rivers. "I'm glad to see you again," Lainie said to her now, and she was, although she felt awkward and grubby with her stringy hair and sand-covered body, in such obvious contrast to Susan's cool perfection.

"Me, too," Susan said easily, giving her a smile that radiated pure friendliness. "I wish we were bringing good news."

"You're not?" Lainie's stomach plummeted, and she saw Griff tense as he set the surfboard down to lean against the fence.

"Nope," Chase said, shoving his hands in his pockets. "Can't get a thing out of LaRue."

"He's still sticking to his story?" Griff asked glumly, rubbing a hand through his wet hair, lifting it in dark blond spikes all over his head.

"Like glue."

Griff said a rude word. "Why do they believe that bastard?"

"I'm not sure they do," Chase said. "I just think they want to blame somebody."

"And you're it," Susan added. "Until we find the real supplier."

"And how the hell do we do that?" Griff snapped. Lainie could see the irritation he had been masking all day begin to eat at him again, and she went to him and slipped her arm around his waist. He tensed for a moment, then shifted his weight and looped his arm over her shoulders, hugging her against his side.

"We're going to question everyone," Susan said. "I know all the players, and Chase knows all the questions. We'll find out who it is."

Griff didn't look convinced, but Lainie heard the steel in Susan's voice and saw the expression of determination on Chase's face. "I hope so," she said fervently.

"So do I." Griff kicked the bottom of the picket fence with his bare toes. "But in the meantime, whatever happened to innocent until proven guilty."

"That doesn't apply to umpires," Chase told him with a wry smile. "Umpires have to be saints. You should have been a reporter, man. Nobody expects anything pure from them."

"I beg your pardon," Susan said sharply, digging him in the ribs even as she smiled.

"Investigative reporter," Chase corrected his statement rapidly. "Not a sports reporter," he added with false meekness. "Susan's as pure as driven snow."

Susan smiled sweetly. "Absolutely," she said in a prim voice that was far from her normal, more sultry tones. But her face turned serious again when she saw Griff's continued scowl. "Don't worry, Griff. I promise we'll get to the bottom of it. Just hang on."

Griff nodded, but he didn't smile, and Lainie felt the weight of his arm across her shoulders as he must have felt the weight of the accusation made against him. She turned her lips and kissed his shoulder.

Then she remembered her manners and asked Chase and Susan, "Would you two like to come in and have a cup of coffee. It won't take a minute for me to change and put a pot on."

Chase shook his head. "No. You don't have to bother. We'll just run along. We were only checking in because we were in the neighborhood and I told you I'd be in touch." He looked at the two of them appraisingly for another moment, then gave Lainie a wink. "Carry on," he said. "It looks like you're doing fine."

Griff gave her a curious, sidelong stare that she ignored, though she knew her cheeks flushed. "All right," she said. "You'll call when you hear something?"

"Of course." Chase took Susan's arm. "Come along, Tonto. Let's see if we can't slay a few dragons or right a few wrongs before bedtime." He led her away up the hill.

"I keep hoping he'll ride off into the sunset," Susan said to them over her shoulder.

"I'd drown," he protested as the last rays of sun descended into the Pacific.

"That, my dear," she told him, "is the general idea."

He seemed to be strangling her gently as they walked off.

"Do you think they're in love?" Lainie asked Griff as they watched Chase drive away.

Griff looked at her as though she had lost her mind. "What?"

"Well, they—" But she couldn't finish, because what she had been going to say was that when Chase and Susan teased each other, they reminded her of the way she and Griff used to be—once upon a time. "Well, it would be nice," she ended lamely.

Griff grunted and picked up his surfboard, then opened the gate and carried it into the yard and up the apartment steps. He didn't like thinking about love. When he did, he felt all kinds of things that he didn't want to feel, like hurt and envy. And that, on top of all the frustration he felt about his baseball situation, irritated the hell out of him. He kicked open the door to the apartment and hauled the surfboard through the kitchen and out onto the tiny enclosed back porch, where he left it. Then he came back, rubbing his hands roughly through his salt-stiffened hair.

"D'you want the shower first?" he asked Lainie sharply.

She looked at him uncertainly. "No, you go ahead."

"Thanks." He grabbed a clean towel out of the narrow wall cabinet in the hall and disappeared into the bathroom. He was ninety-nine percent glad she hadn't made a comment about sharing it with him. It was the other one percent that annoyed him through gallons and gallons of cold water.

When he came out, he had raised the water bill and lowered his blood pressure considerably. "I saved the hot for you," he said magnanimously, and was rewarded with a smile. Then she disappeared into the bathroom.

He fixed himself a cup of coffee and prowled around the apartment restlessly. Chase and Susan's arrival had reminded him forcibly of why he was there in the first place, and he gnashed his teeth. Up until yesterday he had thought that other than Lainie he had his life pretty well under control. Things ran smoothly, not perfectly, but on the whole, all right. And now this. He slammed his hand against the refrigerator and bit down on his lip. Why the hell had LaRue done that to him? Damn.

He wandered back out to the living room, feeling hedged in. A part of him wanted to go for a walk, to get away, to try to solve his problems out on the beach. But for the first time he suspected that there was no way he could solve them. They had told him in Montreal just to go home and wait. And damn it, that was the hardest thing of all—not being able to do anything, giving up control and, especially, living again with Lainie.

He let his mind play back over the events of the past twenty-four hours, thinking about her presence at the airport, her quiet solicitude, her support, her invitation to lunch, their surfing lesson. Then he jammed his fists into the pockets of his jeans and let out a long hissing breath. She was such a Good Samaritan, so willing to help. And it infuriated the hell out of him.

Why, he asked himself.

Because he wanted more, or he didn't wany anything at all. That was the long and the short of it. The water running in the bathroom stopped, and he heard her humming as she moved around the room. In a minute she would be in the living room again, probably ready to hold his hand and comfort him in his distress.

Hell.

He grabbed his coffee cup off the table and dumped it into the sink. Then he went into the spare bedroom and shut the door. It was more than his sanity was worth to face her again this evening. Not the way his mind and emotions were messed up right now.

When Lainie walked back into the living room and found it empty, she thought for a moment that he had left. She stood in the middle of the room, a rising panic welling within her. Then she heard him bang against the spindle chair in the spare room, and she breathed again.

Still, even now that she knew he was there, she couldn't stop the faint tremor in her fingers and the feeling of somehow having just avoided a disastrous accident. It was this continual living on edge, she told herself. She never knew what he would do next, and she was always afraid he would bolt. How on earth could she live this way for days on end? When she had seen Chase and Susan this evening, her emotions had been mixed. A part of her wanted for the whole thing to be over and Griff to be exonerated, but another part protested immediately that it was too soon, that they had barely had a chance to live together again.

But if it was too soon in that way, it was aeons long in others. Every minute she was with him, she wanted to be building a life together. Simply being content to maintain a perilous hold on a very questionable status quo was unnerving. And yet for the moment it was all she had. They were walking a tightrope, the two of them, and at any moment either one of them could make a wrong move and they would both fall off.

She knew she couldn't go to sleep right away, even if Griff had done so. It was only nine-thirty, and all the surfing in the world couldn't have dulled the razor edge of her emotions tonight. Idly, she flipped through a magazine, but nothing in it held her interest. She tried the television, but the comedies were inane and the action shows a bit too full of mayhem for her taste. There was a baseball game on, but she flicked the control past that without even stopping.

She wanted to do something. Her hands itched to be working. If she couldn't talk to Griff, she needed to do something else to work off some of her pent-up emotions. It was then that she remembered the cradle.

It had been a spur-of-the-moment purchase, picked up at an antique-cum-junk store on the Pacific Coast Highway that she had been browsing through to kill time not long ago. She had bought it with the idea of refinishing it for Brendan and Cassie's baby. It would be a good therapy, she told herself. A labor of love for friends that might help her purge some of her envy for them at the same time. But she hadn't been able to face seeing it in the apartment day after day. Not so far at any rate. And so she had stuck it in the locked cabinet in the garage where it was out of sight. It would be, as Brendan pointed out, months and months before the baby arrived.

Well, it might be months and months until then, but Lainie needed something to do right now—tonight—so she let herself out of the apartment and went down the steps to the garage, rummaged through the cabinet and came back up minutes later with the cradle in her arms.

It had been most recently painted a ghastly pink with garish red roses at the head and foot of it. And before that, judging from the layers of paint, it had held babies in green, blue and gray environs. But Lainie suspected it was walnut beneath all the layers, and she intended to strip it down and refinish it to its former glory. Starting, she decided, tonight.

She carried it out onto the back porch and fetched the stripper, steel wool and rags that she would need. Then she opened the windows so she would have some ventilation as she worked. Humming softly, she began to apply the stripper, her mind going willingly to thoughts of how the grain of the wood would look when it was revealed, of how pleased Brendan and Cassie would be with it, because they admired her work and hadn't the faintest idea themselves of how to turn a piece of junk into a family treasure. She even allowed herself small fleeting thoughts of the baby who would one day occupy the cradle, and if once or twice a tear dripped onto the gummy surface of the wood, she told herself it was because the stripper was so strong that it was damaging her sinuses; that was all. She was not crying.

"What's that?"

She had been working for so long that she had a crick in her neck from sitting cross-legged on the floor and bending over the rungs of the cradle as she stripped them one by one. But now she jerked her head around at the sound of Griff's husky, uncertain voice.

She blinked at him, and he cocked his head to one side, puzzlement written on his face as he stood in the doorway to the kitchen, bare chested and wearing only a pair of faded jeans, as he looked at the cradle.

"What is that?" he asked again.

"A cradle." He frowned and scratched his ear thoughtfully.

"For Brendan and Cassie."

His eyes widened with shock.

"Didn't you know they were expecting a baby?"

"No."

Lainie wondered if she imagined the wealth of pain she heard in that one word. She didn't think so. He looked at her, stricken, and she saw him swallow almost convulsively.

"When?" he asked hoarsely.

"Late February, I think."

"Oh. That's nice," he managed, but his voice cracked. He stuffed his hands into his pockets. "I—I couldn't sleep. I'm going for a walk," he said abruptly, and turned on his heel.

Lainie watched him go, heard the door slam, then let out her breath slowly as she strangled the cradle rung in her rubber-gloved hands.

Chaper Eleven

Griff hadn't realized before that it was possible to have a love-hate relationship with an inanimate object. But that was the way it was between him and the cradle.

In some ways it came to symbolize for him all that he wanted and could not have. When he had seen Lainie's hands lovingly smoothing over the now-stripped wood, he wanted to feel her touch on him. And when he thought of the promise of the cradle—of the love and the resulting child who would come forth from that love, of the future that implied—the pain was almost too much to bear.

But he couldn't stay away from it, either. As the days passed and there came no news, good or bad, from either the commissioner's office or from Chase and Susan, he had to fill his days with something. And more often than not while Lainie was at work, he would find himself coming back to the cradle, picking up the pieces she had so carefully marked when she had taken it apart and weighing them in his hands. Then, getting out a piece of fine-grained sandpaper and, working slowly and almost reverently, he would set to bringing out the silken smoothness of the wood.

There was a satisfaction in it, a sense of bringing the future out of the past that was positive and warming. Something, he realized, that could never be done with his own past, so he was glad in one small way that he had a part in someone's future, even if ultimately it was not his own.

He sighed now and pushed a lock of hair off his sun-burned forehead and wrinkled his nose because the perspiration made the sanding dust stick to his skin. It was almost time to get up and fix some supper. The clock said five-thirty, and Lainie would be home soon. She rarely came in past six these days. And she wasn't called out in the evening as much anymore, either. Except for her night class, she was there every evening. He was pleased; it was what he had wanted all along, but it bothered him a little, because he wondered if she was only doing it because she felt obliged to do so. Granted, in other ways she didn't seem to be doing her social-worker act for him, but she didn't seem interested in saving their marriage anymore, either. At any rate, she certainly didn't talk about it.

He unfolded himself from his sitting position on the cramped back porch and cleaned up the mess before he ambled into the kitchen and set the table. He didn't have to fix dinner. She had told him that over and over. But he enjoyed doing it, though he couldn't have explained why. It made him feel as if he were somehow contributing something. But what it was he was contributing to he couldn't have said.

He was chopping mushrooms for the beef Stroganoff when the door opened and Lainie came in. She looked worn out, as if she had been carrying the world's problems all day long, and he longed to go to her and hold her in his arms and comfort her, but he didn't. It would have been presumptuous, out of line. So he simply ached for her—and for himself—and continued chopping the mushrooms, permitting himself to ask only, ''Rough day?''

She dropped her purse on the couch and sank down next to it, kicking off her shoes and putting stocking-clad feet on the coffee table. ''And how.'' She wriggled her toes and stretched out her arms, the material of her knit top tautening across her breasts. He looked away.

"Did you hear anything?" she asked him.

"No."

He had spent the past few days wondering what would happen if he did hear. Sometimes he had lain on the beach in the afternoons, fantasizing about getting the call that said LaRue had named the true supplier and that he was in the clear. But while that moment of exhiliration was always sharp in his mind, what came afterward was hazy. For it meant the end of his life with Lainie, the way things were now. He never let his fantasy get that far. Instead, he always jumped up and ran into the surf, letting his exertion and the pounding of the waves wipe out his fears. By the time he was worn out, he was content to let the police, the commissioner and Chase and Susan take as long as they wanted on the case.

Since the initial shock of his accusation had worn off, he had in fact found a certain comfort in the limbo in which he was living. And while he didn't like having his integrity questioned and the running of his life taken out of his control, at least he had Lainie right now. And that meant a lot.

"Would you like to go to a movie tonight?" he asked her now, hoping to offer her a bit of distraction from the cares of her job.

She raised her eyebrows. "Movie?"

"I just thought you might like to take a break," he said quickly, hoping it didn't sound as if he were asking for a date, as if he were pressuring her.

Lainie smiled and stretched again. "I think that sounds great."

"Good." Griff finished with the mushrooms, pleased that he had asked her. "Check the paper, why don't you?" He dumped the mushrooms into the frying pan, still smiling to himself. It wasn't a date, he reminded himself again. But he couldn't suppress the feeling of gladness, nor did he bother to ask himself why he would even consider such a thing with her again. He only knew that he wanted it. Badly.

The phone rang halfway through the meal, and he felt his stomach tighten. Not tonight. Of all nights for her to be called out, he hoped, it wouldn't be this one. He looked at her expectantly, supposing that she would snatch it up on the first ring. She did not.

"You get it," she said. "It might be Chase."

He wasn't sure right now if he wanted to hear from Chase or not. But he answered the phone. "Hello?" He needn't have worried, he thought, sighing as he handed the receiver to her. "It's for you."

He chewed a bite of Stroganoff slowly while Lainie listened to the woman on the phone. Griff thought the woman sounded more put together than most of Lainie's callers. But whoever she was, she must want something. They always did from Lainie. He watched his wife, surprised when she didn't immediately jump right up and say, "I'm on my way." She had done it often enough in the past.

But tonight she was tapping her plate with her fork, a scowl on her face. "I don't know," she was saying. "Let me talk to my—um, my, er... Just a minute." She covered the receiver with her hand. "This is the college night-school supervisor," she said to Griff. "They want to be sure I can do another session of that effective communications in marriage class again. Starting tomorrow."

Griff did his best to look noncommittal. It wasn't his business what she did from now on. "Do what you want," he said. "I won't be around forever."

Lainie gave him a look that he thought was almost pained, but she turned back to the phone quickly. "Yes, all right," she said, her tone brisk. "Same time as last session." She hung up and resumed eating. Nothing more was said, but he felt lingering disapproval in the air. Now what, he wondered. Had she expected him to object? And what good would that have done?

Serves you right, Lainie told herself, *for getting your hopes up.* Obviously Griff looked at their time together as a simple stopgap, just the place he had to hang around until things got settled and he could move out without causing a scandal to erupt. Damn. She felt tears sting behind her lids and she ducked her head, finishing her dinner with far less enthusiasm that she had begun it. His invitation to the movie this evening had been the first thing he had initiated since he came home. It had given her a moment's exhilaration. And now she was down again. Clearly he had only offered because he felt somehow beholden to her. For her hospitality, she wondered wryly. And was that why he fixed dinner every night, too?

Well, for whatever reason, she was glad he had suggested the movie. It would help her get through the evening without having to say much to him. There seemed, she thought, very little now to say.

"I'll clean the dishes while you change," she told him as she finished carrying the plates to the sink. She could wear what she had worn to work. But Griff still had on a pair of paint-spattered jeans and no shirt, a fact that her eyes had been avoiding for over an hour.

"Okay."

He was just about to head for the spare bedroom when the phone rang again. Chase, he wondered. Or one of Lainie's clients? He paused in the doorway, holding his breath.

Lainie picked up the phone, and her face changed from a smile to a worried frown almost at once.

"Where is he, Claire?" she asked. "Where *are you*?" She raked her fingers through her hair, agitated. Griff knew again the sinking, knotted feeling in his stomach. Lainie hesitated. "What about the boys?"

Griff leaned his hand against the doorjamb and waited. Lainie's eyes flickered from him to the floor and back again. She nodded to whatever Claire was saying, then covered the receiver and said to Griff, "I don't know what to do. Claire Hudson's husband got laid off today. He's—well, he's..."

She didn't have to tell Griff what he was; he knew damned well, and he knew what Hudson would probably do, if he hadn't done it already. He felt the sinking feeling churn into nausea, and his knuckles tightened on the woodwork.

"I know I promised you we'd go to the movie, and—" Lainie began carefully.

"Is Claire all right?" he cut in.

"Yes. So far. I think I can talk to him and—"

"And end up like you did with Dick Leary?" Griff asked bitterly, his voice rising.

"No. Bob's not like that! He—"

"Do you need to go?"

She didn't say anything for a minute, her expression unreadable. Then she nodded reluctantly. "I think perhaps I'd better," she admitted.

"Okay. I'll drive you."

"No." She shook her head vehemently. "You don't need to do that."

"I want to. Tell her we'll be right over."

Lainie looked as if she wanted to protest again, but Griff pushed away from the door and stood in front of her, not moving an inch. Sighing, she took her hand off the receiver and told Claire what he had said. "Stay in the bedroom until I get there," she added, and hung up. "Really, Griff, it's not necessary. I can easily go by—"

But Griff had left her standing there and was in the spare room, stripping off his faded jeans and stepping into a pair of clean ones and buttoning up the front of a pale blue shirt. Stuffing his bare feet into a pair of huaraches, he grabbed his car keys off the dresser. "Come on."

Lainie didn't argue.

"She's not with him now, is she?" Griff asked once they were en route and Lainie had given him directions.

"No. She's locked herself in their bedroom. With the boys."

"What boys?" He slanted her a quick glance.

"They have two sons," Lainie said slowly.

Griff didn't reply. She saw his jaw tighten and his knuckles whiten as he gripped the steering wheel harder. Damn. That was precisely why she hadn't wanted him to come. Hudsons' boys would be living reminders of the hell of his own childhood. But she couldn't have said that to him. She didn't know what she could say to him at all. She lifted her lids enough to peek at him, to try to gauge his reactions, but as usual, most of what Griff was feeling was hidden beneath a stoic exterior. She drew a long, prayerful breath and crossed her fingers.

Neither of them spoke again until they took the freeway off ramp that led them into the quiet residential neighborhood where Claire and Bob Hudson lived. Then Griff suddenly demanded, "What can you do?" and Lainie heard real anguish as well as doubt in his voice.

"I'm not sure," she said honestly. "But they've both been coming to my class ever since the last—the last time he—" her voice faltered.

"The last time he beat her?" Griff finished for her baldly, his eyes raking her for a moment, telling her that he knew far more clearly than she did what this kind of abuse was all about.

"Yes." Lainie wanted to reach over and touch him, but it was as if he were surrounded by an invisible shield that she couldn't penetrate. "I've been trying to help Bob communicate, too," she added.

"Like Dick Leary" Griff snorted.

"No."

"Jeez," he said, shaking his head and rubbing the back of his neck in an effort to relief some of the tension.

"Turn here," Lainie directed. "It's the third house on the right."

It looked just like half the houses on the street, a split-level ranch-style tract house with a basketball hoop above the garage door, a bicycle on the lawn and roses blooming by the door. Lainie got out the moment Griff pulled into the driveway and cut the engine.

"You can wait for me here," she told him, hoping to forestall any more memories he might have.

For a moment he looked as though he might comply. He sat completely still, his hands resting on the bottom of the steering wheel, his head bowed, the blond hair drifting across his forehead. Then he straightened up and looked at her, his eyes dark with more emotions than she could name. "No," he told her in a raw voice. "I'm coming with you."

Lainie wasn't sure what to expect, either from him or from the Hudsons, but she remembered an experienced professor once telling her, "Plunge in; the fire's never much worse than the frying pan." She hoped to God he was right; she suspected that she might well find out. She never knew, walking into a situation like this one, how the people would react. Some men were belligerent, some angry, some frightened, some meek. She hoped that over the past couple of months she had made sufficient headway with Bob Hudson that he had developed enough self-respect and common sense not to do anything rash. She had had great hopes for him and Claire.

When Bob answered her knock at the door, he simply looked beaten and resigned. She breathed a small sigh of relief. Griff was emanating enough tension for all three of them as he stood next to her, his feet braced solidly a couple of feet apart, his hands curled into fists that she knew weren't accidental.

"Claire called me," Lainie said slowly, not moving in on Bob.

He nodded, but his gaze flickered nervously toward Griff. "She's still in the bedroom."

Lainie nodded, relieved, glad that Claire had followed her suggestion. The best thing to do would be to give Bob a chance to cool off and reflect on what he had been about to do. Thank heavens Claire had. And kept the boys away, too. Now maybe they could sit down and talk.

"May we come in?" she asked Bob.

He looked uncertain, and his eyes whisked with brief anger before he stepped back and shrugged, letting them pass.

"Where is the bedroom?" Lainie asked once they were in the modestly furnished living room.

Bob jerked his head toward the back of the house but made no move to show her. He was poised almost like a fighter, his eyes still warily fixed on Griff.

"Oh, excuse me." Lainie took Griff's arm and tried to inject a hint of normal etiquette into the tense situation. "This is my husband, Griff. Bob Hudson."

Whether they spoke or not, she didn't wait around to find out. She knew enough of Griff that whatever he was feeling, he wouldn't show it. All his years as an umpire would have paid off. It was his emotional reaction she was worried about, not the physical threat that Bob Hudson seemed to fear. She found a closed door at the end of the hall and knocked. "It's me, Lainie."

The lock turned, and the door opened cautiously. Claire Hudson, a birdlike woman with pale blond hair just brushing her shoulders, gave Lainie a tremulous smile. "Is he— is Bob all right?" she asked.

"I think so. Calmer."

Claire breathed a sigh of relief. "I was so worried. We've done so well, and now this and—" Her eyes filled with tears, and Lainie reached out and gave her a quick hug.

"Do you want to talk now?" she asked. "I think we can."

"I—I suppose," Claire managed. She shook her head as if the events of the day had drained her completely. "He hasn't been like this in ages. It was being laid off. I know it was. He just started ranting. He—he—" Her voice wavered again, and she stepped aside so that Lainie could see the two boys sitting huddled on the bed. "He slapped Danny. I was afraid—" Claire gave a vague sort of fluttering wave with her hand. Lainie knew exactly what she had been afraid of. "Otherwise, I wouldn't have bothered you," Claire went on, almost apologetically.

"You were right to call," Lainie reassured her. "Come on." She beckoned to Claire to follow her back to the living room.

"Us, too?" the older boy, Danny, asked. He was about eleven, with tousled brown hair, enormous eyes that were red from crying and the remains of a stinging mark on his cheek. His voice came out in a croak, and he looked down, rubbing his nose on his sleeve.

"Wait here just a minute, will you?" Lainie asked him, her voice gentle.

He nodded, and his younger brother hunched back against the pillows on the bed, fear and worry written on his young face.

Neither Bob nor Griff had moved from where she had left them. They reminded her of wolves, circling and wary, about to attack. "This is my husband," she told Claire briskly. She had no intention of clarifying that statement now. The mess her own life was in should have no effect here. And Griff, bless him, showed no inclination to contradict her. On the contrary, he looked ready to spring at Bob Hudson if she should just say the word. She knew with dead certainty that he would do whatever she asked right now. And she knew equally well that what she was going to ask of him would require far more from him than pounding Bob Hudson ever would. She wished she didn't have to, but there was just no other way.

"Griff?"

His eyes left Bob to meet hers quizzically.

"I need to talk with Bob and Claire. I wonder, would you be willing to take their boys out for ice cream or something?"

Griff opened his mouth, but no sound came out. She could see him struggling with her request. Then, eyes shuttered, he closed his mouth and simply nodded his head.

"They're in the bedroom," she told him. "Could you give us about an hour?"

He nodded again and headed for the back of the house. A few minutes later, he came back, followed by the Hudson boys. They looked to their mother for permission, neither of them venturing a glance at their father, who stood next to the television set, his hand drawn into tight fists as he watched, unmoving. Claire shot him a nervous glance, but she nodded to the boys and said softly, "It's all right. I'll be all right. You go ahead with Mr. Tucker." She touched the older boy's arm when he hesitated. "Please, Danny."

"Awright," he mumbled. "C'mon, Todd."

The younger boy blinked, but didn't move. Then Griff rested a gentle hand on his shoulder and drew him toward the door.

"We'll be back soon," he promised. His eyes lifted for an instant, and Lainie saw the stark pain in them, and the knot of misery within her grew. She knew what he was seeing, what he was remembering. She offered him her love with her eyes, but he dropped his gaze and turned to go out the door, Danny and Todd at his heels.

GRIFF COULD SEE IT in their eyes. The pain. The way they avoided looking at him as if he might blame them, might think they had caused it all. God, how well he remembered. His own eyes sought the cool impersonality of the cement driveway, for he was as unwilling as Danny and Todd to face the reality they all knew.

None of them said a word.

He put the car in reverse and backed out of the driveway. His first impulse was to drive straight to the beach. It had been, after all, his solace and comfort when his own parents had behaved like Bob and Claire. Or—he acknowledged bitterly—far worse than Bob and Claire. But, he wondered now, had it actually done him any good? Oh, he had avoided his problems, no doubt about that. But what if he had confronted it, admitted it, talked about it? What if he had shared it?

He glanced at Danny, who was sitting slumped in the front seat next to him. There was a red mark on the boy's cheek. "He hit you," Griff said, his voice low.

Danny's hand went to his cheek instinctively. "No. I—I fell. I—"

"My father hit me, too."

The words came out as if Griff had dragged them from the depths of his soul. In truth, he had. He had never spoken those words to a living person in his entire life. But he couldn't stand seeing Danny trapped in the same solitary hell he had been in. "And he hit my mother."

Danny's eyes lifted, meeting Griff's, full of shock and questions. The heck with the beach and with the ice cream. He pulled the car over to the curb and parked, switching off the ignition. His hand shook.

"It wasn't my fault," he went on raggedly. "And it's not yours, either," he said firmly, his eyes locking first with Danny's, then when the boy made a tiny nod of acknowledgment, with Todd's. "It's not," he repeated.

"He hurt my mother," Todd blurted out.

"Yes." How well he recalled his own mother's pain.

"I hate him!"

Griff bowed his head. "I know."

A tear trickled down Todd's cheek, and he swiped at it. "But sometimes—sometimes, ya know, he's good. I mean, he plays with us and—" He hiccupped.

"I know." The memories were suffocating him, the happy times as well as the bad, the smiles as well as the pain. For years he had shut it all out, pretended that none of it had ever existed. He had lived his life as if it had begun the moment he graduated from high school and left home. Except for Brendan, he didn't permit any holdover from his early years. Only at his wedding, when he had felt secure enough in Lainie's love and unwilling still to share with her his pain, had he allowed his parents into his life. But only for that one day, because he had had a shield around him. He had been too caught up in the present to remember the past or to let it affect him. But it had affected his marriage whether he had wanted it to or not.

He had thought he was doing everything right, minimizing the chances that he would be like his dad, avoiding any situation that might possibly provoke him, putting space between himself and other people except on his own terms, in his life as well as in his job.

But it hadn't worked with Lainie. Because, in spite of himself, he loved Lainie. He couldn't control her, but he couldn't isolate himself from her. To do that contradicted the love he felt. Yet he was afraid to try to do things her way, too. It might mean failing. It might mean becoming like his father. And God help him, he *never* wanted to do that.

He knew, looking at Danny and Todd, that they didn't want that, either. He saw small bodies just aching with love for their parents, and for the first time he overcame his cynicism in a hope that Lainie's optimism was warranted; he hoped to God she would succeed. He hoped she would be able to teach the Hudsons something that his own parents had never learned. And he hoped that he had something to offer their sons.

"I've been where you are," he told them soberly, turning to face sideways so he could see both Danny in the front and Todd in the back. "I've hurt like I see you hurting. I know how you feel."

Danny chewed his lower lip uncertainly, regarding Griff with a somber face that looked far older than his years. His fingers absently stroked the faint red mark on his cheek. Finally, he asked, "Did you ever just want to run away?"

Griff pressed his lips together. "Mmm-hmm."

"Did you?"

"I used to go stay with a friend."

"Did it help?"

"At the time, yes, I think it did. But it's not enough."

Danny frowned. "What do you mean?"

"I mean, I got away, but never solved the problem. I just avoided it."

Danny shrugged and looked skeptical. "Sounds good to me."

"Not in the long run," Griff told him. "Believe me, it comes back to haunt you."

Danny scratched his nose. "So how do you solve it, then? I mean, what can I do?" There was agony in his voice.

"About your parents? Nothing. They have to solve their problems. But you can do something about how it affects you. At least," he amended, "I think you can. I think maybe if I'd had somebody to talk to, somebody I trusted to understand, it would've helped." The time that he had been living with Lainie since he had come back from Montreal had taught him that. Like the situation with his parents, the one with LaRue was out of his control. But just having someone in his corner, someone who knew the painful parts of his life and didn't condemn him for them, helped somehow. He was surprised just how much.

Danny seemed to be considering what he said, weighing it with much the same skepticism that Griff had always weighed Lainie's exhortations to talk, to share his feelings with her. "You think that you might understand, huh?"

"Yeah."

"So I could maybe talk to you?"

"If you wanted to."

Danny mulled that over, then nodded, apparently reaching a decision. "I think," he said slowly, "that sometimes I might."

"IT'S ALL ARRANGED then," Lainie said to Claire as she hung up the phone. "If you want to get some things together, we can go on over as soon as Griff and the boys get back." She looked up and smiled encouragingly at Bob and Claire, then noticed Griff standing in the doorway. "Oh, good, you're here." She didn't dare express the relief she felt. She searched his face for some sign of how things had gone, but as usual, Griff wasn't showing much.

"Mom?" Danny came up behind him and looked at his mother questioningly.

"We're spending the night at some friends of Lainie's," Claire told him calmly. "How about going to your room and getting what you want to take."

"When are we coming back?" Todd wanted to know.

"Tomorrow or the next day."

Todd shot a quick glance at his father, the first time he had looked Bob's way since he had come in. "What about Dad?"

"I'm staying here." Bob spoke quietly and gave his son a wan smile. Then his face sobered as he looked at his other son. "Dan, I'm sorry, I—"

The boy ducked his head and started for the back of the house. "'S'right," he mumbled.

"They're just going for a day or two," Lainie said to Griff. "A cooling-off period." She wanted to ask him if he was all right. Now that he was closer, she could see that he looked pale, shaken, the normal tan of his skin somehow bleached. He didn't seem to be hearing a thing she said.

The boys came back within minutes, and when Claire had got her things, Griff took them out to the car.

"Will you be all right, too?" Lainie asked Bob. He was sitting at the dining-room table, his head in his hands.

"Sure," he choked out, and lifted his head, trying again to smile. "Thanks. I'm uh—I'm glad you came." He rubbed his eyes. "It was good Claire called you. I wouldn't have wanted to—to—" His voice failed, and he bowed his head again.

"We won't leave you alone if you want someone to stay," Lainie told him, aware that Griff had returned and was standing behind her.

"No. I'm okay now." Bob shuddered. "Thank God," he added almost under his breath, and Lainie heard Griff draw in a shaky one of his own.

She turned then and took his arm, drawing him out the door. "We'll meet you tomorrow at my office, then, Bob," she said to him. Looking at Griff, she continued, "Come on. We'll see Claire and the boys safely to the house; then we'll go home."

He followed her mindlessly. He didn't even object when she took the keys right out of his hand and got in the driver's seat herself. She had only to look at him to know he had no business on the freeway. His fingers were icy and trembling.

He never said a word on the drive to the halfway house where Claire and the boys would stay. He sat staring straight ahead, seeing God knew what. Not the taillights of the cars ahead of them, Lainie was certain. He saw the past most likely—the child he had been, the parents he had had, the pain he had known. She reached over and touched his hand where it lay limply on his thigh. Convulsively, his fingers wrapped round her own.

Had it been a mistake to send him with the boys, forcing him into a situation in which he had had to confront their lives, which must in many ways be as his own had been as a child? Had she even had a choice? He had insisted on coming. And having him go with the boys had at least spared him the agony of sitting through the painful gropings and attempts at communication in a marriage that he wouldn't even face in his own.

Griff roused himself long enough to get out of the car when they arrived at the halfway house and Danny and Todd were leaving the car.

"Call," he said to Danny, and scribbled something on a piece of paper that he dug out of his pocket.

Danny looked at the scribbled note, which apparently carried a telephone number. Then he looked up and met Griff's eyes. "Yeah, awright," he said. "Thanks." He stuck out his hand, and Griff took it, shaking it solemnly. Then, when the boy's hand dropped to his side, Griff's lifted and touched the mark on Danny's cheek. Lainie's eyes stung with tears.

Then Griff turned and got back into the car. He was still sitting there, deep in thought, when Lainie reemerged ten minutes later. Neither of them spoke. For once in her life Lainie couldn't think of a thing to say.

When they got back to the apartment, she expected he would turn right around the walk away from her, heading for the beach to work things out as he always did. She was wrong. Instead, he followed her up the stairs, then went and stood by the window, staring out into the darkness for a long, long time.

Almost idly, he reached up with one finger and set the rainbow sun catcher to swaying against the windowpane, its colors muted by the darkness behind it. "Do you think they have a chance, Bob and Claire?" he asked her, turning to look at her over his shoulder.

She stuffed her hands into the pockets of her denim skirt. "Yes. Yes, I do." He pushed the sun catcher again and watched it swing back and forth. "Good."

She wanted to say something more, to thank him for taking care of Todd and Danny. She wanted to ask him what had happened when he was with them. Something had, she was sure. There was a link between Griff and Danny that was almost visible. But it was not, she sensed, something that he would talk about.

He gave the rainbow one last push and turned on his heel and went into the spare bedroom, pulling the door shut behind him.

Lainie didn't stay up much longer herself. It had been a long day, a draining one. Emotionally, she felt as though she had just gone over Niagara Falls—without a barrel. It wasn't unusual for her to feel like this after an evening like the one she had just spent with Bob and Claire Hudson. But she knew it wasn't the Hudsons who were draining her emotions this time. It was Griff.

It took her a long time to fall asleep despite her tiredness. Somebody whose car needed a muffler apparently decided to use the alley behind their apartment for a drag strip. Then there were some jovial late-night joggers laughing their way past the window and a stereo up the hill that was extra heavy on the bass tonight. There were also obvious noises from just on the other side of the bedroom wall. Pacing. Squeaking bedsprings. Coughing. More pacing.

She knew that he was restless. She couldn't blame him. Although he was being pleasant about it, she suspected that he really didn't want to be here with her like this. And after what she had put him through tonight, she imagined that he could hardly wait to leave. She fell asleep, wondering if the odd moments of rapport she felt with him were simply an aberration or if she dared to hope.

THE ILLUMINATED DIAL of the clock on her dresser read 12:47. She couldn't have been asleep for long. But it was finally blessedly quiet except for the soothing rhythm of the surf on the sand. She lay quietly, listening. There was nothing. *Go back to sleep,* she counseled herself. The morning would be all too quick in coming. She tried, rolling over onto her side and clutching the pillow against her breasts, pretending it was Griff.

But knowing that Griff was right on the other side of the wall made the fantasy unbearable, and she lay awake, staring across the room at the curtain blowing in the breeze and listening to the muted roar of the ocean. She didn't know how long she lay there before she could stand it no longer. Flinging back the sheet and thin blanket that had covered her, she got up. Maybe if she made herself some cocoa, she could sleep.

She eased her way out into the living room, noticing that the door to Griff's room was open and that beyond the kitchen, on the porch, there was a light on. Wrapping her cotton dressing gown around her, she crossed the kitchen and peered around the corner of the door to the porch. It was just barely ajar, and she pushed on it tentatively.

Griff was sitting on the floor, leaning back against the wall. His knees were drawn up and his shoulders hunched forward so that his elbows rested on his knees and his arms were crossed. His chin dug into his arm. Though his eyes were open, he didn't even look up at her when she stepped into the room. He was staring at the cradle, which he must have just reassembled, because it sat before him complete in the middle of the floor.

"Griff?" She spoke his name softly, dropping to her knees beside him.

His gaze moved toward her slowly, as if it were costing him great effort, as though he were coming back to her across years. She guessed that he was. He opened his mouth to speak, but no words came. His jaw trembled, and his teeth chattered. She touched his bare arm. He felt frozen.

"Come on," she urged him. "You're like ice."

He didn't resist as she drew him to his feet. He couldn't. The evening had taken too much out of him; he had confronted too many ghosts. He couldn't lift a hand now to stave off her gentleness. Maybe she didn't love him anymore—he wouldn't blame her if she didn't—but at least she was showing him compassion. For now, for tonight, compassion was enough. He would take whatever crumbs she offered him.

She led him into her bedroom, rubbing her hands up and down his bare arm as if she were trying to warm him, to revive him from the cold. And he was cold. He was shaking. His teeth wouldn't stop chattering. He had paced his room forever, facing the memories of his father and mother, seeing their faces as well as Bob's and Claire's, seeing Danny and Todd, then seeing himself as a child and, finally, facing the man he had become. And God, he felt so cold.

Was it too late, or was there hope? If Bob Hudson could change, could he? And if he could, then what? What about him and Lainie?

Finally, one small room hadn't been enough to contain all his feelings. His mind kept going to the future, and he remembered Brendan and Cassie's baby. And the cradle. He crept out to the porch, careful not to make noise and wake Lainie. There he turned on the light and knelt on the floor, picking up the pieces, now complete stripped and sanded, and fitting them together again. When he began, he had no idea of what he was doing. But before he knew what happened, the cradle stood before him on the floor, complete.

And empty.

But Brendan and Cassie's child would sleep in it. A new generation would be born—children like Todd and Danny. But what about his own children? His and Lainie's? He slumped against the wall, then slid down, shivering as he stared at the cradle and the promise that might never come to be.

Lainie unbuckled his belt and stripped the jeans off him, then gave him a gentle shove against his chest so that he sank down on her bed. "Lie down," she said.

He lay. She crossed the room and shut out the light, then came back and slid into the bed beside him, her arms slipping around him to draw him close. For a second he tried to hold out; then her lips touched his eyelids, and he felt them move. Her breath whispered over him.

"Let go," she said, and he did.

All the times that he had huddled alone at the top of the stairs, listening to the fights below, all the times that he had walled himself off so he would be able to say nothing mattered when really it did, every hurt he had held in and never shared, suddenly burst within him. He turned into her, burrowing against her, feeling the strength of her arms as they tightened around him and the tenderness of her lips as they kissed away the tears that streamed down his face.

"I—I'm sorry," he choked when he could speak past the deep, shuddering breaths that shook his chest.

"I'm not," Lainie said softly, her hand ruffling through his hair, soothing him.

He sighed, limp, drained, exhausted.

"Sleep now," she whispered as she snuggled against his chest, her arms still wrapping him tight.

He slept without waking the rest of the night.

Chapter Twelve

The ringing phone woke him. It only rang once before it was snatched up, but he was on the edge of wakefulness, subconsciously aware that the strong arms that had held him through the night had gone. He rolled over in the wide bed, remembering.

He wondered if he ought to feel embarrassed, ashamed of himself for breaking down. It had been years since he had cried, twenty at least. And even then he hadn't shared his tears. Always before he had hugged his pain to himself, showing the world only a silent, inscrutable exterior. But, he thought now, always before he had turned away from actually facing the hurt he had felt as a child, the anguish he had experienced at seeing the two people he loved most in the world try to destroy each other. But last night he had seen his own pain reflected in Danny's eyes and Todd's, and he couldn't deny the reality of it anymore.

When Lainie had found him on the porch, he was in a nether world halfway between the past and the present. Raw and aching on the one hand, yet curiously numb on the other. He couldn't have spoken then if his life had depended on it. Everything about him felt frozen except his emotions; they were consuming him like an unquenchable fire. And Lainie had known it at once. She had taken charge, and he hadn't been able to resist, hadn't wanted to resist. How many times had he hunched miserably on the steps or huddled in his room, listening to the battles that had raged below, and prayed for someone to come to him, to share his pain and soothe him? But no one had ever come. Until last night. Until Lainie.

God, how he loved her. And he needed to tell her so. Now.

She must not have left for work yet. He could hear her voice talking softly to whomever had called. He got up quickly, pulling on his jeans, which he found in a heap on the floor where she had discarded them. He wanted to see her before she left for work, wanted to talk to her, even. He wanted to tell her that something had happened to him last night, that seeing Bob and Claire struggling, that facing himself in Danny and Todd, had given him a faint glimmer of hope. Maybe, he thought, all marriages in which there was abuse were not absolutely doomed to failure. Maybe children with experiences like his did not have to grow into abusive parents like his.

He licked his lips, feeling suddenly nervous. Nervous? Terrified was more like it. He opened the door to the living room slightly. Lainie was standing by the door, her purse in hand, an armload of paperwork resting against her chest as she held the receiver to her ear.

"Not a word," she was saying. "I hope he hears soon, too." She paused, then sighed. "Hell. Sheer hell, Cass. I don't know how much longer I can stand this. Not after a night like last night."

Griff went cold, his knuckles clenching the door.

"Well," she went on, "I hope so, too. And soon. See you for lunch." She dropped the receiver onto the cradle and shouldered her way out the door, never looking back.

Griff felt sick.

LAINIE HADN'T WANTED TO leave him. Not at all. Waking up this morning with Griff in her bed—in her arms—had been a gift from heaven, one that she had been loathe to relinquish. But she couldn't stay home as much as she would have liked to. She had a full schedule of appointments today—Bob and Claire among others—and she had hope, real hope at last, that things might work out with Griff.

Maybe, she tried to convince herself while she got dressed for work, her eyes scarcely straying from the sleeping form of her husband sprawled out peacefully in her bed, it was indeed for the best. With Griff you couldn't rush things. Perhaps a bit of space was what he would need now.

Perhaps she needed some herself. She wanted him desperately. It was almost a relief when the phone rang and it was Cassie calling to see if she would be free for lunch. She had been tempted to forget her obligations and crawl back in bed with Griff. She didn't know how much longer she could stand simply being there with him—helpful and kind—when she loved him so much. And that was exactly what she had told Cassie. Then she had bolted out the door without looking back. Maybe Griff would call her later—unless he was going to try to pretend that last night hadn't happened. But she didn't think he would do that. He had clung to her too tightly last night, had looked too peaceful this morning, for him to deny that something had changed. She crossed her fingers and hurried into the hospital, ten minutes late for work.

It wasn't fair, Griff decided, to taste hope and then have it cruelly snatched away. It wasn't fair to believe finally that you might be able to change and then to realize that your wife no longer cared if you did or not, that, in fact, she could hardly wait until you were gone.

"Hell," he muttered to the empty apartment. "Bloody, bloody hell." He sank down on the sofa and rested his head in his hands and tried to tell himself it didn't matter.

He didn't have much success.

When the phone rang, he almost didn't answer it. It would be Lainie, he knew, sounding caring and solicitous, wanting to know if he was all right.

Hell, no, he wasn't all right. He grabbed the receiver and barked, "Yes?"

"Griff?"

His pounding heart stumbled. "Chase," he acknowledged numbly.

"Good news. We got 'im!"

"What?"

"LaRue's supplier. We got him."

Griff tried to switch gears. "Who? How?"

"It was Huxley. You know, the catcher. Susan nailed him."

"Huxley?" Griff felt as if he were decompressing, coming up from a year at the bottom of the sea. "Tim Huxley?"

"The very one."

"I'll be damned." He couldn't make any sense of it. Tim Huxley had never crossed his mind as a possibility at all. A virtual nonentity, he was the third-string catcher on La-Rue's team. Conscientious and marginally capable, Huxley seemed always on the verge of being sent down. He hadn't been, Griff guessed, because he never caused any trouble. He was always there. Steady, reliable Huxley. "Huxley?"

"You got it." Chase was exultant. "Don't go away. We'll be right over. I'll bring a bottle of champagne, and we can celebrate."

"Yeah," Griff mumbled. Celebrate? "Sure."

He sat there, staring at the receiver in his hand long after Chase had hung up. Huxley? He couldn't have been more surprised if they had proved beyond a doubt that he'd done the supplying himself. He supposed he ought to be feeling pleased. Chase and Susan certainly were. And somewhere, deep inside, he guessed that he probably was.

Lainie would be, he thought suddenly as he recalled her phone conversation, and his mouth twisted into a grim smile. There was no doubt about that. Now there would be no reason for him to hang around any longer. She wouldn't have to "stand it" anymore. She was free; so was he.

He was still digesting that fact when the doorbell rang. Even before he got there to open the door, Chase had wrenched it open himself, and he and Susan burst into the room. She flung her arms around Griff, hugging him tightly, crowing, "We did it! We did it!" while Chase stood back and grinned.

Griff didn't know how to respond, and Susan pulled back abruptly to look at him with concerned, curious eyes. "What's wrong?"

"Nothing." Griff shook his head quickly to deny his feelings. "Nothing at all. Everything's great." He dredged up a smile. Everything was great, wasn't it, he asked himself.

"Did you call Lainie?" Chase asked.

"No."

"Why not?"

Griff shrugged. "She'll be busy right now. Clients, you know. I'll call her at noon," he stalled. He couldn't talk to Lainie, he couldn't tell her the news and listen to her happiness. She would make it sound as though she were happy for him, and he supposed she probably would be. But he knew the real truth—she would be glad she was finally getting out of her life.

"Okay," Chase said, but his expression still told Griff he thought that something was wrong.

"So tell me what happened," Griff said, changing the subject and gesturing toward to sofa, indicating that Chase and Susan should sit down. He took the champagne bottle from Chase and opened it, letting the foaming liquid froth over into the sink before pouring it into glasses and handing each of them one. He declined to drink any himself, not wanting to think about the reason why. "How'd you do it?" he asked, settling himself into the chair opposite them.

"It was Susan mostly," Chase told him, leaning forward, resting his elbows on his knees. "She's more thorough than most investigative reporters are, let alone sportswriters. She went through every one of those interviews with LaRue and all the other people who had said they had seen you with him. She pulled out every name that turned up, and then we started talking to them one by one."

"That would have taken days," Griff protested, amazed at their persistence.

"It wasn't so bad," Susan told him. "Most of the guys were easy enough to dismiss as possible culprits. Fletcher and the rest of your umpiring squad, for example. They're great guys, all of them." She gave Griff an approving smile.

"They are," he agreed. "So how'd you latch on to Huxley?"

"He was one of the guys quoted as having seen you with LaRue. Several guys admitted seeing you, but most of them had to be coaxed. Huxley volunteered the information," Susan told him.

Griff's eyebrows lifted. He could remember now that Huxley had been around LaRue on the plane to New York. But he still found it hard to believe.

"So Susan arranged a private interview with him," Chase said. "We flew to Houston where the team was playing last night. And when we talked to him, she let drop the information that the police were close to having enough evidence to press charges and that they would probably only need a bit more to make an indictment stick. It was all the bait we needed. Huxley bit."

"What's this about an indictment?" Griff demanded. "You're making that up."

Chase sighed. "I'm not, I'm afraid. LaRue seemed only too willing to offer you up. He cited your meeting at the airport with him as an incident of drugs changing hands, and then he pointed out that you were especially hard on him on the field to make it look like you were against him."

He spread his hands. "None of it was terribly damning in and of itself. It's just that, all together, people could see in it exactly what they wanted to see. And they wanted a scapegoat here. They wanted to believe LaRue."

Griff felt suddenly cold, like a man pulled back from sure death who is only just realizing how serious the situation was. "They would have crucified me."

"Yes," Chase agreed, and met his eyes.

"Jesus." Griff rubbed his hands across his eyes, then pinched the bridge of his nose. "He hated me that much?"

"You were handy," Chase said. "And there was no love lost between you, that's for sure."

Griff didn't say anything, just took a deep breath and held it for a long while before he let it out slowly.

"But they didn't indict you," Susan said swiftly. "And they never will. You're clean. Home free. And that's what counts."

"But how'd you get Huxley after he took the bait?" Griff asked.

"He told me you tried to sell to him, too. He was prepared to testify that you had. But I told him I had to see the stuff. I said that if he could provide some, we'd have all the evidence we needed." Susan shook her head, remembering the interview. "We agreed to meet later in the day. He apparently set things up with his own supplier to get something he could say he bought from you. I called Chase, and he tipped off the police. They tailed Huxley and caught him buying. After he was implicated, it wasn't hard to get the whole story from him and LaRue."

Griff shook his head in disbelief. "What'd LaRue say?"

"That he was scared, that the cops were putting pressure on him for his source. He needed a name, and he was pissed off at you. He sure as hell didn't want to be the one to give them Huxley's. That would have touched off a chain reaction that could have left him dead. As it is, we got Huxley and his source, too."

Griff whistled, then rubbed a hand through his hair. "I still can't figure it, though. Why Huxley? He always seemed so harmless. No one paid a bit of attention to him. He was damned lucky to be in the majors at all."

"Too true," Chase agreed. "And he knew it. Everyone like LaRue was able to nail down a big contract. Huxley couldn't. He was living on the edge all the time, and he wanted a piece. If his talent as a ballplayer wasn't going to get it for him, drugs would. And did."

"He was living high, all right," Susan put in, sipping her champagne. "That was one of the things that first made me suspect him. He seemed just a bit too affluent for a man of his limited talents. And you're damned lucky he was, too. If they had come back with an indictment against you, even if you were eventually proved innocent, you'd have had a rough time in the future being the voice of law and order on the ball field."

The way he felt right now, Griff was surprised they hadn't. An indictment was all he would have needed to cap his feelings of hopelessness. *Stop it,* he told himself firmly. *Enough self-pity.* "Thanks," he said to both of them, and swallowing his earlier worries, he looked up to meet their eyes gratefully and unflinchingly.

"Anything for a friend," Chase told him quietly, one corner of his mouth lifting in an almost sympathetic smile.

"The commissioner's office should be calling you soon," Susan said. "They'll be reinstating you as soon as you want. Though I imagine if you want to take a bit more time off and let the whole thing blow over, they'd probably go along with that. What do you plan to do?"

Griff worried his lip reflectively. A very good question. "I don't know."

"I imagine Lainie will have some ideas," Susan said brightly. "You can talk it over with her."

"Yeah." He saw Chase lift a skeptical eyebrow and averted his gaze at once, jumping to his feet and pacing across the living-room floor. "I don't know yet what I'm going to do. I'll have to think about it."

Chase, apparently taking Griff's leap out of the chair as a hint, stood up also and held out his hand to Susan. She carried both their empty glasses and set them on the table, then joined him next to the door where he stood regarding Griff gravely. "Well," he said, offering Griff his handshake. "I'm glad the LaRue bit is settled at least." He clapped Griff on the arm with his other hand and gave him a quick squeeze. "The rest, I reckon, is up to you." His dark eyes held a challenge that was impossible to ignore.

But what the hell can I do, Griff wondered dismally. He watched Chase and Susan all the way down the steps and up the sidewalk to where their car was parked, then went back into the apartment and sank down on the sofa, put his elbows on his knees and propped his head in his hands.

He didn't know how long he sat there, trying to get his life straight. It might have been an hour; it might have been more. But when he stood up and began to move resolutely around the apartment, he knew three things for certain: that he wasn't going to call Lainie and tell her and have to hear her relief over the phone; that he wasn't going to be there when she got home, because there was no way he could face having her tell him to leave; and that despite everything, he still believed in the possibility of their having a future together. He also knew that now it was up to him. He had to prove it to her.

He gathered all his things together, stuffing everything into paper sacks and carrying them out to his car. Then he straightened up the apartment. While he was doing so, the commissioner's office called. Did he want to go back to work immediately, they asked him.

"I'll let you know tomorrow," he said, and crossed his fingers that the answer would be no.

"Well, it's up to you," the secretary told him, her voice offering friendly encouragement that augmented the challenge he heard from Chase a couple of hours before.

Griff sighed and took one last look around the apartment. They were right. Now it was up to him.

"YOU MEAN they found out who was supplying LaRue with drugs?" Lainie demanded. She stared at Cassie over her bacon and tomato sandwich, unsure whether to believe her ears.

"Didn't Griff tell you?"

Lainie shook her head. "He probably tried," she excused him, her mind racing, figuring, rationalizing. "I've been swamped all morning. He might not have been able to get through."

"He could've left a message," Cassie reminded her, supremely reasonable, as always.

"Maybe he did. I'll check with Pam when I get back. So tell me, how did you find out? What happened? Who was it?"

"Chase called Brendan this morning," Cassie told her between bites of chicken salad. "Right after he got back from seeing Griff. Susan uncovered it, actually." Cassie sounded proud of her friend, and Lainie remembered a time when all Cassie had felt was jealousy of Susan Rivers.

"Tell me," she urged.

Cassie did. And all the while she was talking, Lainie was trying to figure out what to do next. There was something distinctly ominous about the fact that Griff hadn't called her and told her. Unless, of course, as she had told Cassie, he had tried and wasn't able to get through. That must be it, she decided. After last night he certainly wouldn't pack up and walk out without mentioning it, would he?

Would he?

No. She rejected the idea immediately. Of course he wouldn't. She wished she felt more certain, though. The rest of the lunch passed in a blur. She supposed she must have eaten her sandwich; she didn't really recall. She scarcely heard all that Cassie told her about Susan and Chase's clever sleuthing, thinking that she would hear it all over again when she finally talked to Griff. *And, damn it, she wanted to talk to him. Now.*

She tapped her fingernails on the edge of her coffee cup while Cassie ate her way methodically through an entire chicken salad, including the parsley, and then ordered a large slice of coconut cream pie.

"Want a bite?" she offered, waving her fork under Lainie's nose.

"No, thanks." Lainie fidgeted irritably. "You're going to be as big as the Goodyear blimp if you eat all that."

Cassie shook her head in denial. "No. I'm eating for two these days, don't forget." She patted her slightly rounded tummy and went on eating.

Lainie hadn't forgotten, but for the first time Cassie's pregnancy didn't send her into complete fits of gloom. She guessed it was because after last night she entertained a tiny sliver of hope that maybe someday she would be eating for two also. Or were her hopes running away with her? Damn it, why hadn't he called?

Finally, Cassie shoved back her chair and sighed. "All right. I'm finished."

Before she had the words out of her mouth, Lainie was paying the bill and heading out the door. The first thing she did when she got back to the hospital was to corner Pam and ask if Griff had called.

"Not that I know of," the secretary replied. "Were you expecting him?"

"Well, no, not exactly," Lainie admitted. "But he might try to reach me this afternoon. If he does, no matter what I'm doing, I want you to put him right through."

Pam's eyes widened slightly, since Lainie usually requested never to be disturbed when she was with a client.

"Whatever you say," she replied. "Your first patient is here," she added, nodding toward the reception area to an older man who was thumbing through a magazine.

"Give me a few minutes," Lainie said. "I have a couple of loose ends from the morning to tie up first."

What she had to do was to call Griff. Her fingers trembled as she punched out the number, and she chewed her lip uncertainly as the phone began to ring. What would she say? "I heard from Cassie that they've found the drug dealer?" or, "I was just wondering if you had heard from Chase?" or, "I just called to say hello and—" But it didn't matter what she decided to say, because the phone rang and rang, and no one was there.

"Damn." Frustrated, she hung up, then paced around her office and wondered what to do next. She would have liked to just lock up and leave for the day, but she didn't dare. Too many people needed her here, starting with the man in the waiting room. *But what about Griff? He needed you last night.* A shiver went right down her spine as she remembered.

But today? She made another circle around her desk. Whether or not he needed her today seemed debatable indeed.

"Ready yet?" Pam's voice interrupted her thoughts.

Lainie sighed and tried to rearrange her mind into some sort of order. "As I'll ever be," she said. "Send him in."

The passing of the afternoon seemed to take years rather than mere hours. Between each appointment Lainie called home, letting the phone ring twenty times or more. But she never got a reply. She thought at first that he might be on his way to the hospital to see her and tell her the news in person. But as time passed and two o'clock turned into three, she had a hard time continuing to believe that.

Then she decided that he had probably just gone for a long walk on the beach. It was exactly the sort of thing Griff would do, especially after the events of last night and to-

day. Besides, she thought, warming to the idea, it would also
be an excellent way to avoid all the curious reporters and TV
newsmen who would be all too eager to invade his privacy
once more, demanding to know his innermost thoughts on
his exoneration. It would also, she concluded, be a good
place for him to remain until she got home from the hospital and he could share the news with her in person.

Yes, she decided happily, smiling at his picture on her
desk, she definitely liked that scenario best. So what if it
seemed a bit too much of a romantic happy ending. After
last night she had a right to dream a little, didn't she? Last
night, after all, he finally opened up to her, finally shared
with her his pain. And the sharing this time, unlike that
which she had provoked in Colorado, had come not out of
anger but out of need. She reached out and touched her
fingers to his picture, letting them trace the gentle, winning
smile she had captured on his face that last day of their
honeymoon in Maui.

They had tasted happiness then. Since then they had had
more than their share of pain. But now they had at least a
toehold on a new beginning. And tonight, with the accusations of LaRue behind him, he would be out of limbo. And,
she prayed, may God let things go right from there.

Putting her hopes in the Almighty, she didn't tamper with
fate anymore by trying to call him again. He might be home,
but she didn't want to ruin his plans by calling in case he
might feel he had to tell her the news over the phone. She
just waited impatiently until her last appointment finished,
then grabbed her sweater and headed for the door.

"Have a good evening," Pam called after her.

I hope so, Lainie thought, crossing her fingers over the
strap of her purse. *Lord, I hope so.* And she practically
sprinted out to the parking lot.

"Hey, Lainie!"

She turned toward the lawn between the wings of the
hospital to see Brendan wave at her just before catching a

Frisbee tossed by his son, Keith. She stopped, and he jogged over, a grin on his handsome face.

"Great news, huh?"

She didn't have to ask what he meant. She simply nodded and tried to smile back at him. "Are you waiting for Cassie?"

"Yeah. What're you going to do to celebrate?"

"I—I don't know yet. Griff hasn't—hasn't said," she finished lamely. She couldn't tell him that Griff hadn't said anything at all!

Brendan laughed, shaking his head. "No, I suppose he wouldn't. He never was one for broadcasting his plans."

"No," Lainie agreed, relieved. How true that was. "But I think I'll stop and buy a bottle of wine for dinner."

"Good idea," Brendan approved, tousling Keith's hair as the boy came up beside him. "If you guys feel like dropping over later, we'd like to have you. We do have a vested interest in all this, you know." He winked at her.

Lainie managed a laugh. "Thanks, but—"

"I know, I know. You'd rather be by yourselves."

"Well, actually," she said, just remembering something, "we can't even do that. I've got to teach that communications class tonight." She grimaced at the thought. *Heavens, tonight of all nights.*

"Well, at least you can tell them how successful at it you are," Brendan comforted, laying an arm across her shoulders as he walked her to her car.

Lainie sighed. "Not without a lot of trial and error, Bren," she confessed. "It isn't nearly as easy as I thought it was."

"You mean it doesn't all just automatically—" he snapped his fingers "—work out?" His face was full of good-natured teasing.

She gave him a rueful grin as she got into her car, then reached out and gave his hand a squeeze. "That's exactly what I mean."

He put one finger under her chin and tilted it up so that she looked directly into his quicksilver eyes. "Ah, yes," he agreed. "But the bottom line, my dear, is that it does." He winked again and touched a finger to her lips. "It does."

Lainie stopped at a liquor store on the way home, asking the man behind the counter for a suitable wine to celebrate.

"To celebrate what?" he wanted to know.

She smiled at him. "A new beginning."

He considered her for a moment, then turned to his shelves of wine bottles and scanned them. Finding what he was looking for in a moment, he plucked it off the shelf and handed it to her. "Try this one, then," he said. "It's the first of a new crop from a very old winery that had several bad years. But this one—" his face lit up with appreciation "—is superb."

"Perfect." Lainie glowed at his words. She paid him and left, humming the "Hawaiian Wedding Song," and counting the minutes until she got home to Griff.

She parked the car in front of the garage door, left her paperwork on the front seat, grabbed the wine and her purse and nearly ran around the corner of the apartment and through the white picket gate and across the small cobbled yard. She took the steps to the apartment two at a time.

Fumbling for her key, she finally got the door unlocked and burst in, calling, "Griff!"

Silence.

She frowned, looking around for a hint of his whereabouts but seeing nothing out of place. In fact, everything looked far neater than it had when she had left that morning. "Griff!" she called again.

But all she got in response was the sound of skateboards scraping on the sidewalk and the distant crash of waves on the shore. Dropping her purse on the couch, she went back out onto the porch and looked up and down the sidewalk as far as she could see. No Griff. Still clutching the wine bottle, she hurried down the stairs, her heart hammering as she headed for the beach. Perching on the low retaining wall that separated the broad sidewalk from the sandy expanse of the beach, she gazed first north, then south. But as far as the eye could see, she could not discern Griff.

The "Hawaiian Wedding Song" had vanished, replaced by the thrumming sound of fear in her head. "No," she whispered, her fingers tightening on the neck of the wine bottle. "No."

Turning back, she forced herself to walk slowly back up the hill to the apartment. She didn't doubt now what she would find. She walked straight through the living room and flung open the spare bedroom.

The narrow bed was neatly made. The few books and magazines that Griff had bought, and which had been casually tossed on the dresser top, were gone. Numbly, she opened the door to the closet. A row of empty hangers stared back at her, and where his shoes had been, she only saw bare floor slightly gritty with sand.

He had gone.

He had actually walked out, taken all his things without one word, and left her. This time there was not even a note. The icy disbelief she had begun to feel the moment she had walked through the door into the silence of the apartment was beginning to thaw, a white-hot anger burning it away.

"Damn you," she railed, the pain, like lava, boiling over inside her, spilling in tears down her cheeks. "Damn you, Griffin Tucker!" And she brought the wine bottle down with a splintering crash on the edge of the dresser.

Then she sank down on the bed and cried.

Chapter Thirteen

Tried and found wanting. Tested and failed.

And it hurt, damn it. It hurt.

And all the tears Lainie cried didn't make it hurt any less. On the contrary, if anything, they seemed to fuel the rage that was growing within her. How could he? How could he simply walk out on her? Share his pain with her, then leave her cold?

She sat up angrily, glaring around the small, now-impersonal bedroom, wanting to berate him, yell at him, kick something. Kick him, she corrected herself, swiping ineffectually at her red-rimmed eyes with the sleeve of her cotton blouse. But he wasn't there. Never would be there again.

"Damn him," she whispered again, her voice raw from the tears. Then she jumped up and in a flurry of activity fetched some rags, the broom and a dust pan and set about mopping up the mess of wine and shattered glass all over the bedroom floor. As an exercise in rage reduction, it didn't take nearly long enough. But for that, she reflected as she stared down at the faint stain that would certainly mar the floor forever, she would have needed to smash a whole case. Or possibly more.

She stalked back out to the kitchen, her eyes searching for something else to tackle. They lit instead on the note she had tacked up by the telephone to remind herself that her night-school class began this evening.

It was enough to make one wonder about the Almighty's sense of humor, she thought as she drew a deep breath. Well, there was no way on God's earth she was teaching a course in effective communication in marriage tonight. Maybe not any other night for that matter. There was only so far that you could push the old adage "Do as I say, not as I do." Lainie figured that she had already pushed it quite far enough.

She rubbed her nose with her sleeve and sniffled, trying to make her voice sound normal before she called the college. Then she picked up the phone and eventually got ahold of the woman in charge of night school classes. She apologized for calling so late, then pleaded illness.

"It's nothing serious, I hope," the woman said.

"No." *Just a broken heart.*

"Take care of yourself, dear."

"I will."

The question was how? Not for her the Griffin Tucker solution to dealing with the ills of the world. She'd be damned if she would go walk for miles on the beach. She'd be steaming if she tried. And while she would have enjoyed taking Griff apart for the benefit of her friends, she had enough sense to know she would hate herself afterward. There were certain things you could talk to your friends about in your marriage and others that were better left undiscussed. What did she always tell her clients? Communicate your anger. Let him know how you feel.

How useful was that, she asked herself sardonically. She picked up the bright yellow communications textbook and weighed it in her hands. Then she flung it at the rainbow sun catcher in the window.

The sound of breaking glass was satisfying somehow, even if the sun catcher itself, barely grazed by the thrown book, only spun dizzily in the air before falling intact to the carpet. For a moment Lainie just stared at the broken glass, her chest heaving with unspent sobs. Then the phone began to ring.

It could not possibly be anyone she wanted to talk to. Everyone she knew well thought she and Griff would be celebrating tonight. None of them would call and interrupt that. And a quote-seeking reporter was the last person she wanted to talk to right now. Pocketing her house key and her wallet, she stepped through the front door and picked her way through the pieces of glass on the porch. She supposed she ought to pick them up. Well, there would be time enough for that later. Lots and lots of time. She went down the steps and walked briskly uptown without looking back. The phone kept right on ringing.

She didn't know how long she spent just wandering around town, losing herself in the midweek traffic of surfers, young execs and off-duty airline personnel who were frequenting the shops and bistros that dotted the main thoroughfares. She simply drifted along the streets, concentrating on the bustle of people, the smells of garlic and frying fish, the sound of talk and laughter and occasional revving of a motorcycle. It was therapeutic in a sense. It forced her to realize that regardless of how miserable she felt, the world would go on. And ultimately she would, too.

Finally, the setting sun and her third invitation to join some tanned, beach-blond young man for a beer and "a chance to know her better" turned her toward home. She certainly couldn't wander the streets all night, and she had got what perspective she could. It wasn't much. Somewhere deep within she was still seething, still hurting, and she suspected it would last for a long time to come. On the outside she simply felt unutterably cold.

She stepped back over the glass shards on her way into the apartment, going to get the broom and dustpan for the second time that night. On her way back out, she took the phone off the hook. She still wasn't in the mood to talk to the press, and she doubted she could talk to her friends, especially Brendan and Cassie, without crying.

She swept most of the glass into a pile, picking up the largest pieces and putting them into the brown paper bag she had put on the welcome mat. Then she knelt in a clean patch of the gray slatted porch and began to whisk the tinier bits into the dustpan while the waning sun's warmth touched her back. She needed it, she thought; it was the only warmth she had. And she shivered when a shadow fell across her, cutting it off.

"What happened?"

She froze at the sound of his voice. Hunched over the dustpan, she didn't move, her fingers clenching the short handle of the whisk broom.

"What happened?" Griff asked again, and she detected a hoarse sort of fear in his voice. "Are you all right?"

That turned her around. *All right? All right? No, by God, I'm not all right!*

"What do you care?" she snapped, her eyes raking over him as she tried to disguise her pain with anger. "Did you forget something?" she continued icily as she stood up, holding the dustpan between them, tempted to fling the whole thing in his face.

"Where were you?" he demanded, ignoring her questions. "They said you were sick."

"Sick?" She didn't know what he was talking about. Who were "they"? "You're damned right I'm sick," she raged. "Sick of you. Sick of what you do to me."

Griff looked stunned; pain scorched his features, and as if she hadn't been so consumed by her own pain, she might have stopped speaking. But her feelings had been bottled up too long. "Just get whatever you forgot and get out of here," she said roughly, and turning her back on him again, she bent down and attacked the porch with renewed fury.

"What happened to the window?" he asked, his voice steady as he shifted slightly against the porch railing.

She felt a faint jolt of surprise. Why wasn't he leaving? He always had before. It was what he did best—leaving. "I broke it," she said baldly, and whacked the gray wooden siding of the apartment with her broom.

"How?"

She turned and glared at him. "I threw a book at it." Setting the broom aside, she placed her hands on her hips. "And I'll tell you why if this is twenty questions we're playing! Because I was—no, I *am*—madder than hell at you!"

Griff flinched, but he still didn't turn. Instead, he met her furious glare with an openness that goaded her even more.

"And if you want to know why I'm madder than hell at you, I'll tell you that, too. Because when I got home today, you weren't here."

He looked at her oddly then, as if he had been smote by a sudden spasm of pain. Then his expression shuttered and he said, "Chase and Susan found the supplier. I didn't have to stay any longer."

"That's the only reason you were here, then? Because you had to be?"

"You didn't want me—" he began, defending himself.

"Didn't want you?" She almost howled the words. "What in God's name do you think I've been trying to do since you walked out of my life that first time except try to get you back?

He shook his head. "At first maybe, but—"

"But nothing!"

"But after what happened in Colorado—"

"What happened in Colorado," she demanded, "other than that you left me again?"

"You know why I left you!"

She didn't say anything to that, just stared at him. Griff glared back, his dark eyes flashing. Then he raked a hand through his hair, turning it into golden fire in the setting sun.

"Why would you have wanted me after I told you about—about my parents?" he asked, his gaze, which had looked with hers, now skittering away.

"Because I loved you."

"I could've hurt you!" he protested.

"You think you didn't?"

"What do you mean? I never laid a hand on you!"

"That's not the only kind of hurt there is." Lainie said in a low, shaky almost tearful voice.

Their eyes met again, and Lainie drew a long, shuddering breath, all her anguish apparent in her eyes. He saw it but shook his head as if to deny it was there. "I was trying to protect you."

She swallowed. "It didn't work."

"No?" His mouth quirked up at the corner in a sad sort of smile; then he gave a weary half laugh and sighed. "No, probably not. Where you're concerned, I don't seem to be able to do anything right." He shoved his hands in the pockets of his jeans and looked down at the toes of his tennis shoes. "I'm sorry."

Lainie felt oddly breathless. She leaned back against the siding for support of two very shaky knees. "I'm sorry, too."

Neither of them said anything else.

Griff watched his toes with absorbed fascination, and Lainie stared past his left ear as though the sunset demanded her entire attention. She didn't breathe—couldn't breathe. At any moment she expected him, apology made, to turn and walk away. She couldn't hope again. How often she had, only to have them dashed. A sea gull flew up and sat down on the windowsill, gawking into the apartment, then tipping his head and looking almost quizzically at them. Still Griff didn't leave.

"Griff?"

He lifted his head, the blond hair falling in a fringe across his forehead.

"Why did you come back tonight?"

He rocked back on his heels, considering his answer. "I was worried about you," he said finally. "I thought something might have happened."

Lainie frowned. "What do you mean? And what was that about my being sick?"

Griff's toe traced the line of the slat beneath his feet. "At night school," he mumbled. "They said you were."

"How did you—"

"Because I'm in your class, damn it!" The tide of red on his neck and face owed nothing to the sunset, and he glared at her defiantly, brown eyes snapping.

"You're—" Surely she hadn't heard him right.

"I'm in your class," he repeated. "You know, six weeks' worth of effective communications in marriage." His voice was rough, angry almost.

"Why?" She still didn't know for sure if she dared to hope, but it was hard not to.

"Why do you think?" He sounded belligerent, not at all the well-measured and controlled man she had lived with all those months.

"But you—"

"What's the matter?" he growled. "Don't you think I can learn anything?"

"I think you can learn whatever you want to learn," she said quickly. "I just never believed that you thought you could..." Her voice died out. She could tell from his expression, though, that he knew exactly what she had been going to say.

"Didn't believe I could change?" His tone altered. The anger vanished, replaced by a sort of hesitant, rueful quality. "You're right. I didn't. And—" he shrugged "—maybe I can't." He sighed and looked down at his shoes again. "But just lately I've been hoping, I guess." He lifted his head and met her eyes, giving her the faintest ghost of a smile.

Lainie's mind was in a whirl. "Are you saying what I hope you're saying?"

"I don't know." He swallowed. "I—I'm saying I'd like to try and make things work, Lainie."

Hope did dawn then and rose, full-born and singing inside her.

"Truly?"

He nodded, his face a mask of uncertainty.

She groped to ask what she still couldn't comprehend. "But why did you leave, then?"

"I thought you wanted me to go."

"No! I never!"

"I heard you say so."

"When? To whom? I never told you that!"

He shook his head impatiently. "Not me. You were talking on the phone this morning. And you said—you said, 'I don't know how much longer I can stand this. Not after—not after a night like last night.'" The stark pain of remembrance was clear on his face, and Lainie, recalling those words in the context in which they were actually spoken didn't know whether to laugh or cry.

Instead, she reached out and touched him, her hand hovering next to his cheek for a single instant before gently making contact with the smooth, freshly shaved skin. "I didn't want to leave you," she told him softly, explaining. "I felt like last night we had finally broken down the biggest barrier. And to have to go on living the way we had been—in limbo—without being able to say if we really had a chance, was more than I could stand. That's what I couldn't take. Not you. Oh, God, Griff, I love you. I always have. I always will." Her voice broke.

For a moment he just stared as if trying to see the truth in her face. Then Griff made a sound that was almost a sob, and his hands jerked out of his pockets, reaching for her, his arms going around her as though she were his lifebelt in a storm-ridden sea. "I love you, too," he mumbled into her hair, his voice trembling. "I love you so much."

Instinctively, she wrapped her arms around him, holding him close, her fingers clutching the muscles of his back, her face buried against his neck, drawing in the warmth and the scent of him, scarcely daring to believe what was happening. Her feelings went beyond need. Now she knew love in its fullest dimensions, hard fought and, she hoped, hard won, an all-encompassing, life-sustaining emotion so powerful it nearly took her breath away.

Apparently, Griff felt the same way, for when he finally broke their fierce embrace and stepped back slightly, he was still trembling as he held her in the circle of his arms. He bent his fair head so that their foreheads touched as he said shakily, "I think we'd better talk."

It was so precisely what she had been saying for months that Lainie almost laughed. In fact, she couldn't help smiling, and Griff grinned back at her sheepishly.

"So I'm a slow learner," he said.

"You and me both," Lainie told him. "Come on. Let's go inside."

She made them a pot of tea and poured it out into mugs, then thought it wasn't substantial enough as it was, so she fetched the bottle of brandy from the cupboard beside the stove and laced each mug liberally. Then she handed one of them to Griff.

He accepted it solemnly, carrying it to his lips and breathing in the potent fumes before taking a sip. "Isn't this what they used on shipwrecked sailors?"

"It could be," Lainie said. She felt like a shipwrecked sailor, more than a little battered and waterlogged but surviving.

"Appropriate," Griff agreed. He took a second swallow and closed his eyes. When he opened them again, he looked directly at her and asked, "Do you really think we might have a chance?"

"I hope so." She remembered Brendan's teasing parting shot about everything "working out" and knew that she wasn't naive enough to believe that anymore. *It only "worked out" if you both worked like hell to make it so and if you came to understand each other.* "A lot of what happened was my fault."

Griff looked as if he wanted to protest, but she held up her hand to shush him. "It was," she insisted. "I put everyone else's needs before yours."

"Maybe," he conceded. "But it wasn't really your fault. I didn't tell you I had any." He shrugged, thinking back. "When I wanted something, I didn't ask you. I just gave orders."

"And I always wanted to discuss the orders," Lainie agreed unhappily.

"I couldn't do that." He looked away, and she knew that the admission had cost him a great deal. She also knew they were fast approaching the most painful topic of his life.

"Your parents," she said gently, acknowledging the unspoken cause of his pain, prepared to gloss over it if he preferred it that way.

But this time Griff didn't deliberately change the subject. Instead, he carried his cup of tea over to the couch and sank down, cradling the warm mug between his palms and staring down at the floor between his feet.

"It was awful," he said, his voice low and rasping, as though he were having to carve the words out of stone. "They fought about everything. A chance remark would escalate into a full-scale battle." He bowed his head as he remembered. His hands clenched on the mug, his knuckles whitening.

Lainie crossed the room quickly and knelt beside him so that her face was on a level with his. She didn't speak at all, just laid her hand on his knee, sharing the pain until he went on.

"And one of the worst things was that on the outside everything seemed so normal. My father was successful. My mother was beautiful. They belonged to the right clubs, had the right friends, went to the right places. And no one ever knew!" He raised his anguished eyes to meet hers, and her fingers tightened on his knee.

"No one?"

He lifted one shoulder in a sort of halfhearted shrug. "No one that mattered. It sure as hell wasn't the sort of thing I wanted to tell my friends. Oh, a counselor here and there knew, I guess. I remember being dragged along to the occasional family counseling session. But that was sheer pain, because my mother's idea of discussing things was just to berate my father. And me," he added softly. "Anyway, nobody seemed to be able to do much. We would go a few times, and then everything would be okay for a while. But, like clockwork, the pattern would start all over again." He shook his head with despair. "I don't even know if they really wanted help!"

"Like Mavis Leary," Lainie said softly.

"What?"

"You remember Mavis?"

"Of course." And she could tell by the look on his face that the memories were sharp. And distasteful.

"She's been in and out of the hospital more times than I can count," Lainie said. "I've sent her to see other counselors. I've got her into halfway houses. I've tried to get her and Dick together for counseling. And for a while things work; then they fall apart again. The same old pattern."

"It could happen to me," Griff said, his voice aching.

"No."

"Why not?"

"Do you want it to happen?"

"Of course not!"

"Mavis wants it to." Lainie rubbed her hand along the soft denim on his thigh. "I think maybe your parents did, too."

"And that's all there is to it?"

"No. It's not always that simple. But wanting to change is a big part of changing. The biggest part. And besides, you're not like that, anyway."

"I get angry."

She smiled. "So do I. I threw a book through a window tonight, remember?"

He let out a long, shaky breath. "I remember. You really wanted me to be here?" The light in his eyes when he asked told her how much he liked the idea.

"You better believe I did. I brought home a bottle of wine to celebrate with."

"So let's celebrate. Where is it?"

Lainie felt an uncomfortable heat rise in her cheeks. "I broke it over the dresser in the spare bedroom," she confessed hesitantly.

"You did what?"

"You heard me! I was furious with you!" And she was embarassed to death right now.

Griff laughed, his eyes tender as he looked at her flushed face. He loosed one hand from its grip on the mug and tangled his fingers in her hair, tugging gently. "Perhaps it's your temper we should be wary of, not mine."

"Could be." Lainie smiled as she felt the soothing motions of his fingers as they tugged on her hair and then rubbed gently against her scalp. Shivers skittered right down the back of her neck, and a delicious warmth was spreading through her. "Probably not, though. If you had been here, it never would have happened." She paused and looked into his eyes. "You are going to be here from now on, aren't you?"

Griff's fingers stilled. "If you want me."

She rested her cheek against his denim-clad thigh. "I'll always want you." she murmured. "I love you. I always have. I always will."

He set the mug down on the coffee table then and reached for her, drawing her up onto his lap and wrapping his arms around her. For long moments he didn't say anything, just held her, luxuriating in the closeness of the woman he loved, the woman who had such faith in him. "It isn't going to be easy, you know," he whispered. "I'm not going to be able to change overnight."

"Neither am I," Lainie replied, snuggling against his chest, feeling the steady beat of his heart speed up as she slid her fingers between the buttons of his shirt and caressed the warm flesh beneath. "I think we're both going to have to keep on trying."

"Like Bob and Claire Hudson?" he asked.

"Yes." She lifted her head to meet his eyes again. "I'm sorry about having to drag you into that. I shouldn't have asked you to go with the boys. I knew what it might do to you."

"It hurt like hell," he acknowledged, and she heard the rough edge grow in his voice. "But it opened my eyes, too. I saw that without someone to talk to, they could grow up into men as afraid of relationships as I was. I didn't want that to happen to them." He hugged her fiercely. "I don't want it to happen to me. To us."

"We won't let it," Lainie promised him. And herself. They had been through too much to let things fall apart now. Now the walls were down between them, and together they would keep them down. She kissed him, making that commitment. And when he returned it, she knew she was receiving his.

She lay her head on his shoulder, smiling, at peace. "Claire told me you gave Danny our phone number," she said softly.

Griff shifted his weight beneath her. "I thought he might want to talk," he said almost sheepishly. When she lifted her head to look up at him, she saw a faint smile touch his lips. "See?" he said. "I'm getting more like you every day."

"God help us," Lainie laughed. "Don't go that far!"

"I'm not going anywhere," Griff assured her. "Except into the bedroom. Coming?"

Lainie pulled away from him and stood up. "Yes. In just a minute."

She crossed the room and bent down, retrieving the rainbow sun catcher from behind the chair where it had fallen. Holding it gently by the nylon filament so that the light that shone through it splashed a rainbow onto the carpet, she carried it across the room to the unbroken window and hung it carefully from the lock. They both watched it swing for a moment against the darkness outside. Then Griff got up and came to stand behind her. She could see him reflected in the window glass, lithe and strong and capable, as he padded across the rug and slipped his arms around her, lacing her fingers with his against her waist. She leaned back against him, letting his love envelope her as, at the same time, she loved him.

"Is that what you were aiming at?" he asked softly. "With the book?"

"Yes." Her admission was the barest whisper, nothing more.

"I'm glad you missed," he said huskily.

"So am I."

"We've come a long way since Maui." His lips brushed against the softness of her hair.

"Farther than many couples do in a lifetime."

"And we've got a long way to go."

She turned in his arms then and held him tightly. "Years and years, I hope."

"Do you suppose we have a chance for a few more rainbows?" he asked.

Lainie smiled and lifted her eyes to his, thinking about the years ahead that were sure to be filled with sunlight and storms. "I think, my darling," she told him in a voice brimming with love, "that I can almost guarantee it."

Harlequin Intrigue

Because romance can be quite an adventure.

Available wherever paperbacks are sold or through

Harlequin Reader Service

In the U.S.
Box 52040
Phoenix, AZ
85072-2040

In Canada
5170 Yonge Street,
P.O. Box 2800, Postal Station A
Willowdale, Ontario M2N 6J3

INT-6

Take 4 books & a surprise gift FREE

SPECIAL LIMITED-TIME OFFER

Mail to   **Harlequin Reader Service**®

In the U.S.
2504 West Southern Ave.
Tempe, AZ 85282

In Canada
P.O. Box 2800, Station "A"
5170 Yonge Street
Willowdale, Ontario M2N 6J3

YES! Please send me 4 free Harlequin American Romance® novels and my free surprise gift. Then send me 4 brand-new novels as they come off the presses. Bill me at the low price of $2.25 each —a 11% saving off the retail price. There are no shipping, handling or other hidden costs. There is no minimum number of books I must purchase. I can always return a shipment and cancel at any time. Even if I never buy another book from Harlequin, the 4 free novels and the surprise gift are mine to keep forever.

Name   (PLEASE PRINT)

Address   Apt. No.

City   State/Prov.   Zip/Postal Code

This offer is limited to one order per household and not valid to present subscribers. Price is subject to change.   DOAR–SUB–1

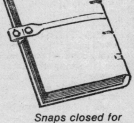